This book is due for return on or before the last date shown
above: it may, subject to the book not being reserved by
another reader, be renewed by personal application, post, or
telephone, quoting this date and details of the book.

HAMPSHIRE COUNTY COUNCIL
County Library

 100%
recycled paper

H.Q.
Account

THE CONVICT
AND OTHER STORIES

THE CONVICT

AND OTHER STORIES

James Lee
BURKE

ORION

Grateful acknowledgment is made to the following publications, in which the stories listed originally appeared: *Atlantic* (June 1980), 'Uncle Sidney and the Mexicans'; *Southern Review* (Summer 1982), 'Taking a Second Look'; *Quarterly West* (Winter/Spring 1980), 'Hack'; *Cimarron Review* (October 1983), 'We Build Churches, Inc.'; *Antioch Review* (Spring 1975), 'When It's Decoration Day'; *Kenyon Review* (Spring 1985), 'The Convict'; *Southern Review* (Summer 1991), 'Texas City, 1947'; *Epoch* (1992), 'Winter Light'; *Writer's Yearbook* (1993), 'Jailhouses, English Departments, and Electric Chairs'; *Epoch* (Winter 1994), 'Water People'.

First published in Great Britain in 1995 by
Orion
An imprint of Orion Books Ltd
Orion House, 5 Upper St Martin's Lane, London WC2H 9EA

A CIP catalogue record for this book is available
from the British Library

ISBN 0 75280 165 1 (cased)
ISBN 0 75280 164 3 (trade paperback)

Printed in Great Britain by
Clays Ltd, St Ives plc

For my children
Jim, Jr., Andree, Pamela and Alafair

Contents

THE CONVICT
AND OTHER STORIES

Introduction: Jailhouses, English Departments and Electric Chairs

O ut of the tank! You know the drill! Shake, rattle and roll!' the jailer yelled into the large stone room that served as the main holding area for the parish prison. Inside the room was an enormous cast-iron box, a room within a room, perforated with square holes, subdivided into tiny four-man cells, that served as the 'tank' or lock-down area from 5 in the evening until 7 the next morning, when a mixed bag of drunks, or 'stewbums,' traffic offenders, bad-check writers, small-time boosters, barroom knife fighters, armed robbers, and a rapist or two would empty out into the bullrun and form a long line against one wall, while the trusties wheeled in the carts that were stacked with stainless-steel caldrons of grits, coffee and link sausage.

We filed out of the tank, across the corridor, into another holding area, where Claude Vidrine had spent his last hours on earth.

'See that stain yonder on the cement?' a toothless old man next to me said. 'They say he puked up his last meal there.'

On the floor, right under a barred window whose wire

mesh had been recently unbolted and removed, was a reddish-brown area almost the color of dried blood.

'The cocksuckers are lying,' Willie, the old man, said. 'Claude wasn't no sissy. The trusty told me the leather gag slipped off his mouth, and his insides come up. Like burnt cork, he told me.

'Claude Vidrine was standup. He'd spit in their faces. You bet.'

At noon sharp the jailer shot back the huge bolt on the door to the tank and pushed it open to let in the trusties with the food carts. The meal was spaghetti and white bread, all that you could eat. But there would be no more food until 7 the next morning. Nineteen hours.

'You ain't gonna eat?' Willie said.

'No, I don't think so,' I said.

'You still feel sick?'

'A little bit.'

'You sure stunk when they brung you in here. You're too young for this bullshit, son. Eighteen ain't old enough to fuck yourself up. Get in the line.'

'What for?'

'Suit yourself. I don't give a shit.'

While the others ate, I sat by myself on top of a black steam pipe that ran alongside the wall. Then I took a shower and washed out my shirt under the spigot. While I was wringing out my shirt, I looked up and saw a narrow-shouldered man watching me, his face disjointed, his eyes riveted on my loins.

'Get away from there, Pookie,' another man said.

His name was Deek. His shirtless body looked like it was fashioned from coat hangers. His skin was as white as a fish's belly and seemed to crawl with vertebrae and rib protrusions when he moved.

'Set down on the pipe here a minute,' he said.

We were alone between the wall and the tank, but down by the end window five men were watching us.

'We're a family here,' he said. 'A guy don't want to eat,

that's his business. But you load up your plate, you pack it down with your spoon, then you load it up some more, and you give it to the guys who heat up the stinger before lock-down. It ain't a big deal, but it's the way we do it here.'

I nodded and didn't reply.

'Them guys ain't gonna hurt you. Some guys are just fucked up in the head, you know what I mean?'

'Yeah, sure.'

'We ain't got broads or money in here. Outside of cigarettes, all we got is scarf.'

'What?'

'Food. It's valuable. Look, I don't want to hurt your feelings, but where the fuck you been, man?'

When I was in my second semester of college English, at a small school in south-western Louisiana before the era of creative writing programs, Irving Stone was on campus one day, visiting a friend who taught English there. I still remember every statement he made about the craft of fiction, as well as the advice he gave us about pursuing it for a career. He was the first professional writer I had ever met, but over the years I've found that every observation he made that day about fiction writing was correct.

One student asked if a writer should be willing to compromise with the market, 'to sell out,' as he put it.

'Oh no, I wouldn't think that way about it,' Stone said. 'Look, if you write a story to pay the rent, you'll never pay the rent. Just write it for yourself, write it as well as you can, and take pleasure in doing it. That's reward enough. If you do that, the publications and the checks will follow.'

I never forgot his advice. But I also found that integrity in your art, like choices between good and evil in your life, can be an ongoing and contentious affair.

I also discovered, at least in my case, that aesthetic vanity and stubbornness could mask themselves as artistic probity.

I finished the rewrite of my first novel, *Half of Paradise*, two weeks after my 24th birthday, in December 1960. I thought I only needed to send it to an agent, and somehow the mysterious process of publishing would take care of itself.

Wrong.

For openers, I couldn't get an agent, not at gunpoint. So I submitted the novel to publishers directly, unsolicited. I wrote eloquent cover letters to accompany the manuscript. I added many more printed rejection slips to my collection.

The novel was in limbo for four years. During that time I wrote another book, began a third one, taught English a while, became a land surveyor in Colorado and a social worker on skid row in Los Angeles. Then I met a writer who introduced me to the agent Kurt Helmer in New York.

Kurt sold *Half of Paradise* to Houghton Mifflin, and I began my first experience at revising a book-length manuscript with a literary editor. But I had a problem. I believed I had shot my way into Dodge City, and no one, by God, was going to tell me what I should change in my art. When the editor marked out lines or scenes, I typed them right back in. I told her that 'revising at someone else's request was like shooting dice with a cup.'

I considered my attitude one of artistic integrity. I persevered, I got my way. I also won the right to live with mistakes that became cut in stone.

I wrote another novel, *To the Bright and Shining Sun*. I loved this book, a story about the Kentucky coal fields and the people of the Cumberland Mountains, and was convinced that it would remain as one of the best things I ever wrote. I received a solid advance from Houghton Mifflin to work on the revisions, which took two months. This time I believed that I had done everything reasonable in the way of editorial changes, and I sent the manuscript back

to the publisher, confident that a fine future lay in store
for it.

Wrong. Big time.

Two months passed with no response. When I finally
telephoned the publisher, I was told there were serious
problems with the book and that I needed to go back,
chapter by chapter, and begin a far more dramatic revision.

I was stunned and angry. I broke the contract, asked for
the novel back and, in so doing, incurred a large financial
debt, because I had already spent the advance.

The following year was a dreary one. My first novel was
out of print, I was without a publisher again, and I now had
three book-length manuscripts that I couldn't sell. I also
did not get tenure at the university where I was teaching,
and my wife was pregnant with our fourth child.

I sent out 212 letters of application for teaching positions and received one affirmative reply, from a junior
college in Florida.

Then, after 14 rejections, Bruce Carrick at Charles
Scribner's Sons bought *To the Bright and Shining Sun*, as
is, with no requests for even minor revisions.

Today I am convinced that if I had made the editorial
changes asked by Houghton Mifflin, I would have dest-
royed the novel.

But during the rewrite of my next novel, *Lay Down My
Sword and Shield*, I refused to listen to Bruce's suggestion
that I cut some of the profanity in the dialogue and the
wiseguy cynicism of the narrator, and once again I won the
right to live with the consequence of refusing to listen to
an intelligent and friendly voice.

By age 34 I had published three hard-cover novels in New
York, with a fair amount of critical success, and had been
given a Breadloaf Fellowship for *To the Bright and Shining
Sun*. I thought I had arrived.

Wrong.

It took 13 years before I published again in hardcover.

It wasn't an easy time. A major literary agent, one with whom I had been for seven years, returned all my material. The best novel I had written to date, *The Lost Get-Back Boogie*, was rejected by virtually everyone in New York publishing. (It received about a hundred editorial rejections over nine years, before it was finally published by Louisiana State University Press and nominated for a Pulitzer Prize.)

I used to have a peculiar dream when sliding off the edge of delirium tremens.

The dream took place in a darkened, third-floor room that smelled of mildew, wet stone, a cement floor that had been scoured with antiseptic. The wire-mesh screen had been unbolted from the single barred window, and you could smell the coldness of a storm and ozone and salt and wet trees in the wind and the fecund odor of humus in a swamp. In the south, the clouds pulsed with veins of lightning, like heated wires that flickered on and off. From below in the street, hillbilly music and the sound of people laughing rose from a jukejoint.

Claude Vidrine's freshly shaved head was running with sweat when they sat him down in the straight-back reenforced oak chair and began buckling the straps across his calves and forearms. Men whom he had never seen before, against whom he had no grievance, nor had harmed in any way, rubbed electrode paste on his ankles, wrists and temples, used ropes to hoist the rubber power cables through the barred window from far below, set metal pins in the skull cap that was about to be lowered on his head, spun wing nuts into place, carefully tightened a Phillips screw close by his neck, all with a singleness of purpose and a level of certainty that made him want to interrupt their work, to tell them that certainly a mistake had been made, that he was only one man and could not be this important in the scheme of things.

Then there was another smell, too, even greater than

the foul odor of sweat and fear that drifted from his armpits.

It ain't my fault. They wouldn't give me time to use the toilet. I ax them, he wanted to say.

But they had already fitted the leather gag across his mouth, bulging his eyes, wrenching his head back against the leather pad on the chair.

He wanted to signal them, to tell them that he forgave or that he didn't forgive them, to leap inside the collective mirror of their eyes, to live a little longer in the strangled reflection that he saw there.

But a tall man in polished cowboy boots and a pearl-gray Stetson flipped a black cloth over Claude Vidrine's face as though he were closing a fly trap.

Did he hear someone say *You got to be standup, Claude?* Did his colon constrict when he felt his own excrement sliding down his buttocks and thighs? As his heart thundered in his chest, did he imagine, behind the face cloth, that he saw a single bolt of lightning leap from the black vault of sky overhead to the Gulf's watery horizon, or for just a second did he actually feel the electric arc that cooked his brain and exploded his insides and caused his body to buckle and vibrate with such energy that his executioners involuntarily stepped back from him?

In 1978, through my cousin Andre Dubus, I met my current agent, Philip Spitzer. He worked out of his house, used only a part-time assistant, and often represented literary writers off whose work he made little in the way of commissions. But he worked seven days a week, never gave up if he believed in a manuscript, and never wavered in his personal loyalties.

I knew that I had the right man. I didn't drink anymore, either. And I had a new job, as an associate professor in a graduate creative writing program.

But I still couldn't sell a book.

I wrote *Two for Texas*, a historical novel about the Texas Revolution of 1835–36. When no one wanted to publish it in hardcover, Philip began offering it to mass-market paperback companies. I wondered if I was selling out.

Then I wrote *Heaven's Prisoners*, a novel about a young boxer from New Iberia. I thought it was a fine book. Philip did, too.

No one was interested.

I wrote a long allegorical novel, set in modern-day Texas, about the search for the Holy Grail. I was sure that this time I had written a publishable book. So was Philip.

Wrong. My letters of rejection were reaching into the hundreds.

Then, in the summer of 1984, a novelist friend of mine, Rick DeMarinis, and I were fishing on the Bitterroot River in western Montana.

'Why don't you try writing a crime novel?' he said.

'Why?'

'You've written everything else. All you've got to do is write one good chapter, and you can get an advance on it.'

That fall I again went back to work in earnest. I rewrote *The Lost Get-Back Boogie* a third time, began putting together a short story collection, and wrote two chapters of a crime novel titled *The Neon Rain*. I liked the two chapters, but they were obviously within a genre that was not considered literary. Was I selling out, I asked myself.

Then I asked myself another question: How is it possible to sell out when the fact is you can't *sell* anything?

The following year Louisiana State University Press published my collection of short stories under the title *The Convict*. They also accepted *The Lost Get-Back Boogie* and told me it was perhaps the best novel ever to come across their desks. I completed *The Neon Rain*, and Philip submitted it to three New York publishing houses. I prepared myself for more rejection letters.

All three houses made bids for the book.

I had been worried over the years about literary compromise. But like the venial sins I would confess as a child and which would fill me with such angst, I discovered that my concerns about aesthetic integrity were the stuff of self-manufactured illusion.

The real enemy was much closer at hand.

When I recall my university teaching experience, I like most to remember those fall mornings when maple leaves swirled across the lawns between red-brick buildings, and I walked to my lit class with a genuine feeling of expectation and happiness about the day that lay ahead.

But I learned another reality about university life. When money becomes short, when jobs are endangered, a pervasive and abiding fear can engender itself in the faculty and cause them to behave in a manner that you would not associate with higher education.

Don't get involved, I would tell myself. *It's their bailiwick, stay out of it, you'll only lose.*

Sometimes I took my own counsel. Often I did not. And I lost every time. I had forgotten the lesson from that parish prison of years ago. I had forgotten that collective fear can make murderers of us all.

Fear was the enemy, I thought. Fear allows the ape to be reborn in us. It kills all joy and charity in our lives. It gives us the memory of Claude Vidrine and the memory of the man he murdered. It alone was responsible for almost every mistake in my life, even my grandiose desire to impose what I thought was academic integrity on those around me. My frustration and anger were based on vanity and the desire to control, and my vanity and presumption of righteousness were so great I was even willing to let them damage my art.

Even though I no longer kicked over baskets of snakes in

my mind with whatever kind of alcohol was at hand, I had found another way that worked just as well.

I think Claude Vidrine was probably standup. He had to be, or he would have taken his own life before the night they shaved his head and rubbed the electrode paste on his skin with wood spatulas because they considered him so different from themselves they didn't want to unnecessarily touch his person.

When he heard music drift up from the street far below and the laughter of people who would go home that night and make love, when he smelled the cold, ozone-laced odor of the impending storm, I wonder if he learned a secret that he wanted to whisper to us from behind that black face cloth.

I suspect that he did.

Uncle Sidney and the Mexicans

Billy Haskel and I were picking tomatoes in the same row, dropping them by the handful in the baskets on the mule-drawn wood sled, when the crop duster came in low over the line of trees by the river and began spraying the field next to us.

'The wind's going to drift it right across us,' Billy Haskel said. 'Turn away from it and hold your breath.'

Billy Haskel was white, but he made his living as a picker just like the Mexicans did. The only other white pickers in the field were a couple of high school kids like myself. People said Billy had been in the South Pacific during the war, and that was why he wasn't right in the head and drank all the time. He kept a pint of wine in the bib of his overalls, and when we completed a row he'd kneel down below the level of the tomato bushes as though he were going to take a leak and raise the bottle high enough for two deep swallows. By midafternoon, when the sun was white and scalding, the heat and wine would take him and he would talk in the lyrics from hillbilly songs.

My woman has gone
To the wild side of life
Where the wine and whiskey flow,
And now my little boy
Calls another man Daddy.

But this morning he was still sober and his mind was on the dust.

'The grower tells you it don't hurt you to breathe it. That ain't true. It works in your lungs like little sparks. They make holes in you so the air goes out in your chest and don't come back out your windpipe. You ain't listening to me, are you?'

'Sure I was.'

'You got your mind on Juanita over there. I don't blame you. If I hadn't got old I'd be looking at her too.'

I was watching her, sometimes without even knowing it. She was picking ahead of us three rows over, and her brown legs and the fold of her midriff where she had tied back her denim shirt under her breasts were always in the corner of my eye. Her hands and arms were dusty, and when she tried to push the damp hair out of her eyes with the back of her wrist, she left a gray wet streak on her forehead. Sometimes when I was picking even in the row with her I saw her look at her shirtfront to see if it was buttoned all the way.

I wanted to talk with her, to say something natural and casual as I picked along beside her, but when I planned the words they seemed stupid and embarrassing. I knew she wanted me to talk with her, too, because sometimes she spoke to Billy Haskel when he was working between us, but it was as though she were aiming through him at me. If only I could be as relaxed and easy as Billy was, I thought, even though he did talk in disjointed song lyrics.

It was raining hard Saturday morning, and we had to wait two hours on the crew bus before we could go into the

12

field. Billy was in a hung-over stupor from Friday night, and he must have slept in his clothes because they smelled of stale beer and I saw talcum powder from the poolroom on his sleeves. He stared sleepily out the window at the raindrops and started to pull on a pint bottle of urine-yellow muscatel. By the time the sky cleared he had finished it and started on a short dog, a thirty-nine-cent bottle he bought for a dollar from a Mexican on the bus.

He was in great shape the rest of the morning. While we were bent over the tomatoes, he appointed himself driver of the sled and monitor of our work. He must have recited every lyric ever sung on the 'Grand Ole Opry.' When we passed close to a clump of live oaks, he started to eye the tomatoes in the baskets and the trunks of the trees.

'Some of these 'maters has already got soft. Not even good for canning,' he said. 'Do you know I tried out for Waco before the war? I probably could have made it if I hadn't got drafted.'

Then he let fly with a tomato and nailed an oak tree dead center in a shower of red pulp.

The preacher, Mr. Willis, saw him from across the field. I watched him walk slowly across the rows toward where we were picking, his back erect, his ironed dark blue overalls and cork sun helmet like a uniform. Mr. Willis had a church just outside of Yoakum and was also on the town council. My Uncle Sidney said that Mr. Willis made sure no evangelist got a permit to hold a revival anywhere in the county so that all the Baptist soul-saving would be done in one church house only.

I bent into the tomatoes, but I could feel him standing behind me.

'Is Billy been drinking in the field again?' he said.

'Sir?'

'There's nothing wrong with your hearing, is there, Hack? Did you see Billy with a bottle this morning?'

'I wasn't paying him much mind.'

'What about you, Juanita?'

'Why do you ask me?' She kept working along the row without looking up.

'Because sometimes your brother brings short dogs on the bus and sells them to people like Billy Haskel.'

'Then you can talk with my brother and Billy Haskel. Then when my brother calls you a liar you can fire him, and the rest of us will leave too.'

Both Mr. Willis and I stared at her. At that time in Texas a Mexican, particularly a young girl who did piecework in a vegetable field, didn't talk back to a white person. Mr. Willis' grey eyes were so hot and intense that he didn't even blink at the drops of sweat that rolled from the liner of his sun helmet into his brows.

'Billy's been picking along with the rest of us, Mr. Willis,' I said. 'He just cuts up sometime when it's payday.'

'You know that, huh?'

I hated his sarcasm and righteousness and wondered how anyone could be fool enough to sit in a church and listen to this man talk about the gospel.

He walked away from us, stepping carefully over each row, his starched overalls creasing neatly behind the knees. Billy was at the water can in the shade of the oaks with his back to Mr. Willis and was just buttoning his shirt over his stomach when he heard or felt Mr. Willis behind him.

'Lord God Almighty, you give me a start there, Preacher,' he said.

'You know my rule, Billy.'

'If you mean chunking the 'mater, I guess you got me.'

Mr. Willis reached out and took the bottle from under the flap of Billy's shirt. He unscrewed the cap and poured the wine on the ground. Billy's face reddened and he opened and closed his hands in desperation.

'Oh, sweet Lord, you do punish a man,' he said.

Mr. Willis started walking toward his house at the far end of the field, holding the bottle lightly with two fingers and swinging the last drops onto the ground. Then he stopped, his back still turned toward us, as though a thought were working itself towards completion in his head, and came back to the water can with his gray eyes fixed benignly on Billy Haskel's face.

'I can't pay a man for drinking in the field,' he said. 'You had better go on home today.'

'I picked for you many a season, Preacher.'

'That's right, and so you knew my rule. This stuff's going to kill you one day, and that's why I can't pay you while you do it.'

Billy swallowed and shook his head. He needed the work, and he was on the edge of humiliating himself in front of the rest of us. Then he blinked his eyes and blew his breath up into his face.

'Well, like they say, I was looking for a job when I found this one,' he said. 'I'll get my brother to drive me out this afternoon for my check.'

He walked to the blacktop, and I watched him grow smaller in the distant pools of heat that shimmered on the tar surfacing. Then he walked over a rise between two cornfields and was gone.

'That's my fault,' Juanita said.

'He would have fired him anyway. I've seen him do it to people before.'

'No, he stopped and came back because he was thinking of what I said. He couldn't have gone to his house without showing us something.'

'You don't know Mr. Willis. He won't pay Billy for today, and that's one day's wage he's kept in his pocket.'

She didn't answer, and I knew that she wasn't going to talk the rest of the afternoon. I wanted to do something awful to Mr. Willis.

At five o'clock we lined up by the bus to be paid. Clouds had moved across the sun, and the breeze was cool off the river. In the shadow of the bus the sweat dried on our faces and left lines in the dust film like brown worms. Billy's brother came out in a pickup truck to get Billy's check. I was right about Mr. Willis: he didn't pay Billy for that day. The brother started to argue, then gave it up and said, 'I reckon the sun would come up green if you didn't try to sharp him, Preacher.'

Juanita was standing in front of me. She had taken her bandanna down, and her Indian hair fell on her shoulders like flat star points. She began pushing it away from the nape of her neck until it lay evenly across her back. Someone bumped against me and made me brush right into her rump. I had to bite my teeth at the quiver that went through my loins.

'Do you want to go to the root beer place on the highway?' I said.

'I never go there.'

'So tonight's a good time to start.'

'All right.'

That easy, I thought. Why didn't I do it before? But maybe I knew, and if I didn't, Mr. Willis was just about to tell me.

After he gave me my check he asked me to walk to his car with him before I got on the bus.

'During the summer a boy can get away from his regular friends and make other friends that don't have anything to do with his life. Do you know what I mean?' he said.

'Maybe I don't want to know what you mean, Mr. Willis.'

'Your father is a university teacher. I don't think he'd like what you're doing.'

My face felt dead and flat, as though it had been stung with his open hand.

'I'm not going to talk with you anymore. I'm going to get on the bus now,' I said.

'All right, but you remember this, Hack — a redbird doesn't sit on a blackbird's nest.'

I stepped onto the bus and pulled the folding doors closed behind me. Mr. Willis' face slipped by the windows as we headed down the dusty lane. Somebody was already sitting next to Juanita, and I was glad because I was so angry I couldn't have talked to anyone.

We got to the produce market in Yoakum, Juanita gave me her address (a street name belonging to a vague part of town with clapboard houses and dirt yards), and I drove Uncle Sidney's pickup out to his house in the country.

My mother was dead and my father was teaching southern history for the summer at the university in Austin, and so I lived with my Uncle Sidney. He raised tomatoes, melons, beans, corn, and squash, and anything he planted grew better and bigger than any other crop in the county. He always had the fattest turkeys and best-fed Angus and Brahmas, and each year his preserves won a couple of prizes at the county fair.

But he was also the most profane man I ever knew. When provoked he could use obscenities in combinations that made people's heads reel. My father said Uncle Sidney used to drink a lot when he was younger, and when he got drunk in a beer joint in Yoakum or Cuero, it would take six policemen to put him in jail. He had been a marine in the trenches during World War I and had brought tuberculosis home with him and over the years had had two relapses because he smoked constantly. He rolled cigarettes out of five-cent Bull Durham bags, but he would roll only two or three cigarettes before he threw the bag away and opened another one. So there were Bull Durham sacks all over the farm, stained brown with the rain and running into the soil.

When Uncle Sidney was serious about something, it came out in a subtle, intense, and unexpected way that embedded itself under the skin like a thorn. One day two summers earlier I had been hunting jackrabbits on his place with his Winchester .22 automatic and I hadn't had a shot all afternoon. I just wanted to shoot something, anything, and hear the snap of the rifle and smell the cordite in the hot air. A solitary dove flew from a grove of blackjacks, and I led her with the rifle and let off three quick shots. The third one snipped her head off right at the shoulders. It was an incredible shot. I carried her in my pocket back to the house and showed her to Uncle Sidney, the fact that I had killed a dove two months out of season far from my mind.

'You think that's slick, do you?' he said. 'Are you going to feed her young in the nest? Are you going to be there when their hunger sounds bring a fox down on them? You put my rifle in the rack and don't touch it again.'

I pulled the pickup truck into the yard and cut the engine, but the cylinders continued to fire with postignition for another fifteen seconds. The pickup was actually a wreck without two inches of the original paint on it in one place and with the World War II gas-rationing stickers still on the cracked windshield even though it was 1947. I walked around behind the house and took the chain off the windmill, undressed, and began pulling the ticks off my body in the jet of water that pumped out of the pipe over the trough. Some of the ticks that had been on me since early morning had worked their heads deep into the skin and were as big as pennies with my blood. I shivered each time I dug one out with my fingernails and popped it in a red spray.

'I'll be goddamn go-to-hell if it ain't ole Satchel-ass,' Uncle Sidney said from the back porch.

Sidney's battered straw hat, curled up at the brim and slanted sideways on his head, and his cowboy boots, which were worn down at the heels, always made him look like he was rocking when he walked. He was all angles: elbows stuck out as though they were about to cave a rib cage, knees askew from the direction of his boots, a quizzically turned head, a crooked smile. His skin was burned and cracked by the sun, and he had a grip and callouses that could shale the edge off of old brick. He had ridden in rodeos when he was younger and had been

18

slammed into the boards so many times by Brahmas that every bone in him popped when he got out of a chair.

I chained the blades on the windmill and started into the house to finish my bath in the tub.

'Can I use the pickup tonight?' I said.

'Sure. But you don't look too happy about wherever it is you're going.'

'It's that damn Mr. Willis.'

'What did he do to you?'

'He didn't do anything to me. He fired Billy Haskel.'

'Was Billy drinking in the field again?'

'It was the way he did it. He treated him like a child.'

'Billy's a grown man. He can take care of himself.'

'That's just it. Billy was fighting the Japs while Mr. Willis was cleaning up selling to the government.'

'Satch, what you done in last Saturday's ball game ain't worth piss on a rock.'

An hour later I was driving down the blacktop in the mauve-colored evening, my hair combed back wet, the smell of the fields blowing cool in my face. Rain clouds hung like bruised fruit on the horizon, and the crack of dying sun on the edge of the land sent long shafts of spinning light across the sky. The breeze bent the corn along the tops of the stalks, and jackrabbits sat in the short grass by the side of the road with their ears turned up in vees. Dead and salted crows had been nailed to the cedar fence posts to keep the live ones out of the field, and their feathers fluttered like a bad afterthought.

I didn't understand the feeling I had, but it was like both fear and guilt and at the same time neither one. I had never thought of myself as being afraid of other people, but maybe that was because I had never been in a situation when I had had to be afraid. Now people whom I had never thought about came into my mind: boys at school who never called Mexicans anything but pepper-bellies, the café owner who would turn a Mexican around in the door before he could even reach the serving counter; the theater manager in Cuero who was suddenly sold out of tickets when anyone with skin darker than a suntan came to his box office.

I saw her sitting in a swing on her front porch. She wore a white blouse with a round collar and a full flower-print skirt, and she had put a red hibiscus in her hair. She closed the truck door, and we banged over the ruts and drove out on the highway toward the root beer stand.

'I talked with my father about Billy Haskel,' she said. 'He's an organizer for the pickers. He's going to try to get him on in another field.'

'Your father's in that?'

'Yes. Why?' She turned her head at me, and the wind blew her hair across her cheek.

'Nothing. I just heard some things the growers say about it.'

'What do they say?'

'I don't know, they're communists, stuff like that.'

'My father's not a communist. None of them are.'

'I don't care about that kind of stuff, Juanita.'

'Your uncle is a grower.'

'He's nothing like Mr. Willis, or some of the others. He doesn't hire wetbacks and he wouldn't fire somebody for drinking in the field.'

Up ahead we saw the lights of the root beer stand and the cars and pickups with metal trays on the windows parked in the gravel under the canvas awning.

'Are we going inside?' she said.

'I don't care.'

'Let's get it in the truck.'

'Sure, if you want to.'

'Hack, you don't have to take me here. We can just go for a drive.'

'What's the big deal about a root beer stand? I should have asked you to the show, except they're still playing Johnny Mack Brown.'

'You don't have to prove something for me. I know

you're a good person.'

'Don't talk like that. We're just getting some root beer.'

But while we waited for the waitress to walk out to the pickup, my hands were damp on the steering wheel and I was conscious of the conversations and the glow of cigarettes in the cars around us. The waitress in red-and-white uniform set the tray on the window and looked at me for the order, then her eyes went past my face into Juanita's.

'What, say it again,' she said.

'Two root beers. One root beer and then another one on the same tray,' I said.

The waitress went away and then looked back over her shoulder at us.

'Don't be sarcastic with her,' Juanita said.

'I know that girl. She's got tractor oil in her head.'

I picked up one of the heavy ice-filmed mugs and handed it to Juanita. When I reached back for mine, I saw a boy from my baseball team walking past the window toward the rest room.

'Hey, Hack. You keeping your arm in shape for next year?' He looked into the truck, his eyes full of light and curiosity.

'I throw a few every evening against a target on my uncle's barn.'

'This man's a mean motor scooter on the mound,' he said to Juanita. 'He's got a Carl Hubbell screwball that wipes the letters off a batter.'

'Yeah, I'm so good I dusted three guys in our district game.'

'That don't matter. Those guys thought sheep-dip didn't stink till you put their noses in it.'

'I'll have better control next season. Look, we'll see you later, Ben.'

'Sure. Take it easy, Hack.'

A minute later he backed his car around to leave the lot, and I saw the white oval faces of two people looking out the back window at us. He burned out onto the highway in a scorch of gravel.

*

A week later Johnny Mack Brown was still playing at the theater in town, so I took Juanita to the double feature at the drive-in. I parked the pickup to the side of the concession stand, and when the lot darkened I put my arm around her shoulders. Her eyes were still on the screen, but when I lowered my head against hers she turned her face up at me with her lips parted. She laid her wrist on the back of my neck when we kissed and brushed her lips sideways on my mouth. I put my face in her hair and could smell the soap and baby powder on her shoulders.

The cab of the pickup had not been designed for romance. The floor stick, even jammed into reverse, stuck up between us like a convent wall, and our elbows and knees banged against the dashboard, the windows, the door handles, and the gun rack. By intermission I had another problem, too: what we used to call the hot rocks, a thick ache in the genitals that made you think someone had poured concrete in your fly. Usually the only way to get rid of it, besides the most obvious way, was to get out and lift the truck bumper. This went on all the time back on neckers' row, but I waited for the intermission and just sat quietly behind the steering wheel for five minutes and then headed for the concession stand.

That was a mistake.

When I went into the men's room – a hot, fetid place that reeked of disinfectant and urinated beer, with an exhaust fan on one wall – a dozen high school boys were inside, leaning over the troughs and passing around a bottle of sloe gin in a paper sack. Someone was throwing up in the toilet cubicle. The room was almost silent while I waited for my turn at the trough.

'Hey, Hack, who's that girl in your truck?'

'Just a friend.'

'Is she a Mexican?' It was the same boy, and his question

was almost innocent.

'It's none of your damn business what she is.'

There was no sound except the dirty noise of the exhaust fan. Then, from a tall kid in cowboy boots, blue jeans, an immaculate white T-shirt, and a straw hat, who leaned against the wall with one foot propped behind him:

'Is is true that Mexican fur burger tastes like jalapeño?'

A left-handed pitcher has certain advantages on the mound, but so does a left-handed fistfighter, because your opponent instinctively watches your right hand as the area of potential damage. I swung upwards from my left side and caught him on the mouth and knocked his head in the cinder-block wall. When he wrenched his head straight again, his fists already flying out at me, I saw the blood in his teeth like a smear of food dye. We fought all over the room (someone shot the bolt on the door so the manager couldn't get in), careening against bodies and troughs and trash cans, and I got him twice more in the face and once so hard in the throat that spittle flew from his mouth, but his arms were longer than mine and he clubbed me into a corner between the toilet cubicle and the wall and I couldn't get my elbows back to swing. His fists, white and ridged with bone, seemed to appear and explode against my face so fast that for a moment I thought someone else was swinging with him.

But the other person turned out to be the manager, who had broken the door jamb and was pulling the tall boy off me.

The boy relaxed his arms and caught his breath.

'The next time you bring a greaser to the drive-in, you better be able to take it,' he said.

I wanted to hit him again, but I was finished. I walked out into the parking lot past groups of people who stared at my torn and blood-streaked clothes and the long strip of damp toilet paper that was stuck to one of my loafers. I got into the pickup and slammed the door. Juanita's mouth opened and her fingers jerked up toward her face.

'Forget it,' I said. I started the engine and bounced out into the aisle, then I heard glass snap and heavy iron smash against the rear fender. I had forgotten to remove the speaker and had torn the pipe and concrete base right out of the ground, which was all right, but I had also broken off the top half of Uncle Sidney's window.

Uncle Sidney started attending the meetings of the Growers' Association. They met on Tuesday nights at the Baptist church, and if you drove by and saw the pickups parked in the grove of oak trees, the fireflies sparkling in the summer dark, and the heads of men through the lighted windows, you thought only that a church meeting was going on and a group trip to Dallas or a new building was being planned. But beyond the noise of the cicadas they were talking about the Mexican farm workers' union and communists, their minds melding together in fear, their vocabulary finding words that were as foreign to their world as peasants' revolutions in Russia.

'Why do you have to go there?' I said to Uncle Sid. He was sitting on the porch step in his shiny suit with the trousers tucked inside his boots. The fire of his hand-rolled, brown-streaked cigarette was no more than a quarter inch from his lips.

'Why shouldn't I go there?'

'Because they're dumb people.'

'Well, there is a couple that was probably playing with their knobs when God passed out the brains. But some-times you got to stick together, Satchel-ass. If these Mexicans are serious about a strike, they can do us some real harm.'

I watched him drive down the road in the dusty twilight, past the pond where under the surface the late sun was trapped in a red ball as motionless and dead as my heart.

But I should have had more faith in Uncle Sid. I should have known he was too angular to fit very long with a bunch like the Growers' Association. The next Tuesday night, when I had gotten Juanita to come over for dinner, he came back from the meeting so mad that you could have lighted a kitchen match by touching it to his face.

'What happened?' I said.

'That little whipsnip of a preacher stood up in front of the meeting and said I was working a couple of Mexicans that was communists. And anybody that kept communists on his payroll after he knew about them might just stand some looking into himself. Then a couple other of them mealymouth sons of bitches turned around and looked at me and said maybe every grower ought to make out a list of who was working for him.'

'Mr. Willis likes to put a finger in your eye if he can.'

'Juanita, I got to hire on six more men next week. You ask your daddy to send me a half dozen of them union Mexicans or nigras or whatever they are. I don't bargain on wages, I pay by the piece, but they'll get more than they will from the likes of that preacher. Just make sure your daddy gets me six hard workers that ain't welcomed nowhere.'

It was a strange collection that showed up at the house the next week: two old men, a boy, a one-armed man, a Negro, and Billy Haskel.

'When did you get in the union, Billy?' Uncle Sid said.

'I figured it wouldn't do no harm. I ain't worked nowhere since Mr. Willis run me off.'

'Is that you, José? I thought you were in the pen.'

'They let me out.'

'Well, all right, boys. You can pick up your baskets at the barn. Come back to the house at noon for your lunch.'

Uncle Sid watched them walk across the lot, his hat tilted sideways on his head.

'Damn, is that the bunch that's got people spraying in their britches all over the county?' he said.

Two nights later it was hot and breathless, and dry lightning was flashing on the horizon. I kept waking up every hour, caught between bad dreams and the hot

25

silence of the house. Toward morning I felt the heat begin to go out of the air, and as my eyes closed with real sleep, I saw the lightning patterns flicker on the wallpaper. Then something in my sleep told me that the color was wrong – the cobalt white had been replaced by red and yellow, and there was a smell of rubber burning.

I heard Uncle Sidney walk from his bedroom to the gun rack in the kitchen and then open the front screen door.

'What is it?' I said, pulling on my Levis.

'Look there. It was done by somebody with experience. They nailed strips of tires along the wood to give it extra heat.'

The cross was fifteen feet high and burning brightly from top to bottom. Strings of smoke rose from the crosspiece like dirty handkerchiefs, and in the distance I saw a flatbed truck roaring down the dirt road toward the blacktop.

Uncle Sid shaved, put on a fresh pair of overalls, and sat down at the kitchen table with a coffee cup and note pad.

'What are you doing?' I said. Outside, the light had climbed into the sky, and I could hear a breeze rattle the windmill blades.

'Making out a list of genuine sons of bitches and possible sons of bitches. While I'm doing this, Satch, see if Billy Haskel's here yet, and you and him put that cross in the back of the pickup. It probably won't fit, so get a boomer chain out of the barn.'

Billy and I loaded up the charred cross and propped the top end against the cab and stretched a chain across the shaft. I hooked on a boomer and locked it down tight.

'The sheriff ain't going to be too happy when your uncle drops this smelly thing in his office,' Billy said.

Uncle Sidney walked out of the house with his note pad in his shirt pocket. He had on his new short-brim Stetson hat, a cigarette twisted in the side of his mouth. His knees rose against his stiff overalls.

'What are we doing?' I said.

'Cutting a notch in their butts. You boys hop in.'

We drove out to Mr. Willis' farm and saw him in the field not far from the road. He tried to ignore us at first by looking in the other direction, but Uncle Sidney began blowing on the horn until every picker in the rows had stopped and was staring past Mr. Willis at us. His face was tight when he walked over to us.

'Somebody left this in my front yard last night and I want it to get back to the right place,' Uncle Sidney said. 'You reckon I ought to leave it here?'

'I don't have any idea of what you're talking about.'

'I don't blame you for lying. It ain't easy to sit in your own shit.'

'You can leave my property, Mr. Holland.'

'I will, in just a minute. But first, my nephew tells me you beat Billy Haskel here out of a day's wage. Now, Billy's a poor man and I think you ought to dip down in your billfold, Preacher.'

Mr. Willis' face grew tighter and he tried to hold his gaze on Uncle Sidney's eyes. Then his hand went woodenly to his back pocket as though he couldn't control it.

'I'll pay him just to get you off my place.'

'No, you'll pay him because I told you to. And the next time you send thugs around my house, I'm going to catch you in town, out in public, and you're not going to want to live around here anymore.'

We drove out to Zack's on the blacktop, and Uncle Sid bought two six-cartons of Lone Star and filled the cartons with cracked ice to keep the bottles cold. Then we headed for the house of the next farmer on the list, and by noon we had worked our way across the county to the town. Warning must have gotten there ahead of us, because the hardware-and-feed store was locked, a farmer who hadn't been home earlier almost ran to his truck when he saw us, and a deputy sheriff's car began to follow us through the streets. People stared from the high concrete sidewalks at

27

the blackened cross in the bed of the pickup while Uncle Sidney sat casually behind the wheel with his arm in the window, his beer bottle filled with amber sunlight. At the traffic light a man in a straw hat, colorless denims, and laced boots stepped off the curb and walked over to the running board.

'Mr. Holland, I'm a member of the Association, but I didn't have nothing to do with this business,' he said.

'I didn't figure you did, Mr. Voss.'

Mr. Voss nodded and crossed the street.

'This is so much fun we ought to do it all over again,' Billy Haskel said.

That afternoon Uncle Sidney told me to drive the cross down to the creek bed and dump it, but I replied that I'd like to keep it in the truck until the weekend. On Saturday evening I picked up Juanita and took her to the drive-in movie, ignoring her argument and her glances through the back window at the cross vibrating under the boomer chain. People whom I hardly knew said hello to us, and during the intermission some boys from the baseball team gathered around the truck and drank warm beer with their feet on the running boards. The truck became not only the respected center of the parking lot for every group there but an excoriated symbol of difference that ennobled the individual who was allowed to stand in the circle around it. The beer cans rattled on the gravel, the laughter rose louder, people crawled and banged around on the cab roof, and finally the manager threw us all out. That was in 1947, the year I pitched four shutouts and learned not to think about them.

Losses

for Philip Spitzer

S trange things happened to me in the fifth grade at St. Peter's Catholic School in 1944. One morning I woke up and felt guilty because I had thoughts about the breasts of the Negro women who worked in the lunchroom. Then I started to feel guilty about everything; an idle or innocent activity of only a few days ago now became a dark burden on my soul. I had looked at a picture of a nude statue in a book, repeated profane words I'd heard older boys use down at the filling station, noticed for the first time the single woman next door hanging her undergarments on the clothesline.

I confessed my bad thoughts and desires to Father Melancon but it did no good. I felt the light going out of the world and I didn't know why. My sins throbbed in my chest like welts raised by a whip. When I lay in my bed at night, with the winter rain hitting against the window glass, my fists clenched under the sheets, my mind would fill with fearful images of the war and eternal perdition, which somehow melded together in an apocalyptical vision of the world's fiery end.

Out on the Gulf southeast of New Iberia, Nazi submarines had torpedoed oil tankers that sailed unescorted out of the mouth of the Mississippi. Shrimpers told stories about the fires that burned on the horizon late at night and the horribly charred sailor that one skipper had pulled up in his shrimp net. I knew that the Nazis and the Japanese had killed people from New Iberia, too. When the war broke out, families hung a small flag with a blue star on a white field in the window to show they had a boy in service. As the war progressed, many of those blue stars were replaced by gold ones; sometimes the lawns of those small wood frame houses remained uncut, the rolled newspapers moldered in the flower beds, the shades were drawn and never raised again.

I believed that a great evil was at work in the world.

My mother, who was a Baptist from Texas and who did not go to church, said my thoughts were foolish. She said the real devil in the world lived in a bottle of whiskey. She meant the whiskey that made my father drunk, that kept him at Broussard's Bar down on Railroad Avenue after he got fired from the oil rig.

I heard them late on a Saturday night. It was raining hard, lightning jumped outside the window, and our pecan tree thrashed wildly on the roof.

'You not only fall down in your own yard, you've spent our money on those women. I can smell them on you,' she said.

'I stopped at Provost's and shot pool. I put some beers on the tab. I didn't spend anything.'

'Empty your pockets, then. Show me the money I'm going to use for his lunches next week.'

'I'll take care of it. I always have. Father Melancon knows we've had some bad luck.'

'Jack, I won't abide this. I'll take him with me back to Beaumont.'

'No ma'am, you won't.'

'Don't you come at me, Jack. I'll have you put in the parish jail.'

'You're an evil-mouthed woman. You're a nag and you degrade a man in front of his son.'

'I'm picking up the phone. So help me. . . . I won't tolerate it.'

I don't think he hit her; he just slammed out the door into the rain and backed his truck over the wood stakes and chicken wire that bordered our Victory garden. My arms were pinched on my ears, but I could hear my mother crying while the water kettle screamed on the stove.

My fifth-grade teacher was Sister Uberta, who had come to us from the North that year. Her face was pretty and round inside her nun's wimple, but it glowed as bright as paper when she was angry, and sometimes she shouted at us for no reason. Her hands were white and quick whenever she wrote on the blackboard or helped us make color-paper posters for the lunchroom walls. She seemed to have an energy that was about to burst out of her black habit. Her stories in catechism class made me swallow and grip the bottoms of my thighs.

'If you wonder what eternity means, imagine an iron ball as big as the earth out in the middle of space,' she said. 'Then once every thousand years a sparrow flies from the moon to that iron ball and brushes one wing against its surface. And by the time that bird's feathery wing has worn away the iron ball to a burnt cinder, eternity is just beginning.'

I couldn't breathe. The oaks outside the window were gray and trembling in the rain. I wanted to resist her words, what they did to me, but I wasn't strong enough. In my childish desperation I looked across the aisle at Arthur Boudreau, who was folding a paper airplane and never worried about anything.

Arthur's head was shaped like a light bulb. His burr haircut was mowed so close into the scalp that it glistened like a peeled onion. He poured inkwells into fishbowls, thumbtacked girls' dresses to the desks, put formaldehyde frogs from the science lab in people's lunch sandwiches.

'Claude, are you talking to Arthur?' Sister Uberta said.

'No, Sister.'

'You were, weren't you?'

'No, Sister.'

'I want you to stay after school today.'

At three o'clock the other children sprinted through the rain for home, and Sister Uberta made me wash the blackboards. She put away her books and papers in her desk, then sat down behind it with her hands folded in front of her. Her hands looked small and white against the back folds of her habit.

'That's enough,' she said. 'Come up here and sit down.'

I walked to the front of the room and did as she said. My footsteps seemed loud on the wooden floor.

'Do you know why Arthur misbehaves, Claude?' she said.

'I don't think he's that bad.'

'He does bad things and then people pay attention to him. Do you want to be like that?'

'No, Sister.'

She paused and her large brown eyes examined my face from behind her big, steel-rimmed glasses. She made me feel funny inside. I was afraid of her, afraid of what her words about sin could do to me, but I felt a peculiar kinship with her, as though she and I understood something about loss and unhappiness that others didn't know about.

'You didn't buy a scapula for Sodality Sunday,' she said.

'My father isn't working now.'

'I see.' She opened the bottom drawer to her desk, where she kept her paint set, and took out a small medal on a chain. 'You take this one, then. If your father buys you one later, you can give mine to someone else. That way, you pass on the favor.'

She smiled and her face was truly beautiful. Then her mouth turned downward in a melancholy way and she said, 'But, Claude, remember this: there are people we shouldn't get close to; they'll cause us great trouble.

Arthur is one of them. He'll hurt you.'

A week later I was back at the confessional with another problem. The inside of the church was cool and smelled of stone and water and burning candles. I looked at Father Melancon's silhouette through the confessional screen. He had played bush-league baseball before he became a priest, and he was still thin and athletic and wore his graying hair in a crewcut.

'Bless me, Father, for I have sinned,' I began.

He waited, the side of his face immobile.

'Tell me what it is, Claude.' His voice was soft but I thought I heard him take a tired breath.

'Sister Uberta says it's a sin to use bad words.'

'Well, that depends on . . .'

'She said if you heard somebody else use them, you have to tell on them or you're committing a sin, too.'

Father Melancon pinched the bridge of his nose between his eyes. I felt my face burn with my own shame and weakness.

'Who did you hear using bad words?' he said.

'I don't want to tell, Father.'

'Do you think it's going out of this confessional?'

'No . . . I don't know.'

'You've got to have some trust in me, Claude.'

'It was Arthur Boudreau.'

'Now you listen to me. There's nothing wrong with Arthur Boudreau. The Lord put people like Arthur here to keep the rest of us honest. Look, you're worrying about all kinds of things that aren't important. Sister Uberta means well but sometimes . . . well, she works too hard at it. This might be hard for you to understand now, but sometimes when people are having trouble with one part of their lives, the trouble pops up someplace else that's perfectly innocent.'

I only became more confused, more convinced that I was caught forever inside my unexplained and unforgivable guilt.

'Claude, spring and baseball season are going to be here soon, and I want you to think about that and try to forget all this other stuff. How is your daddy?'

'He's gone away.'

I saw his lips crimp inward, and he touched his forehead with his fingertips. It was a moment before he spoke again.

'Don't be too hard on him,' he said. 'He'll come back one day. You'll see. In the meantime you tell Arthur to get his fast ball in shape.'

'Father, I can't explain what I feel inside me.'

I heard him sigh deeply on the other side of the screen.

That night I sat by the big wood radio with the tiny yellow dial in our living room and listened to the 'Louisiana Hayride' and oiled my fielder's glove. My mother was ironing in the kitchen. She had started taking in laundry, which was something done only by Negro women at that time in New Iberia. I worked the Neetsfoot oil into my glove, then fitted a ball deep into the pocket and tied down the fingers with twine to give it shape. The voices of the country musicians on the radio and the applause of their audience seemed beamed to me from a distant place that was secure from war and the sins that pervaded the world. I fell asleep sitting in the big chair with my hand inside my fielder's glove.

I awoke to an electric storm, a huge vortex of air swirling around our house, and a static-filled news report about waves of airplanes that were carpet-bombing the earth.

Spring didn't come with baseball season; it arrived one day with the transfer of Rene LeBlanc from boarding school to my fifth-grade class. Her hair was auburn and curly and seemed transfused with light when she sat in her desk by the window. Her almond eyes were always full of light, too, and they looked at you in a curious, open way that made something drop inside you. Her cream-colored pleated skirt swung on her hips when she walked to the blackboard, and while she worked an arithmetic problem with the chalk, her face thoughtful under Sister Uberta's gaze, I'd look at the smooth, white curve of her neck, the redness of her mouth, the way her curls moved with the air from the fan, the outline of her slip strap against her blouse, and in my fantasies I'd find ways to sit next to her at morning mass or in the lunchroom or maybe to touch her moist hand during the recess softball game.

But even though she was French and Catholic, she didn't belong to the Cajun world I came from. She lived in a huge, pillared home on Spanish Lake. It had a deep, green lawn, with water sprinklers turning on it in the sunlight, a pea-gravel drive shaded by rows of mossy oaks, and a clay tennis court and riding ring in back beyond which the blue lake winked through the cypress trees. Some of the other kids said she was a snob. But I knew better. Silently I gave her my heart.

I never thought a time would come when I could offer it to her openly, but one fine spring afternoon, when the air was heavy with the bloom of azalea and jasmine and myrtle and the wind blew through the bamboo and clumps of oaks along East Main, Arthur Boudreau and I walked home from school together and saw Rene, alone and under siege, at the bus stop.

A gang of boys who lived down by Railroad Avenue were on the opposite side of the street, flinging pecans at her. The pecans were still in their wet, moldy husks, and they thudded against her back and rump or exploded against the brick wall behind her. But her flushed, angry face had the solitary determination of a soldier's, and she wouldn't give an inch of ground. Her little fists were crossed in front of her like a knight-errant's.

Arthur Boudreau was not only a terror in any kind of fight, he had a pitching arm that could make batters wince when they saw a mean glint in his eye. In fact years later, when he pitched Class-C ball in the Evangeline League, people would say he could throw a baseball through a car wash without getting it wet.

We scooped up handfuls of pecans, Arthur mounted a garbage-can lid on his arm, and we charged the enemy across the street, slamming one pecan after another into their bodies. They tried to resist but Arthur had no mercy and they knew it. He nailed one boy in the back of the neck, another flush on the ear, and drove the garbage-can lid into the leader's face. They turned and ran down a side street toward the south side of town, one of them impotently shooting a finger and still shouting at us.

'Come around again and I'll kick this can up your hole,' Arthur yelled after them.

Rene brushed at the green stains on her blouse. There were still circles of color in her cheeks.

'We'll walk with you tomorrow in case those guys come back,' I said.

'I wasn't afraid,' she said.

'Those are bad guys. One of them beat up Arthur's little brother with a stick.'

But she wasn't buying it. She'd let those guys throw pecans at her every afternoon before she'd ask for help. She was that kind, a real soldier.

'I have a nickle,' I said. 'We can get a twin Popsicle at Veazey's.'

Her face hesitated a moment, then her eyes smiled at me.

'There's three of us,' she said.

'I don't want one. My mother always fixes something for me when I come home,' I said.

'I have some money,' she said. 'It's my treat today. Look at the scratch on your arm. You can get lockjaw from that. It's terrible. Your jaws turn to stone and they have to feed you through a tube in your nose.'

She wet her handkerchief with her tongue and wiped at the red welt on my forearm.

'I'm going to get some bandages at Veazey's and some

36

iodine and alcohol, and then you should go to the hospital later for shots,' she said. 'Here, I'll tie the handkerchief on it to keep out infection till we can wash it off. The air is full of germs.'

The three of us walked down to the ice-cream parlor next to the drawbridge that spanned Bayou Teche. Cypress trees grew along the banks of the bayou, and on the other side of the bridge the small gray-stone hospital run by the sisters was set back deep in the shade of the oaks. Purple wisteria grew on the trellises by the adjacent convent, and I could see some of the sisters in their white habits working in their Victory garden. Rene, Arthur, and I sat on the bridge and ate ice-cream cones, with our feet hanging over the water, and watched a shrimp boat move slowly down the bayou between the corridor of trees and bamboo. I knew that long, cypress-framed ribbon of brown water eventually flowed into the salt, where I believed Nazi submariners still waited to burn and drown the good people of the world, but on that spring afternoon, with the wind blowing through the trees and ruffling the water under our feet, the red and yellow hibiscus blazing on the convent lawn, the war had ended for me like heat thunder dying emptily over the Gulf.

Small drops of water started to dent the dust on the school playground. Through the bamboo that grew along the bayou's banks I could see the brown current being dimpled, too. We were a group of five boys by the corner of the school building, and Arthur Boudreau had a thin, cellophane-wrapped cardboard box enclosed in his palm.

'Hold out your hand,' he said. The other boys were grinning.

'What for?' I said.

'Put out your hand. What's the matter, you afraid?' he said.

'You put chewing gum in a guy's hand one time.'

'Well, you better not chew on these,' he said, grabbing

37

my wrist and pressing into my hand the thin white box with the image of a black Trojan horse on it.

I stared at it numbly. Both my hand and face felt dead. The boys were all laughing now.

'This is crazy. I don't want something like this,' I said, my voice rising, then catching in my throat like a nail.

'Sorry, they're yours now,' Arthur said.

I tried to push the box at Arthur. I felt wooden all over, my skin tainted with something loathsome and obscene.

'I found them behind Provost's pool hall. They got a machine there in the men's room,' Arthur said.

I was swallowing hard and my heart was clicking in my chest. My face rang with the kind of deadness you feel after you've been slapped.

'You're my friend, Arthur, but I don't want in on this kind of joke,' I said. I knew my voice was weak and childlike, and now I felt doubly ashamed.

'I don't want in on this joke because I'll piss my little diapers and my mommie will be mad at me,' one of the other boys said.

Then a second boy glanced sideways and whispered, 'Sister's looking!'

Thirty yards away Sister Uberta watched us with a curious, even gaze, her body and the wings of her habit absolutely motionless.

'Oh, shit,' Arthur said, and shoved the bunch of us around the corner of the building. I tripped on my shoes and revolved in a foolish circle, my hand still trying to give him back the box.

'Gimmie that,' he said, and slipped it into the back pocket of his jeans and walked hurriedly toward the opposite end of the building in the soft rain. His tennis shoes made stenciled impressions in the fine dust under the trees.

'Fling it in the coulee,' one of the boys called after him.

'Like hell I will. You haven't seen the last of these babies,' he answered. He grinned at us like a spider.

*

It was raining hard when we came back into the classroom from the playground. The raindrops tinked against the ginning blades of the window fan while Sister Uberta diagramed a compound sentence on the blackboard. Then we realized we were listening to another sound, too – a rhythmic thumping like a soft fist on the window glass.

Sister Uberta paused uncertainly with the chalk in her hand and looked at the window. Then her eyes sharpened, the blood drained from her face, and her jaws became ridged with bone.

Arthur Boudreau had filled the condom with water, knotted a string around one end, and suspended it from the third story so that it hung even with the window and swung back and forth against the glass in the wind. It looked like an obscene, bulbous nose pressed against the rain-streaked pane.

Some of the kids didn't know what it was; others giggled, scraped their feet under the desks in delight, tried to hide their gleeful faces on the desk tops. I watched Sister Uberta fearfully. Her face was bright and hard, her angry eyes tangled in thought, then she opened her desk drawer, removed a pair of scissors, lifted the window with more strength than I thought she could have, and in a quick motion snipped the string and sent the condom plummeting into the rain.

She brought the window down with one hand and the room became absolutely still. There was not a sound for a full minute. I could not bear to look at her. I studied my hands, my untied shoelaces, Arthur Boudreau's leg extended casually out into the aisle. A solitary drop of perspiration ran out of my hair and splashed on the desk top. I swallowed, raised my head, and saw that she was looking directly at me.

'That's what you had out on the playground, wasn't it?' she said.

'No, Sister,' I said desperately.

'Don't you compound what you've done by lying.'

'It was just a box. It wasn't mine.' I felt naked before her words. Everyone in the class was looking at me. My face was hot, and through my shimmering eyes I could see Rene LeBlanc watching me.

'Somebody else put you up to it, but you did it, didn't you?' she said.

'I didn't. I swear it, Sister.'

'Don't you swear, Claude. I saw you on the playground.'

'You didn't see it right, Sister. It wasn't me. I promise.'

'You took the box from Arthur, and then you made everybody laugh by bragging about what you were going to do.'

'I didn't know what was in it. I gave it –'

'You ran around the corner with it when you saw me watching.'

I looked over at Rene LeBlanc. Her face was stunned and confused. I felt as though I were drowning while other people watched, that I was hideous and perverse in her eyes and in the eyes of every decent person on the earth.

'Look at me,' Sister Uberta said. 'You weren't in this by yourself. Arthur put you up to it, and he's going to wait for me in Father Melancon's office at three o'clock, but you're going to stay here in this room and tell me the truth.'

'I have to help my daddy at the filling station,' Arthur said.

'Not today you don't,' Sister Uberta said.

Until the bell rang I kept my eyes fixed on the desk top and listened to the beating of my own heart and felt the sweat run down my sides. I couldn't look up again at Rene LeBlanc. My moment to exonerate myself had passed in failure, the class was listening to Sister talk about the Norman Conquest, and I was left alone with my bitter cup of gall, my fear-ridden, heart-thudding wait in Gethsemane. The three o'clock bell made my whole body jerk in the desk.

The other kids got their raincoats and umbrellas from the cloakroom and bolted for home. Then Sister sent

Arthur to Father Melancon's office to wait for her. I looked once at his face, praying against my own want of courage that he would admit his guilt and extricate me from my ordeal. But Arthur, even though he was ethical in his mischievous way, was not one to do anything in a predictable fashion. Sister Uberta and I were alone in the humid stillness of the classroom.

'You've committed a serious act, Claude,' she said. 'Do you still refuse to own up to it?'

'I didn't do anything.'

'All right, fine,' she said. 'Then you write that on this piece of paper. You write down that I didn't see you with something on the playground, that you don't know anything about what happened this afternoon.'

'I hate you.' The words were like the snap of a rubber band in my head. I couldn't believe I had said them.

'What did you say?'

My face was burning, and my head was spinning so badly that I had to grip the desk top as though I were falling.

'Stand up, Claude,' she said.

I rose to my feet. The backs of my legs were quivering. Her face was white and her eyeballs were clicking back and forth furiously.

'Hold out your hand,' she said.

I extended my hand and she brought the tricorner ruler down across my palm. My fingers curled back involuntarily and the pain shot up my forearm.

'I hate you,' I said.

She stared hard, incredulously, straight into my eyes, then gripped my wrist tightly in her hand and slashed the ruler down again. I could hear her breathing, see the pinpoints of sweat breaking out on her forehead under her wimple. She hit me again and examined my face for pain or tears or shock and saw none there and whipped the ruler down twice more. My palm shook like a dead, disembodied thing in her grip. Her face was trembling, as white and shining now as polished bone. Then suddenly I saw her eyes break, her expression crumple, her mouth drop open in a moan, and she flung her arms around me and pulled my head against her breast. Her face was pressed down on top of my head, and she was crying uncontrollably, her tears hot against my cheek.

'There, there, it's all right now,' Father Melancon was saying. He had walked quietly into the room and had put his big hands on each side of her shoulders. 'Hop on down to my office now and wait for me. It's all right now.'

'I've done a terrible thing, Father,' she said.

'It's not so bad. Go on and wait for me now. It's all right.'

'Yes, Father.'

'You're going to be all right.'

'Yes, yes, I promise.'

'That's a good girl,' he said.

She touched her tears away with her hand, widened her eyes stiffly, and walked from the room with her face stretched tight and empty. Father Melancon closed the door and sat down in the desk next to me. He looked tall and strange and funny sitting in the small desk.

'Arthur told me he's responsible for all this,' he said. 'I just wish he'd done it a little sooner. She was pretty rough on you, huh?'

'Not so much. I can take it.'

'That's because you're a stand-up guy. But I need to tell you something about Sister Uberta. It's between us men and it doesn't go any farther. Understand?'

'Sure.'

'You know, sometimes we look at a person and only see the outside, in other words the role that person plays in our own lives, and we forget that maybe this person has another life that we don't know anything about. You see, Claude, there was a boy up in Michigan that Sister Uberta almost married, then for one reason or another she decided on the convent instead. That was probably a mistake. It's not an easy life; they get locked up and bossed around a lot

and those black habits are probably like portable ovens.'
He stopped and clicked his fingernails on the desk, then
focused his eyes on my face. 'Last week she got a heavy
load to carry. She heard his ship was torpedoed out on the
North Atlantic, and well, I guess her sailor boy went down
with it.'

'I'm sorry,' I said.

'So let's show her we think she's a good sister. She'll
come around all right if we handle things right.'

We sat silently for a moment, side by side, like Mutt and
Jeff in the two desks.

'Father, I told her I hated her. That was a sin, wasn't it?'

'But you didn't mean it, did you?'

'No.'

'Claude, think of it this way . . .' His face became
concentrated, then he glanced out the window and the
seriousness faded from his eyes. 'Look, the sun's out.
We're going to have ball practice after all,' he said.

He rose from the desk, opened the window wide, and the
rain-flecked breeze blew into the room. His eyes crinkled
as he looked down on the playground.

'Come here a minute,' he said. 'Isn't that Rene LeBlanc
standing down there by the oak trees? I wonder who she
might be waiting for.'

Two minutes later I was bounding down the steps,
jumping over the dimpled puddles under the trees, and
waving my hand like a liberated prisoner at Rene, who
stood in the sunlight just outside the dripping oak
branches, her yellow pinafore brilliant against the
wisteria and myrtle behind her, her face an unfolding
flower in the rain-washed, shining air.

Sister Uberta went back North that year and we never
saw her again. But sometimes I would dream of an infinite,
roiling green ocean, its black horizon trembling with
lightning, and I'd be afraid to see what dark shapes lay
below its turbulent surface, and I'd awake, sweating, with
an unspoken name on my lips – Sister Uberta's, her

drowned sailor's, my own – and I would sit quietly on the side of the bed, awaiting the gray dawn and the first singing of birds, and mourn God's people for just a moment lest our innocence cause us to slip down the sides of the world beyond the tender, painful touch of humanity.

The Pilot

Some people around the south Louisiana oil patch say my pontoon plane is just a rust-streaked, window-cracked, baling-wire special, fit only for a winehead pilot or one of those south-of-the-border guys who sniff too much of their own nose candy before they go into Colombia. But it can float like a goose in eight-foot seas, and it's got an engine that can whip a lake into a dry mud flat. I can juice it and slip sideways on a layer of hot air and set down on a wet handkerchief when I want to. I crop-dusted all over Texas and skywrote in California, and for that reason flying out to offshore wells and doodlebug companies and skimming in on a bayou isn't anything to me.

For example, take the day I dropped out of a hot, blue sky, gunned over the trees, and drifted like a paper kite onto Bayou Teche just outside of New Iberia, where I kept my two-story houseboat moored next to a bank thick with cypress. She wasn't expecting me, at least not straight out of the sky, blowing water in my back draft all over the windows and the wash, entertaining the black people who were cane fishing in the trees. I guess I thought I'd catch her, see her pull on her blue jeans over her flat stomach, watch him try to mix a casual drink at my drain-board and tell me he had another job for me in Belize.

But she was shelling crawfish and drinking Jax out of the bottle at the kitchen table instead. The far door was open, and the outline of her body seemed to shimmer in the brilliant shatter of light off the bayou.

How do you tell your wife that the guy who's diddling her is a Nazi war criminal?

'Klaus Stroessner is what?' she said. Her curly blonde hair was sunburned on the tips, and she didn't wear a bra under her knit shirt. She had long legs like a dancer, and her arms were tan and smooth and her hands always quick and confident when she worked. Through her knit shirt I could see the small American flag tattooed above her heart.

'Here's the picture from *Life* magazine. He's not from Argentina. He was a guard in Dachau. That's him standing next to the gallows.'

She studied the photograph, clicking her nails on the beer bottle. She folded her legs and rubbed the top of a bare foot.

'How do you know it's him?' she said.

'He didn't even change his name. And look at that arrogant profile. Even thirty-nine years couldn't change that.'

'It's a coincidence and you're imagining things again. Klaus is a gentleman and he grew up on a ranch in the pampas. His mother still lives in Buenos Aires. He's very attached to her.'

'I know that –'

'What do you know?'

'I know that –'

he pulls you on top of him in the Holiday Inn at Lafayette, buys you lobster at the Court of Two Sisters in New Orleans, rubs his hands over you in the surf in Biloxi while you drip with foam and moonlight and wreaths of laughter.

'I dropped those geologists off at Morgan City early. I

46

thought we might –'

'What?' she said. Her eyes looked at the willow trees wilting in the heat on the far side of the bayou. Her eyes were blue and empty.

'Maybe go to –'

'What is it you want, Marcel?'

'Maybe go out to eat.'

'I'll change clothes.'

She went into the bedroom and closed the door, and I leaned with my head on my arm against the icebox.

Klaus Stroessner swims a mile a day in his kidney-shaped, turquoise pool, and his skin has the smooth tautness and color of the inside of a clam shell. He glows with health. His gun-metal hair is oiled and combed straight back; the three pale dueling scars glisten dully on the top of his forehead; he smells of chlorine, cologne, imported soap, Bordeaux wine, the South American cuisine he eats, the countries he has occupied; he smells of my wife.

I'm a Louisiana coonass raised on *boudin* and *couche-couche*, rice and garfish balls. What does that mean? I'm short and thick-bodied, overweight from too much beer and crawfish; I'm restless and lonely whenever I leave the Bayou Teche country; I think slow; maybe I'm dumb.

I stood on the patio by his pool, the turquoise water winking at us in the morning sun, and watched him eating soft-boiled eggs in his seersucker suit. His expensive clothes crinkled with their freshness.

'I have friends who've seen you,' I said. 'I've got the room-service bill she signed for you in Lafayette.'

'You drink too much at night, Marcel, then you have these fears and delusions in the morning. If you drink, take vitamins and aspirin before you sleep.' The *Times-Picayune* was folded to the stock-market section by his elbow, and he read while he spooned the eggs into his mouth.

'Do you know what diddling another man's wife can get you around here? I could grease you and walk right out of it. Besides, you're a Nazi war criminal.'

'Marcel, Marcel,' he said patiently, 'sit down and have some coffee and stop talking this nonsense. Do you want to make another run for me to Belize?'

'You were only nineteen when that picture was taken, but it's you and you're in this country illegally and I'm going to expose you.'

'No one cares about those things, except maybe a few ancient Jews that nobody pays any attention to.'

'Uncle Sam cares. Wait till they send your butt back to Germany.'

'I'm a citizen and businessman, Marcel. Would you like me to dial friends of mine in the State Department so you can talk with them? It would make you feel better, I think.' He smiled at me and his rimless glasses were full of light. His dueling scars looked like a small gray bird's claw at the top of his brow. 'You know the businesses I represent. Would they hire a Nazi? Ask yourself that.'

'Try this one for size, Klaus – I've got a nine-millimeter Luger at the houseboat, probably one your pals used to execute some partisans. You try to cook some barbecue with Amanda again and I'm going to stick it in your mouth and turn your brains into marmalade.'

'She said she's worried about you. I think you should talk to a psychologist. I know several in Lafayette. I'll lend you the money if you need it.'

I left and drove in my pickup to a bar out in Bayou Teche and got drunk and listened to all the Cajun records on the juke-box. I was all bluff with Klaus. I didn't own a gun, and I never broke the law in my life except when I was a kid and I got those eight months on Angola farm in 1955 for running a bunch of whiskey up to north Louisiana. I was just full of guilt, that's all, and sick inside because of Amanda. I love this damn country. The Nazis are supposed to be in old black-and-white newsreels. Why is one in New Iberia diddling my wife?

Because I allowed it. I flew for him.

*

The Pilot

He said it was machine parts for Belize. But the Nicaraguan he put on the plane with me in Miami waved me right on through Belize into Guatemala. I started to get mad at this Nicaraguan because I'd been had, then one of the port engines on the DC-6 started to misfire and shudder and blow oil back on the wing, and I had to feather it before the prop sheared off, which meant I had to feather the corresponding engine on the starboard wing, which meant we were carrying about three boxcar loads of metal-filled crates over the mountains at night with half power.

The moon was full and the black-green jungle-covered crests of the mountains were coming up fast, and I was leaning back on the stick and juicing it with everything I had while Klaus's man whimpered beside me with his fist against his teeth. The downdrafts were hammering on the wings, and I heard stuff busting loose and sliding around in the hole, and I knew we'd either rip apart at the joints in midair and rain down on the jungle like an exploding junkyard or nose straight into a rock wall and fill the sky with thunder and yellow light.

But I believe a lot in prayer, and sure enough I dropped through a deep cut between two mountains, saw the valley open up before me, saw a long shining river bordered by coffee plantations, and wiped my palms on my windbreaker while the flat, geometrical, moonlit landscape moved by predictably a thousand feet below.

'Relax, podna,' I said to Klaus's man, the Nicaraguan. 'You look as uncomfortable as an ice cube in a skillet. That's the strip where those truck flares are burning, isn't it?'

His face was white and sweating in the instrument lights, and he twisted his head back at the rolling clatter of noise behind the cabin, his mouth too dry and pinched with fright to speak.

'That stuff's not going anywhere,' I said. 'If it didn't punch out the ribs a few minutes ago, it's not going to do it now.'

'Three-point-fives,' he said.

'What?'

'Bazooka rockets. Dey already unstable. I seen dem blow up with my cousin in back of yeep.'

I took a deep breath, held it, and eased down on the dirt runway that was lit by two rows of hissing flares spiked into ground. The runway was short, and I was standing on the brakes by the time I reached the wall of eucalyptus trees at the far end. A large crate crashed into the bulkhead right behind my seat.

'That Klaus is one entertaining fellow,' I said.

Short Indians in tiger-striped fatigues and U.S. Army steel pots off-loaded the whole store. Stroessner's traveling dry goods included flamethrowers to polish a face into a roasted egg, Garlands and Thompsons to blow hearts and lungs all over the trees, grenades, mortars, and rockets that could make dog food out of a whole village.

I decided to let the Guatemalans keep Klaus's DC-6, with its bum engine and its cargo hole that smelled of death, and I would catch a commercial flight back to Miami or New Orleans. The major, who was a friend of the Nicaraguan, gave me a ride into the village in his jeep. The air was warm and smelled of the low rows of coffee trees that stretched away toward the encircling mountains in the moonlight, and I could see the river winking through the thick groves of bananas that grew along its bank. We reached the village just as the dawn rimmed the mountain crests in the east, and the air was so hushed in the rock streets, in the graying light that slowly revealed the glistening tile roofs, the rust-colored, dew-streaked adobe houses, the colonnades and stone horse troughs in the square, that it was hard to believe that these people lived in the iron sights of the guns that Klaus sold to moral dimwits.

I thanked the major, a compact, moustached little man who looked like a streetcar conductor, and asked where I could catch a bus to a town with an airport.

'No, no, you stay here till plane fixed,' he said, waving his small hand like he was swatting at flies. 'It very dangerous for you out there. The communists kill many people along the road. You safe here.'

And he locked me in the village jail.

For two weeks I watched a war through my barred window. Each morning trucks full of soldiers would drive down the crushed rock street and out into the hills. I'd see them advance up a switchback on a mountainside, small-arms fire would start popping like strings of fire-crackers, then the shadows of two gun-ships would streak across the village, the chopper blades beating in the glassy blue sky. The soldiers would flatten out behind the switchback while the door-gunners opened up on the tree line, then the rocket launchers would kick smoke, and balls of orange flame would balloon out of the jungle.

One afternoon the soldiers came back with six prisoners roped together by their hands in the back of an army truck. They were barefoot, covered with dust, and sweat ran in clear lines down their faces. The soldiers marched them by my jail window; one of them fell, and a soldier kicked him and then pulled him erect by his hair.

'What's going to happen to those guys?' I asked one of the alcoholic thieves who shared the cell with me.

'Dey tie him up on phone crank.' He began giggling and pumping his fists in circles like he was working invisible bicycle pedals. 'When dey call up a communist, he always answer.'

I never saw the prisoners again and I don't know what happened to them. But three days before I got out, I saw the handiwork of the death squads. An American priest driving an old flatbed truck brought in the bodies of sixteen Indians who had been shot in a ditch outside of town. The police tied handkerchiefs across their noses and put the bodies in a line under the colonnade. It was a burning hot day and I could hear the blow-flies droning in the shade. The thumbs of the dead were tied behind them with wire, and the cop who had to snip them free was sweating heavily behind his bandanna. There were two fat, middle-aged women among the victims. Their faces were painted with blood. The wind blew their dusty dresses and exposed their underwear and swollen thighs. The priest took a torn piece of striped canvas awning from inside his truck and covered their lower parts.

The alcoholic thief began to giggle next to me at the window. When the others pulled me off him, his tongue was almost halfway down his throat.

Amanda is brushing her hair in front of the dresser mirror. Her red mouth points upward with each stroke. She wears an orchid-colored nightgown I've never seen before and smells of a new perfume. It's like the odor of four-o'clocks opening along the banks of the bayou in the evening. I put my hands on her shoulders, rub the back of her neck. She neither resists nor acknowledges me. The muscle tone of her skin is perfect, smooth as sculptured soapstone.

I feel my resolution, my respect for myself, draining into an erection. I begin to touch her everywhere.

'Don't, Marcel.'

My hands turn to wood.

'It came early this month,' she says.

I don't believe you. You got it on with Klaus this afternoon.

'What?' she says. She flips her head when she starts brushing again.

'We could see a marriage counselor,' I say. 'Lots of people do it. You talk it out with a third person there.'

'I think behavior like that is silly.'

Her accent changes. Her daddy was a gyppo logger, and she grew up from Montana to Maine in the back of a rig. She once belonged to a fundamentalist religious cult in Florida, but when I met her she was waiting tables in a Galveston bar that was one cut above a hot-pillow joint.

'You think maybe I ought to boogie on down the road and find a sweet young rock and roller?' I say.

'It's not your style, Marcel.' She bites off a hangnail and examines it.

'You're right.' But at one time *our* style was to fly out over the Gulf in my pontoon plane, set down on a patch of floating blue ink, and drink Cold Duck and fish out the doors for gaff-top and speckled trout. Then when the sun boiled like a red planet into the watery horizon, I would inflate the air mattress and make love to her on the cabin floor, rocking in her embrace, which was deeper and more encompassing than the sea.

'I'm going up to the colored beer joint and listen to some *zydeco*,' I say. Then I grin at her. 'But I'll leave you with a thought.'

'What's that?'

'If I catch you with him, I'll ice the pair of you.'

Her face freezes in the mirror and her eyes look at me like blue marbles.

I started my own national beautification project the next morning: KEEP AMERICA CLEAN, DEPORT YOUR LOCAL NAZI GEEK AND GRIME BAG TODAY. But the man I talked with on the phone at the Immigration Department thought I was drunk, and the wire service in New Orleans told me they'd already done a story on Klaus – about his collection of South American Indian art.

'Lampshades?' I asked.

'What?' the wire reporter said.

'He was one of the Katzenjammer kids that threw them through the oven doors.'

The reporter hung up on me.

But the FBI man I called was a good listener. So I unloaded on him, told him everything, even about flying illegally into Guatemala. I felt as if a fish bone had been cleaned out of my throat.

He paused when I finished, then said, 'What do you

want us to do?'

'Arrest him. Pack him in a Wiener-schnitzel can and ship him to Nuremberg.'

'What for?'

'He was SS. I've seen the lightning bolts tattooed in his armpit.'

'It's not against the law to wear a tattoo, pal. Bring us something else. In the meantime spell your name for me and tell me a little more about this fun-in-the-sun trip you took to Guatemala.'

'Adios, amigo,' I said, and looked with a beating heart at my sweaty handprint on the dead phone receiver.

But I couldn't just give up. It was a beautiful gold-green morning, with a cool breeze riffling the bayou and the cypress trees, and I could smell the four-o'clocks that were still open in the damp shade. It was a day for boiling crawfish, for *zydeco* music and barbecue and baseball; it wasn't a day for surrendering to the likes of Klaus or some government and newspaper guys who didn't take me seriously.

My daddy, who trapped every winter at Marsh Island, used to say, 'Son, if it ain't moving, don't poke it. But if it starts snapping at you, wait till it opens up real wide, then spit in its mouth.'

I figured Klaus started snapping at me the first time he put his manicured, slender hand on top of Amanda's forearm at the Petroleum Club cocktail party in Lafayette. It was just a touch, a rub of the hair, a light gesture that an older, fatherly man could get away with. Except for his eyes. They sliced through tissue and bone, linkage and organ.

I'd read in the *Daily Iberian* that a large garden party was planned for Klaus that afternoon in New Orleans. Yes, I thought, and I put a city map, my field glasses, a thermos bottle of water, and two ham-and-onion sandwiches wrapped in wax paper into my canvas flight bag and filled up at the gas dock. Within an hour I was lifting above the long, flat expanses of dead cypress and salt marsh into the blue summer sky, the wonderful smell off the Gulf, the wind currents that the great pelicans ride on high above the spreading coastline of Louisiana.

A friend of mine owned an aerial sign service outside of New Orleans, and I'd already called him to set up the letters on a big black-and-yellow tow and to string the pickup wire across the strip, so all I had to do was come in low with my hook down, snag the tow, and juice it back into that shimmering blue-white sky that always pulls on me a little like eternity.

I could feel the heavy canvas drag of the sign behind me as I flew across Canal and followed the streetcar tracks down St Charles Avenue. The street was thickly lined with oak trees, and palm trees grew on the esplanade and groups of black people waited in the shade on each corner for the streetcar. I saw Audubon Park and the old stone buildings of Tulane University ahead, and I veered toward Magazine, which separated the colored slums from the Garden District, and passed right over a lawn party that was in progress between two beautiful, white pillared, iron-scrolled homes that were surrounded with oak and mimosa trees. It was like a fortress of wealth down there. Japanese lanterns hung in the trees, waiters carried trays of drinks around the clipped lawn, swimmers dived into an emerald pool with barbecue pits smoking on the flagstones. Two blocks away on the other side of Magazine were several square miles of paintless, dilapidated shacks on dreary, narrow streets that had always been set aside for New Orleans' Negroes. That had to be Klaus's crowd down there on that lawn.

So I went in for a closer look, several hundred feet under the FAA minimum. Sure enough, Klaus looked up at me from a deck chair where he was lying in a bikini and shades while a blonde gal rubbed oil on his chest. I made a slow turn so that the sign arched around the party like an angry yellow jacket: HELLO TO LT. KLAUS STROESSNER, DACHAU CLASS OF '44.

I kept it up for twenty minutes. They started moving around down there like ants on a burning log. They carried their drinks and paper dinner plates into the trees, but I flushed them out with a power dive that almost clipped some bricks out of a chimney. They tried to hide under the veranda and I circled wide so that my engine sounded like I was headed out toward the Mississippi. Then I flattened her out and roared in full throttle like I was on a strafing run and blitzed the sign through the tree-tops and showered the lawn and pool with leaves and broken twigs.

I almost didn't hear the police helicopter whipping through the air on my starboard wing. But that was all right – I'd gotten my message across. And to make sure I did, I pulled back on the stick, wobbled over them one more time, released the hook, and floated the sign down on the rooftops and lawns like a gutted snake.

I spent two days in the New Orleans jail before I could make bail. The *Times-Picayune* ran a story about an ex-convict pilot 'with a known drinking history' who had buzzed the Garden District. The *Daily Iberian* wrote that not only had I been in Angola but I had an irregular work record and federal authorities thought I'd done time in Latin America. People around town weren't going out of their way to be seen with me that week.

I figured Klaus had won again. I'd dropped the dime on him with the feds and the wire service, plastered his name and his crime all over the sky, and ended up in the lock with a good chance of my license being yanked. Maybe the Catholic brothers were wrong when they taught us the bad guys lost the war.

But a couple of Klaus's friends blew it for their man. When I boxed Golden Gloves at New Iberia High, I learned to swallow my blood, to never show the other guy I was bleeding behind my mouthpiece. Klaus should have boxed.

Two of them caught me outside the colored beer joint. They didn't touch me; they just stood real close to me while my back hit up against my truck door. One of them had the kind of bad breath that comes from rotted teeth.

'You been telling some lies about a friend of ours,' he said. 'Do it again and we'll feed you into your own propeller.'

I smiled with the happiness of a man who knows the world might turn out right after all.

'Hey, I can understand you guys worrying over your friend, but you really shouldn't be here,' I said. 'Those three black dudes behind you are my friends, but the one with the barber's razor is hard to control sometimes.'

We learned to fight from the Indians. You can do a lot more damage shooting from behind a tree than charging uphill into a howitzer. My tree was the telephone.

'Hello, my name is Klaus Stroessner,' I said into the receiver, my feet propped up on the sunny deck rail of my house-boat, 'and I'd like my utilities turned off for the next three months. Now, my brother-in-law will probably call you up and tell you he's me and try to get you to turn them on again, but if you do I'm not paying one cent on the bill. The fact is, I'll sue you for helping him occupy my house.'

Then I called a wrecker service and had Klaus's Cadillac towed to a garage 110 miles away in Lake Charles, told a fertilizer company to spread a dumptruckload of fresh cow manure on his lawn, informed the parish health office he had AIDS disease, ran an ad with his phone number in a newspaper for sexual degenerates.

'Have you lost your mind? What are you doing?' Amanda said from the kitchen door. She was dressed to go to town. Her designer jeans looked sewn to her skin. Her breasts were huge against her yellow silk cowboy shirt.

'I've got an errand or two at the post office,' I said. 'Stay here till I get back.'

'Marcel, when did you think you could start talking to

57

me like this?'

'Make some chicken-and-mayonnaise sandwiches and put some Cold Duck in the icebox. I'll be back in an hour. Turn on the window fan in the bedroom.'

I left her there with her lips parted, her tongue barely touching her teeth, her blue eyes caught with a curious pause.

In town I bought a box of envelopes, a package of writing paper, and a pair of skintight rubber gloves. I wrote the letter in the typing room of the public library, then dropped it, still using the gloves, from my truck window into the mailbox outside the old red-brick post office on Main Street. It was a perfect south Louisiana summer morning. The sun was shining through the moss-hung oaks overhead, the wind smelled of rain and flowers, and the lawns in front of the nineteenth-century homes along Main were filled with yellow hibiscus and flaming azaleas.

As an afterthought, I went inside the post office, filled out a change-of-address card, and had Klaus's mail forwarded to general delivery in Nome, Alaska.

A light, warm rain was denting the bayou when I got back to the houseboat. I parked my pickup under the cypress, undressed on the bank, and walked naked into the kitchen. Amanda dropped the jar of mayonnaise to the floor.

'I'm calling the sheriff's office, Marcel,' she said.

'Good idea,' I said, and jerked the telephone out of the wall and handed it to her. Then I loaded her across my shoulder and carried her into the bedroom. The window fan hummed with a wet light from the bayou.

'I'll file charges. They'll send you back to Angola,' she said.

'They won't have time. They're going to be busy investigating Klaus.'

I set her down on the bed. Her face was quiet, motionless on the pillow.

'What do you mean?' she said.

'I wrote a letter to the president of the United States and signed Klaus's name.'

'I don't believe you.'

'It goes: "Dear Gipper, I liked that film you and Errol Flynn played Nazis in. I was one myself. I'd like to get together with you and have a chat about the Russians and those UFOs that have been flying around the White House.'

'You did that?'

'The feds will go through his life with a garden rake. And wait till he tries to explain some of the phone calls he made today.'

'You really did that?'

'You don't need to believe me, Amanda. But I don't think we'll be seeing Klaus around New Iberia for a while. In the meantime your mainline daddy's meter is running.'

I slipped my arms under her cowboy shirt, up her back, and leaned my face close to hers. Her blue eyes, like a schoolgirl's, looked unblinkingly into mine. Then I felt her slender fingers slide across my shoulders and rest on my neck.

We made love on the bed, on the floor, in the porch hammock behind the bamboo shades while the rain sluiced off the roof and danced on the bayou. I started to go to the icebox for the Cold Duck.

'Don't you dare move, you bad ole alligator man,' she said.

And I lay with my head on her breast, her heart beating under the tattooed flag of my reclaimed country.

Taking a Second Look

He looked out the bar window at the lighted baseball diamond in the park across the street while he waited for the bartender to bring him another manhattan. He didn't know if it was the alcohol working in his head or his present mood of reverie that made him see for the first time the similarity between this baseball field and Cherryhurst Park, where he had played ball as a boy in Fort Worth. Just a minute ago he had been telling the bartender about the Cheerio and Duncan yo-yo contests that were held on street corners all over the country during the 1940s. He hadn't thought about them in years. Why now? The bartender was old enough to remember them but said he didn't. However, that wasn't surprising. Few people today invested much in memory.

In fact, he often felt that he was the only person he knew who cared about remembering things. It was a self-indulgent attitude, he realized, but then again sometimes there were instances when he truly knew that he was an anachronism, alone, and surrounded by people who had no conception of history, even the most casual form of it. That afternoon at the English department meeting he had done a stupid thing: broken his own rule, yielded to his vitriol, confusing the younger members of the faculty and boring the others. The discussion had gone on interminably about 'meeting the needs of the community' until finally he had said, 'The people who would let the community plan a college curriculum probably would also think that the finest form of government in world history was the French general assembly under Robespierre.'

Then he had left the meeting early and had gone to the bar, disgusted with his cynical vanity. The bar was his Friday afternoon place, but it was no longer afternoon and he had been there two other nights during the week, each time sifting out his anger and discontent, chasing each thought down like a snapping dog that he had to bludgeon to death. Yet he wondered if his unhappiness with his job at the city college, his tilting with the educational behaviorists and the administration, wasn't just a means to avoid the feeling of loss that would overcome him suddenly and leave him so weak that he couldn't put sentences together, focus on the change of a light at an intersection, or remember what he was reading on an examination paper.

He had devised several ways of disguising or explaining those moments when they happened in front of other people, but sometimes the numbness was so thick, so devastating to his mind, that he didn't care whether he appeared the fool or not. His son had been killed at Khe Sanh three years ago, and although he knew that his loss was not unique, the grief that it brought seemed to be, because it did not obey its own nature and cauterize itself with time, and he was not sure that it ever would. He thought possibly he had come to understand the axiom *You just live with it.* Yes, he thought, you don't confront and overcome it; you don't accept it stoically; you just carry it around like a tumor and ignore the black lines that spread along the veins.

'Oh, here, Doc, I'll fix you another one. I shouldn't have set the glass so close to the edge,' the bartender said.

'That's all right, Harold. I'll take you up on it the next time in.'

He left the bar and cut across the park towards his apartment building. The field lights were off now, but the moon was full over the mountains, and the rounded details of the ball diamond had the soft half-lighted quality of memory. It *was* just like Cherryhurst Park: the chicken-wire backstop, the thin in-field grass, the wood bleachers that were weathered gray and sagging in the center. The trees on the edge of the field were elms and maples instead of pin oaks, but the dusty black-green leaves moved with the same summer breeze, made the same cove of shadow where high-school girls once waited to be held and kissed after a game.

He tapped the leather sole of his shoe on home plate, then began running toward first base, his necktie and starched collar like a metal band around his throat. He pivoted on the bag and turned away from the infield, breathing deeply and pulling off his coat. That was a single, he thought. Now for the steal against an overconfident left-handed pitcher. He led off the bag, one arm pointed deceptively back to it, then dug out for second, his head low, his thighs pumping, while the ball sped from the catcher's extended-crouch throw and came in too high for the tag. He stood up from the slide in an explosion of dust and headed for third. The infield was in a panic and the throw to the third baseman was in the dirt. He never slowed down. He rounded the bag, the coach's arm swinging in a circle in the corner of his vision, and sprinted for home. Why not? Jackie Robinson had done it and won the pennant. His leather sole clacked across the rubber plate, and he collided into the chicken-wire back-stop, his chest heaving, his head thundering with whiskey and his own blood.

His heart was clicking inside him and his breath rasped uncontrollably in his throat as he walked over to pick up his coat. He thought he was going to throw up. His pants knee was torn, and he flinched when he touched the dirty red scrape through the cloth. He wondered if forty-six was a sufficient age for one to pare away the confines of reason from his life.

The next morning he made breakfast, which he had enjoyed doing on Saturday mornings even when he was married, and put on a pair of old slacks, a sweatshirt, and his tennis shoes and headed for the park. The spring weather was wonderful. The mountains were blue west of town and the air was clear and bright and every detail of the park seemed etched in the sunlight. He jogged around the circumference of the park, breaking his stride when he went through the trees by the ball diamond, and watched a junior-high team in gold-and-green shirts taking batting practice. His wind wasn't as bad as he had thought it would be. He made two laps before he had to sit for a moment on the bleachers, the sweat drying on his face in the cool air. Then he started around the backstop again, increasing his speed all the way around the park until finally each breath came like a sliver of glass in the lungs and he had to walk with his head held back as though he had a bloody nose. But that's all right, he thought. Each gasp is a piece of smoke gone from the chest and some measure of converted alcohol out of the liver and brain. In two weeks it could all be gone. Why not? The body of his youth was buried in him somewhere. It was only a matter of burning away the softness until he found it.

He sat on the grass behind third base and watched the batting practice. The kids on the team were Mexican, black, and working-class white, and they talked and played rough and broke up double plays with elbows and knees. Pete Rose wouldn't have anything on this bunch, he thought. When the regular pitcher went in to take his turn at bat, a crippled boy took his place on the mound. The boy's left leg was wasted as though he had had polio, and although he had a strong arm he threw flat-footed from the rubber like an infielder. Come over with your arm and put your weight into it, the professor thought. Get it down, too. Don't float them by the letters. Oh, good Lord, duck!

The batter crashed a high outside pitch behind the first-base line and made the professor tumble over backward in the grass. As he sat up laughing he saw a police car pull to the curb under the shade of an elm tree. An enormous policeman in sunglasses, with a freshly lit cigar, filled the driver's window.

With no warning the first baseman casually turned toward the squad car, shot the finger, and said, 'Hey, Pork Butt. Stuff this.'

The policeman opened the door and raised his massive weight out of the car. The butt of his revolver and the brass bullets on his belt glinted in the sun as he walked toward the diamond. The first baseman had turned back to the game and was hitting his glove as though nothing had happened.

'Get your ass in the car, Gomez.'

'I'm busy.'

'You'll either get your ass in the car or I'll put it in there with my foot.'

'You're just going to look like a dumb shit running a kid again.'

'That's it.' The policeman pulled the boy off his feet by his arm and walked him to the car as though he were a crippled bird. He closed the back door on him, made a call on his radio, and then turned out into the traffic.

'What's he going to do with him?' the professor said to the boy who had walked over to play first.

'Take him down to juvie and call his old man so he'll get a whipping.'

'Why did he shoot the cop the finger?'

'Everybody gives Pork Butt the finger. He's a turd. He runs in guys all the time.'

Twenty minutes later the policeman drove down the

street again, alone, and parked in the same shady spot under the elm. On the window rested a fat arm with a cigar between two thick fingers. His mouth was partly opened, but because of the dark green sunglasses the professor couldn't tell if he was asleep or not. Incredible, he thought, a grown man investing his day in monitoring the public morality of fifteen-year-olds. Ah, there's nothing like the moral vision of a nation that can send a whole generation to Viet Nam and then worry about an upraised middle finger.

He crossed the street to the hardware store and bought an ice pick with a cork stuck on the tip. He put the ice pick in his pocket and walked down the street toward the park house, then circled back through the trees and approached the police car.

'Excuse me, Officer. The rec director in the park house is having trouble with a kid and would like for you to walk over there.'

'Is it a big colored kid?'

'I think so.'

'All right.' The policeman put on his cap and walked across the diamond toward the park house, oblivious to the pitch he interrupted.

The professor sat on the curb by the squad car's front tire, unscrewed the valve cap, and picked up a rock from the gutter. He inserted the ice pick into the valve and hammered the point deep into the tire. The kids on the diamond had stopped playing and were staring at his back, dumbfounded. The air rushed out instantly. How's that for meeting community need, he thought, and rose to his feet, the wind cool on his face, his mouth grinning in the roar of applause from the field. Then he jogged with a high step down the tree-shaded sidewalk toward his apartment building.

The boys were playing a practice game when he went back to the park the next morning and began his laps. As he jogged through the trees behind the backstop, he saw the crippled boy sitting alone in the bleachers, his fielder's glove strapped through his belt.

'Why aren't you playing?' the professor said.

'I just play in the work-up games and help out at batting practice.' The boy looked away from the professor when he spoke. Then he smiled. 'Say, that was great yesterday. You should have seen Pork Butt when he saw his tire. I thought he was going to brown his pants. Then he broke a lug off trying to change the tire. When he left we all gave him the bird.'

'Forget about that. Let's talk about pitching. You've got a good arm, but you're not using your leg right.'

'Oh yeah. What am I supposed to do with it?'

'You've got a bad leg there, so you don't pretend it's a good one. You take what's wrong with it and make it work for you. See, a pitcher's left leg isn't good for anything except weight. You throw it out in front of you, and then bring your arm and hip over with your delivery. Let me tell you about a guy who used to pitch in the old Texas League when I was a kid. His name was Monty Stratton, and he threw nothing but gas, then he went rabbit hunting one day and blew his left leg off with a shotgun. So he was finished, right? Well, wrong, because he learned to pitch with an artificial leg, throwing it out in front of him and swinging his weight around with his arm.'

'What happened to this guy?'

'He had to hang it up eventually, but not before he went to the Dixie Series. My point is that the best thing on a pitcher's side is his intelligence. He knows what pitch he's going to throw and the batter doesn't. So you give them the whole buffet: curves, sliders, fast balls, spitters, in-shoots, and then a fork ball at the head in the interest of batter humility.'

'Why don't you get your glove and play with us?'

'I don't have one.' The professor formed a pocket of air in his jaw and looked at the diamond. 'But I'm going to get one. I'll be back before the inning is over.'

But the sporting-goods store on the corner was closed Sundays, and he had to jog almost a mile to the shopping center to find a store that sold gloves. He brought a catcher's mitt and a fielder's glove, a green-and-gold cap, a ball in a cardboard box, and a can of Neetsfoot oil. He wore the cap low over his eyes as he jogged back to the park. Tonight he would fold the crown down into a crease and cup the bill with tape to give the cap the only proper shape for a ballplayer. There were a lot of things he could teach the boys. For example, it was no accident that Sandy Koufax didn't shave before he pitched and wore his cap darkly on his brow. And what oil and pocket shape meant to a glove and a fielder's ability with it. Tonight he would work the oil deep into the leather and then fold the fingers and thumb over the ball and tie them down with the thick twine. There were all the illegal things he could teach the boys, too: how to hide Vaseline under the belt buckle or the bill of the cap, wetting down the ball with a sponge the second baseman kept inside his perforated glove, blocking the bag with a folded knee that left the runner senseless.

When he got back to the park the boys were gone and the diamond was startlingly empty, as though it had been vacated by elves in a dream. He sat for a half hour in the empty bleachers, watching the dust blow in the wind, and then walked home just as the rain broke over the mountains.

But at three-thirty the next afternoon they were back, whipping the ball around the diamond, their faces electric with energy in the spring air. These boys weren't made for school-rooms, he thought, or leather shoes when the days turned warm or new clothes still stiff from the box. They were intended for wash-faded blue jeans and dusty elbows and knees and hands grimed with rosin from the bat. They were heroic in a way that no school could teach them to be. The catcher stole the ball out from under the batter's swing, the third baseman played so far in on the grass that a line drive would take his head off, the base runners sanded their faces off on a slide.

He crouched on his knees in the bullpen and caught for the crippled boy. Every third or fourth pitch he reminded the boy to throw his leg out and come over with his arm, and after a half hour he had the boy burning them into the mitt, one delivery after another, hard, low, and inside.

'Those are real smokers, partner,' the professor said. 'And now we're going to teach you the change of pace. All you got to do is hold it in the back of your palm and pull the string on it and you'll make a batter's scrotum come out his mouth.'

'You really think I'll get good enough to start in a game?'

'You're good enough now, pal.'

When the boy's arm tired they joined a pepper game, and the professor bunted the ball across the grass to a row of five boys, all of whom knew him only as the guy who had flattened Pork Butt's tire. As he threw the ball up and knocked it shorthanded into a fielder's glove, he felt a pleasure that he hadn't known in years. What was more natural, he thought, than playing baseball with boys?'

But what was more unnatural, he also thought, than his Tuesday morning general-literature class? The students had changed and he didn't understand them anymore. Or maybe the problem was that there wasn't much out there to understand. They were bored with the material, bored with him, bored with themselves. If they had a common facial expression, it was a remoteness in the eyes and a yawn that not even the apocalypse could disturb. They wanted to be court reporters, cops, and computer programmers, but few of them could explain why. On some mornings when it was obvious that no one had read the material, he tried to talk about other things: trout fishing, baseball, folk music, clean air, mental health. But there was no way to violate that encompassing yawn.

On this morning he was discussing 'The Charge of the

Light Brigade.' He wanted to be fair to Tennyson, but this particular poem always bothered him because its content had nothing to do with the reality of war, and it was this kind of romantic blather that replaced memory and provided the delusions that the manipulators used so well. But he contained his feelings and simply said, 'Tennyson was a great craftsman, and actually a great poet, but the sentiment in this poem is what made some critics accuse him of intellectual poverty.'

Then the hand went up from one of the three boys in class who wore ROTC uniforms.

'If he was a great poet, how could he be intellectually poor at the same time?' the boy said.

'Sometimes Tennyson wrote for newspaper publication, and he didn't invest a lot of thought in what he said.'

'What is intellectually poor about this poem?'

'Namely that there's nothing grand in sending hundreds of men to die in an artillery barrage.'

'They had a choice, didn't they? Maybe they felt they were giving their lives for something.'

'My point is that Tennyson does not describe what actually took place on that field. He doesn't write about the scream of the chain and grape in the air or the men who are disemboweled in the saddle or the fear that makes their urine run down their thighs.'

He was going beyond the limits of the classroom now, and he swallowed and tried to hold back the words that were breaking loose like lesions in his head.

'Okay, but they were there for a reason,' the boy said. 'Why does a poem have to be antiwar to be good?'

'Forget about this damn poem.' The professor leaned over the podium and pointed his finger at the boy. 'When you put on that uniform, that costume, you help another man dig your grave.'

He could hear his own breathing in the room's silence. He swallowed again and looked out the window at the blueness of the mountains. 'Hey, it's spring. You guys go drink beer in the park today or watch the tulips grow, and I'll see you Thursday,' he said.

He made a pretense of putting his papers together and prayed that nobody would stop by the desk so that he would have to raise his eyes.

Two hours later the department secretary handed him a message. The dean of humanities would like to see him at one o'clock.

The dean was a heavy man both physically and mentally. He tried to keep his weight down by playing handball, but he only got more thick-bodied as a result, and the black hair on his arms and chest made him look simian behind his desk. He was a pragmatist, and no matter how irrational the current educational psychology was, he quickly acclimated to it and made it his. Certificates of administrative merit and student art work that could have been painted by blind people were hung all over his office walls. The professor thought of these as appropriate symbols for the dean's ability to collect everything that was worthless in modern education.

'Well, I got another complaint,' the dean said.

'From an ROTC kid in my general-lit class.'

'No, this one's from two girls, but they're in the same class.'

At least the ROTC kid is a stand-up guy, the professor thought.

'They say you use the class for your own ideas and you run people down.'

'Do you believe that?'

'I have to deal with the complaint.'

'Is it possible that those girls got a low grade on their mid-terms or that they have oatmeal in their heads?'

'It's the fourth complaint to go into your folder this semester.'

'You're actually keeping those things on file?'

'They're part of an official record. Look, let's talk

honestly a minute. It's my feeling that you should see the school psychologist.'

'I'll be damned if you're going to talk to me like this.'

The dean pushed a ring of keys around on the desk top with his finger.

'It's either that or taking leave without pay after this semester,' he said. 'I'm not in the business of mental health. That's a problem you're going to have to deal with yourself.'

The professor stood up and put his hands in his slacks pockets and clicked his change a moment against his thigh.

'Some situational philosophers I know have a good epigram for your kind, Dean. Stuff it, Pork Butt.'

'I'll ignore that because frankly I think you're losing your mind.'

'Well, you just keep on playing with your keys and maybe you'll have your own file one day.'

The dean flattened his fingers on the desk top and kept his hand motionless.

That afternoon the professor was still thinking of his conversation with the dean when he walked to the park to watch the boys play a league game. He knew that he was finished at the college, that even if he wasn't fired the administration would only keep him on in a capacity that was suspect and shameful. And there weren't many other teaching jobs around, particularly when one's recommendation from his previous position stated that he was a lunatic. It was going to be tough to start over again at his age, but then what was numerical age anyway? He was forty-six and considered old by some, but maybe he had thirty years on earth ahead of him. A boy of nineteen about to step on a Claymore mine set in the middle of a jungle trail had been much older in his lifespan than he. And that boy had never wavered or pitied himself or complained about the time that had been allotted him.

The professor bought a hot dog from the wood stand under the elm trees and sat in the bleachers behind third base. His team had its two best pitchers knocked off the mound in the first five innings, and then the manager sent the crippled boy out from the bullpen. Think Monty Stratton, pal, the professor said to himself. Give them sliders and in-shoots that make the navel shrivel up and hide.

But they cut the boy to pieces. They crashed line drives through the infield and drove home runs all the way to the street. It looked like batting practice rather than a game. The professor walked out onto the field and motioned the umpire for time.

'Who the hell are you?' the umpire said. The umpire's face looked like a baked apple under his black cap.

'I'm their coach from the college. You new to this league or something?'

The professor put his arm over the boy's shoulders and bent down toward his ear.

'Throw at their heads,' he said. 'After you dump one or two of them in the dirt, they'll rattle and back off from the plate.'

But it was no use. The boy didn't have the killer instinct, the professor thought. His best delivery was waist-high and down the middle, and each batter hit it so hard that runs were crossing the plate faster than the scorekeeper could change the numbers on the board. No, this one was not a killer, the professor thought, and maybe thank heaven for that.

After the next inning the umpire called the game because the visiting team's lead was so great that a continuation would be a humiliating travesty. As the boys wandered off the diamond toward the bicycle racks and the park house, the professor bought two hot dogs from the concession stand and gave one to the crippled boy.

'We're going to have to put some weight on you before your next game,' he said.

'Oh, I ain't pitching again.'

'Sure you will.'

'Nope.'

'In a couple of days you'll see this game correctly in your mind, and you'll know what you did wrong, and you'll go back out there throwing gas.'

'Maybe.'

They sat down in the empty bleachers and ate the hot dogs. The mountains were so blue against the sky that they hurt the eyes.

'Do you mind if I ask you something?' the boy asked.

'Go ahead.'

'Sometimes you look real happy when you watch us play. Then you look real sad. Is it because we mess up or something?'

'My son was killed three years ago at Khe Sanh.'

'Was it in a car accident?'

The professor smiled and turned the boy's cap sideways.

'No,' he said.

In the silence the boy looked straight ahead, his eyelids blinking.

'Hey,' he said, and took a folded leaflet out of his back pocket. 'Did you hear about these Cheerio yo-yo contests they're going to have in front of the drugstore? They're giving away maple-leaf badges and sweaters and all kinds of crap.'

'Partner, you're looking at the guy who wrote the book on Cheerio yo-yo contests. I think we'd just better toggle on over to the drugstore and buy us a couple of those babies.'

They walked off through the trees toward the street. In the dappled light they looked out of step with their own shadows.

Hack

From where he sat in his straight-back wicker chair on the front porch, he could dimly see the green river and the sloping hills and the oak trees on the crests. But his pale blue eyes, frosted with cataracts, really didn't need to see them. He could smell the land, the water, and the trees in the hot July wind, and sometimes when he slipped into memory again, he could even smell the herds of cattle moving seventy years ago to the rail pens in San Antonio. He was ninety-four today, or at least that was what they told him, and it had been years since he had stopped caring about losing his sight. Memory and the lucid, bright dreams of sleep provided everything he needed.

His son Jack had dressed him in his low-topped brown boots, his Oshman's western suit, a soft shirt buttoned at the throat, and the pearl John B. Stetson that he always wore when he sat on the front porch. The flower boxes on the railing were filled with showers of purple and white petunias, and Jack had hung twists of red and white bunting all over the latticework. When Hack, the old man, looked at the colored paper, he became confused about the reason for the party. Was it July the Fourth or really his birthday? They often lied to him or even made up stories about him. They said he did things he hadn't. Only moments ago he heard them talking about him through the screen. They talked about him as though he were a deaf or a drunk man who couldn't hear.

He found the whiskey under the cupboard and set the bed on fire with his pipe. He would have been burnt up if my nigras hadn't seen the smoke.

The wind blew across the tall yellow grass in the field below the house and bent the limbs of the pin-oak tree in the Holland family cemetery. The whitewashed markers were dappled with shadow and light, and as the vision of the cemetery slipped with him into sleep, he smelled the hot, drowsy odor of wild poppies in the wind.

His sleep took him many places, where all the people and towns and the elemental sweep of Texas were unchanged. Each dream brought it back into focus, without distortion, as though he had stepped away from it just a moment before: the drunken New Year's party with the other Texas Rangers in the El Paso saloon and bordello where John Wesley Hardin was killed in 1895; racing his horse into the Rio Grande in a shower of mud and water, the reins in his teeth, while he fired one shot after another from his Winchester carbine at three Mexican rustlers headed for home; and the beautiful childlike faces of the Mexican girls who groaned under him after he came back from a raid on Pancho Villa's troops.

He heard more pickup trucks and cars banging up the corrugated road to the front lot, then the voices of people who passed him on the porch and let the screen slam behind them. Someone threw a pair of socks partly wrapped in white tissue paper and ribbon into his lap. The voices inside were like a whiskey hum in his head in the hot shade of the porch, senseless and too many to understand. He heard the screen slam again, the wood boards bent with someone's weight close to him, and he looked into the face of his son-in-law, the history professor at the University in Austin, who was leaning over as though he were trying to see around something. It was a stupid face, one that went with a tape recorder and a half pint of Jim Beam and patronizing questions.

'How are you, Hack? I gave Jack a little bottle of red-eye for you.'

'Bring it out on the porch.' His words were full of phelgm and still caught somewhere in afternoon sleep.

'Well, I don't know about that,' the son-in-law said slowly, smiling, his eyes grinning with wrinkles at his wife. 'Jack says you've already raised too much hell this week.'

'Give me a cigarette,' Hack said.

'The doctor says you're supposed to stay off smoking tobacco, Hack. Maybe I can get you a twist to chew on from inside.'

Hack looked away at the yellow haze on the fields, the burst of red blood drops in the tomato acreage, and thought he could smell the poppies again in the wind.

'Bonnie says you told her you knew Frank Dalton. Is that true?' the son-in-law said.

'I knew Frank and I knew Bob Dalton, too.'

'Grandpa, you've got it mixed up,' Bonnie, his daughter, said. 'It was Wesley Hardin you locked in jail over in Yoakum. You never knew the Daltons.'

'There was eight of them rode into the lot. Emmett and Bob and Frank was in front. They wanted water from the well for their horses, and Bob Dalton had a brace of pistols hung over his pommel. They was shot all over the street in Coffeyville, Kansas, two months later.'

'Are you sure that's not just a story, Hack?' the son-in-law said.

'You're a fool,' Hack said.

The stupid face of his son-in-law drew away from him, and he felt the boards of the old porch creak back into their natural level, then the gentle outline of the hills and the blackjack oaks took shape again against the infinite blue, hot sky, and he thought he heard a rumble of horses and a train whistle in a field just beyond the line of his vision.

As he looked with his mind into the brilliant haze, he knew where his sleep was about to take him. There was a low, brown mountain, with a high-banked railway grade at its base. The tracks shimmered wetly in the early morning light, and the sage and stunted mesquite at the bottom of the grade were blackened by passing locomotives. Hack heard the train beyond the curve, and he and the other rangers formed their horses into an advance line and started at a walk through the field of wild poppies. The dried poppy husks brushed back over the horses' forequarters and rattled like a snake about to strike. The horses shook their heads against the sawed reins, their eyes wide with fright, and tried to cant sideways. Captain McAlester hit his sorrel between the ears with his fist.

'Hold, you shit hog, or I'll cut your nuts out,' he said.

One by one they pulled their carbines from their saddle scabbards. Hack propped the butt of the Winchester against his thigh and slipped the leather thong off the hammer of his Colt revolver. The wind was blowing strong across the field, and his sweat felt cold in his hair. He bit off a piece of plug tobacco, and it made a hard, dry outline in his jaw.

'Put your star outside, gentlemen,' Captain McAlester said. 'We want to make goddamn sure they know who done this to them. Satan will go to church before this bunch of Mexicans ever raids in Texas again.'

They slipped their ranger stars out of their shirt pockets and pinned them on their coats. They weren't supposed to be in Mexico, but after Villa's last raid across the river they had ridden two days, wearing dusters over their pistols and carbines, talking to no one, eating jerky and dried corn out of their saddlebags, until they made camp in a grove of juniper trees at the edge of the field last night. While they sat drinking whiskey and coffee out of their tin cups in the firelight, the captain told them how they would take the train: they would simply take it. He was a tall, fine-looking man, Hack thought, but in the wavering light of the fire his face looked as though it had been shaped in a forge. They would attack the train just the way Sam Houston had attacked and defeated the Mexicans at San Jacinto in 1836 when he sent Deaf Smith to burn the bridge behind the enemy. Once the battle was joined, there would be no retreat for anyone. They would fight under a black flag, the captain said, and give no quarter and ask none in return.

Hack took the dry lump of tobacco out of his mouth with his fingers and put it back in his pocket.

'I bet this is more fun than throwing John Wesley Hardin in the DeWitt jail,' the captain said.

'At least that was a fair fight,' Hack said, and they both laughed.

'Here them sons of bitches come,' a man down the line said.

The locomotive pulled around the curve, the white smoke blowing back over the bending line of box and cattle and flat cars, all of them loaded with small, dark men in brown uniforms. Hack squinted his eyes and saw a machine gun set up on a tripod just behind the engineer's cab. Mexicans sat up on the spine of the cars, their rifles in jagged silhouette, and legs hung down through the slats of the cattle cars as though there were no bodies attached. It looked more like a refugee train than part of an army en route to another campaign.

'All right, let's fry them in their own grease,' the captain said, and kicked his horse into a trot.

It wasn't really necessary for him to give orders, because each man knew what the captain would do before he did it. Each of them was leaned partially forward in the saddle, the reins wrapped around one fist and the carbine held upward, his thighs posting easily with the horse's motion, the stomach muscles drawn tight, the genitals tingling lightly with expectation. The captain would have made a good cavalry officer, Hack thought. The sun was at their backs and the Mexicans still weren't sure who they were. Also, the captain knew that in a charge their quarter horses were good only for a few hundred yards, and if they began their attack at too long a distance, their horses would be spent early, their carbines would be ineffective against the train ('Them thirty-thirties would hit them cars like birdshit on a brick,' he had said), and the 9-millimeter Mausers and .30–.40 Kraigs that the Mexicans used would cut them into piles of rags.

'I think they're about to sniff us. Git it!' he shouted.

Hack flicked his roweled spur into the ribs of his Appaloosa, leaned into the pommel and tightened his legs at the same time and felt the power of the horse swell up under him. He was a dead shot, even from horseback, and he loaded his own soft-nosed X-cut bullets with enough grains of powder to knock down a barn door. He rose in the stirrups each time he fired, ejected the smoking brass casing with a flick of three fingers in the lever action, and fired again. The explosion in his ears and the acrid smell of the burnt powder made the blood beat in his temples, and he drilled shot after shot into the tangle of soldiers caught in the cattle cars, then swung his rifle into the men on the spine who were trying to fire back from a sitting position without falling from the train.

The Winchester snapped empty, and he turned the Appaloosa into an even gallop with the train, the reins loose over the pommel, while he slipped the cartridges from the leather hoops of his bandolier into the magazine of his rifle. Two cartridges spilled from his hand, and when he tried to catch them he saw that his trouser legs were white with the beaten pulp of poppies. He felt the spring of the magazine come tight when he pushed in the last shell with his thumb, and he wrapped the reins in his fist again and leveled his rifle across his forearm to fire into any of those small men in their dirty, brown uniforms.

But he had forgotten the machine gun mounted on the

flat-car behind the engineer's cab. He was abreast of the locomotive, and while he looked into the terrified face of the engineer through the square iron cab window and tried to swivel backward in the saddle, he knew that it was simply too late. The man on the machine gun had turned the barrel right at him and was hammering up the elevation with his fist, his face like a twisted monkey's paw under his cap. Hack tried to extend the Winchester with one hand at a backward angle and fire at him; but it was a comic gesture, he thought, even as the Lewis gun's barrel flashed at him out of the sunlight, a waving of a silly wand in front of eternity.

He heard the bullets thunk into the rib cage of the Appaloosa, then the horse's weight went out from under him as though it had been hit between the ears with a sledge. Hack landed on the tall poppies, the reins still tangled around his fist, and felt the hot back draft of the train blow over him. Blue coils of entrail pressed out the stitched wound in his horse's side. He flung the reins from his hand and ran after the flatcar, heedless of the bullets crisscrossing through the air around him, and emptied the cylinder of his single-action Colt .45 at the machine gunner. He was firing too fast, and the recoil brought the rounds high, each of them whanging into the iron plate of the engineer's cab. His hammer snapped on a spent shell casing, and he stared after the receding face of the machine gunner.

Remember what I look like, you son of a bitch, he thought, *because I'll be back to get you.*

Then he felt his coat jump and saw a neat horizontal tear along the cloth.

Get up, Hack.

It was the captain, and he was having trouble sawing the bit back in the sorrel's teeth. The horse's neck was covered with foam, and there was a green froth at its mouth.

'Forget that goddamn Mexican. Swing up behind me. You hear me?'

The captain pulled his boots out of one stirrup, and Hack grabbed the back of the saddle and swung his weight up on the sorrel's rump. The last of the wooden cars clicked away past them, and in the sudden quiet and the sweep of the wind through the dry poppies, Hack looked back down the track at the small, brown men strewn along the embankment.

The next night back in Juarez they drank and whored until dawn. The girls came to him in succession all during the night and mounted him on the down mattress, his pistols hung on the brass bedstead, holding his sex tightly between their hands before they pressed it inside, as though they drew some power themselves from the blood of their own kind that he had spilled that day. There was a bottle of tequila and a saucer of salt and red peppers and sliced limes on the night table next to his head, and each time he finished with one girl he took another drink, with a bite of pepper in his teeth and a salted lime for a chaser, and he felt the heat swell up through his erection again.

'*Get up, Hack.* They're going to cut the cake,' his daughter Bonnie was saying.

He saw the green river again in the afternoon haze and the soft hills that looked like women's breasts.

The cake was covered with white lace and candy roses, and his name, Hackberry Holland, and the numbers nine and four were written on top in pink icing. Someone had placed nine and then four candles on each number. They sat him in the chair at the head of the table, from where he could see his face reflected in the mahogany-framed mirror on the dining-room wall. In the glow of pink candles he didn't recognize the face, the white hair that stuck out from under the Stetson, the toothless mouth that made his lips a crooked line, the incongruous baby quality of the skin against the white whiskers.

'I'll blow them out for you, Grandpa,' Bonnie said.

'Where's little Hack? Where's Satchel-ass at?' he said.

'He's in the service now, Hack,' his son Jack said.

'Why ain't he here?'

'He's fighting in the war in Korea, Grandpa,' Bonnie said.

'He's got more sense than all of you.' For just a moment he saw his grandson, barefoot in his overalls, following the mule sled through the rows of tomato plants, picking the blood drops out of the leaves and dropping them into the baskets, the sun hot on his freckled shoulders.

'I gave him that name Satchel-ass,' he said. 'He looked just like a nigra washwoman bent over in the row.'

But they weren't listening to him now. They were drinking bottles of Lone Star and Pearl and talking loudly about things the way younger people did, as though no one had lived them before. Someone put a piece of cake on a paper plate with a fork in front of him. A burnt candle lay flat in the icing.

'Give me my whiskey.'

'One glass,' his daughter said.

'Bonnie,' Jack said.

'Let him have a glass, for God's sake,' she said.

He saw her pour out of the Jack Daniels bottle into the cup in front of him. The whiskey shimmered with brown light in the sun's glare through the window. He raised the cup with both hands and felt the bourbon spilling over his mouth onto his shirt front, clicking over his tongue, burning through his throat. His eyes blinked slowly like a bird's when the heat hit his stomach and ticked with a sharp fingernail at his loins. His hand went out toward the warm, amber light inside the bottle.

'Tomorrow, Hack,' Jack said.

'That's right, Grandpa,' his son-in-law said, squatting by his chair. 'Bonnie and I are spending the weekend, and I want you to tell the story about locking Wesley Hardin in jail. I brought the tape recorder and a nip for both of us.'

'You have the face of an idiot,' Hack said.

He wasn't sure whether he fell asleep on the porch again or

in his bed in the side room. Wakefulness came to him once during the middle of the night when he urinated into the metal pan he held between his naked thighs, and while the drops congealed between his fingers and the pin-oak tree bent outside in the wind, he slipped into a dream as bright and clearly etched in its sequence as a Lucifer match touching a candle.

He and his grandson little Hack stood in the ruins of the old county jail. The ceiling and one of the adobe walls had collapsed, the roofing timbers hung down like broken teeth, and there were broken bottles and used condoms in the corners. The little boy ran his fingers over the worn, nail-scratched inscription on the wall: WES HARDIN WILL KILL HACKBERRY HOLLAND FOR NIGGER MEAT.

'Is that where you chained him up, Grandpa?'

'Yes, but Wes didn't write that. He didn't send a message when he shot somebody. He just come at you with his pistol already out.'

He looked into his grandson's face and saw his own face there, and before the boy could ask, he told the story again about how he had put the most dangerous man in Texas in jail. When Hack was sheriff and justice of the peace, he had put out word for John Wesley Hardin never to come into DeWitt County again. A week later Hardin rode drunk all night from San Antonio and came into the lot just at sunrise, his black suit streaked with sweat and mud and whiskey. He had a navy Colt revolver propped on his thigh and a shotgun tied down to the saddle. He drilled five rounds from the pistol into one of the wood columns on the front porch, cocking and firing, while his horse reared and sawed against the bit.

'Get out here, Hack, and I'll give you a rose petal between the eyes!'

But Hack was in the barn with one of his mares that was in foal, and he waited until Hardin's pistol snapped on an empty chamber, then stepped into the lot with the Winchester that he always kept in the leather scabbard nailed inside the barn door.

'You goddamn son of a bitch,' he said. 'Start to untie that shotgun and I'll put a new asshole in the middle of your face.'

Hardin laid his pistol against his knee and turned his horse in a half circle.

'You come up behind me, do you?' he said. 'Get your pistol and let me reload and I'll pay them nigger deputies for burying you.'

'I told you not to come back to DeWitt. Now you shot up my house and probably run off half my Mexicans. I'm going to put you in jail and wrap chains all over you, then I'm taking you into my court for attempted assault on a law officer. Move off that horse.'

Hardin looked back at him steadily with his killer's eyes, then brought his boots out of the stirrups, slashed his spurs into the horse's sides, and bent low over the neck with his fingers tangled in the mane as the horse charged for the front gate. But Hack leaped forward at the same time and swung the Winchester by the barrel with both hands, as though he were chopping with an ax, and caught Hardin squarely across the base of the neck. Hardin pitched sideways out of the saddle and landed on his back, and when he tried to raise himself to his feet, Hack kicked him full in the face with his boot. Then he threw him unconscious into the bed of a vegetable wagon, put manacles on his wrists, wrapped him in trace chains and nailed the end links down to the boards.

'What did he say to you when he was in the cell?' his grandson said.

'He wouldn't say anything. He'd spit in his food and throw it out on the floor and look at me with them eyes that was like a slow match burning. He didn't need to say anything else.'

But he hadn't told his grandson the rest of the story, the part that had bothered him through the years, not because it was singular in itself, but instead because it was not –

something that was in him that he had never come to understand.

On the way into Yoakum, with Hardin chained in the back of the wagon, the blood kept beating in his temples, his chest expanded with each breath that he drew, and he whipped the mules over holes that could have broken a wheel. Hardin was conscious, his manacled hands clasped on the front of his black coat like a preacher's, his body swaying under the chains as the wagon bounced over the ruts, and when Hack looked back into his blood-flecked eyes, he felt a strange relationship with him that was based on neither fear nor hatred.

'You want to stop the wagon and do it proper between us?' Hardin said.

'I don't want to see you get knocked off your own horse and go to hell in the same day.'

'If you just lock me in jail, you know you ain't going to sleep tonight, Hack. You make the rules. Pistols or knives or shotguns.'

'Tell me, did you really kill them forty men?'

'Some of them was federal niggers, like your deputies. That don't really count,' Hardin said. 'I tell you what. Take these shackles off me, and we'll use one pistol and you can hold it. That'll make it even.'

'You're a shit hog, Hardin, and that's what I'm going to use you for in my jail. You're going to clean slop jars and spittoons until I send you up to Huntsville pen.'

But even after he threw Hardin headlong into the cell and turned the key on him, the blood still hummed in his head, and his face was hot to his own touch. He left the mules in harness behind the jail and rode his deputy's horse back to the house. He slipped the cinch on the saddle and let it fall to the ground, pulled the bridle over the horse's head, and slapped its rump toward Yoakum. The Mexican woman (he thought her name was Marta) was at the back of the barn, mixing molasses and feed in a nose bag for the mare that had just given foal. There were dried flecks of blood and gossamer wisps of membrane in the hair of her forearms. She started to smile, then turned toward the stall when she saw his face. Her breasts were too large for the man's denim shirt she wore, and her thighs were thick from doing stoop labor in the fields. Her flat, Indian face and obsidian eyes looked back at him again, and she tried to bend over into the stall and slip the straps of the nose bag around the mare's ears before his hands took her shoulders and pulled her back. He pressed her down on the feed sacks, lifted her peasant dress over her hips, and pulled her bloomer underwear down over her legs. She went through it without choice, her face turned away toward the stall, and after he reached that heart-rushing moment and labored with his head pressed between her breasts, she pushed up softly at him with her palms.

'She'll bite the foal if she don't eat,' she said.

'No. Again,' he said, and felt the heat burn inside him throughout the morning.

It was a brilliant morning on the front porch, and the blowing clouds left deep areas of shadow, like bruises, on the soft, green hills in the distance. His daughter ran her comb through his hair and touched at it with her fingers as she might at a child's, then placed the Stetson back on his head and moved a white strand away from his eyebrow.

'You look right handsome, Grandpa,' she said.

'But we don't want you chasing women when we get to town,' his son-in-law said.

He felt them take him by each arm and help him into the yellow convertible, then the front gate went by and the Angus grazing through the short grass in the front pasture, the wind-mill ginning in the hot breeze and the water pumping out over the trough, and finally the long, white fence that bordered the field where his son kept his thoroughbreds. The rocks clicked under the fenders, then the car rumbled over the cattleguard, and he heard the tires hiss along the soft tar surfacing of the road. The pines and oak trees were thickly spaced along the road, and he could smell the dry needles on the ground and blackjack burning in someone's smokehouse. Somewhere beyond a watery pool on the bend of the road a train whistle was blowing.

'Where did you say Satchel-ass was at?' he said.

'In Korea, Grandpa. Don't you remember when he sent the medal home?' his daughter said.

It's inside him, too, he thought. *It didn't go into any of the others.*

The road wound out of the woods and dropped over a hill, then the country flattened out into small farms and neat, white houses with tin roofs and rose gardens. The billboards and the huge signs painted on the sides of barns flashed by him, the drive-in root-beer stand and the trailer park, then the prefabricated houses in a bulldozed field, and he tried to call back into memory what that part of the county had looked like before, but the convertible was going too fast.

His son-in-law pulled the car into the high-banked side-walk with the old tethering rings set in the concrete and put a coin in the parking meter. It was Saturday, and the sidewalk was crowded with Mexicans, Negroes, and farm families, and most of the merchants had rolled out the awnings in front of their stores and put wood chairs by their doors. The sun was hot on the leather seat of the convertible. Hack looked through the front glass into the dark interior of the poolroom straight ahead. He could hear the click of the billiard balls and the laughter of drunk farmhands and cedar cutters and almost smell the bottles of beer set along the bar.

'We're just going in the dime store, Grandpa,' Bonnie said.

He saw them walk away through the brightness into the awning's shadow. A drop of perspiration ran out from under his hat and caught in his eyelash like a diamond. It was too hot in the car and he wanted to urinate. Then a large, gray man, with square shoulders and eyes as blue as a butane flame, was standing next to the car door.

'Why, hello, Mr. Holland, how are you today?' he said, and picked up Hack's hand with his own. 'Can I get you a glass of beer from the bar?'

'They won't give me nothing to drink at home.'

'Well, I don't expect Bonnie will mind. You wait here and I'll be right back.'

The tall man stepped back on the high sidewalk in his cowboy boots and went inside the darkness of the poolroom. A moment later he returned with a mug of beer, the foam and ice slipping over his hand.

'After you finish this, Mr. Holland, just wave and I'll bring you another one.'

'My grandson little Hack is fighting across the big water.'

'Yes sir, we heard about it. They give him the navy cross, didn't they?'

'He's a Holland. He's the only one of the bunch that's got the same thing inside him.'

'Well, OK, Mr. Holland, you let me know when you're ready.'

Hack raised the mug to his mouth with both hands, his frosted eyes staring into the brassy bead of the beer, and drank it all the way to the bottom. He felt the foam dripping off his chin and a wetness start to run down his trousers into his half-topped boots. He pushed the mug up on the dashboard and waved at the dark opening of the poolroom. The people inside moved around like shadows in the noise of the billiard balls and the jukebox. The leather seats burned his hands and the odor from his trousers sickened him. He knocked with his knuckles against the front windshield, his collapsed mouth opening and closing like a fish's.

Then, suddenly, there was a tall man who looked cut out of burnt iron by the side of the car. His silhouette seemed to break the murderous sun in half.

'Why, hello, Hack. How have you been?' the man said.

Hack thought he heard a branch of the pin-oak tree at home snap in the hot wind like a rifle shot.

'I didn't expect to see you here, Captain McAlester,' he said. He shook the captain's extended hand, squeezing it, the board roughness biting into his palm, and felt a resilience and strength swell into his arm.

'We haven't had any fun together since we killed all them Mexicans and spent the night in that hot-pillow house in Juarez,' the captain said. 'You remember when you turned the key on Wes Hardin? He said he was going to gun you soon as he come out of Huntsville.'

'He didn't get a chance, though,' Hack said. 'Old John Selman put a ball through his eye first.'

'It's too hot out here, Hack. Let's take a walk and have a cigar.'

Hack opened the door and stepped up on the sidewalk in the shade of the awning, his shoulders erect inside his open coat, an unlit Havana cigar between his teeth. He popped a kitchen match on his thumbnail, cupped his hands in the warm breeze, and drew in on the smoke. He felt a physical power and confidence in his body that he hadn't known since he was in his prime as a middle-aged man.

He and the captain walked the full length of Main Street, tipping their hats to the women and politely refusing invitations for a drink from men who wanted to be seen at the bar with two of the best law officers in south-central Texas.

At the edge of town he leaned against the wood colonnade in front of the feed-and-tack store and looked out into a deep field that was burned sear by drought. In the distance was a low, brown mountain covered with summer haze. He could smell the drowsy odor of the poppies blowing across the field.

'This is where we go, ain't it?' he said.

'Let's just walk on into the field, Hack.'

He heard the dried husks of the poppies rattle around him and the whistle of a locomotive somewhere beyond the curve of the mountain as he went deeper into the field with the captain, this time without resistance or heat or fear of a machine gunner's twisted, monkey-paw face.

On the far edge of the field he saw an old adobe jail set back in a grove of juniper trees, and he could hear a man railing in his chains. Was that John Wesley Hardin screaming in there, or was it himself or his grandson, he thought.

'No sir, that's Satan you chained in that cell,' the captain said.

Then he saw the train come around the curve of the mountain, the smoke blowing back over the line of cars and the men sitting on the spine, and for just a moment he thought he could hear the laughter of Mexican girls in a roar of hooves.

We Build Churches, Inc.

Across the frozen rice fields the brown North Korean hills were streaked with ice and pocked with craters from our 105s. It was cold and bright, and the concertina wire we had strung around our perimeter was half-buried in the snow, looping in and out of the surface like an ugly snake that had been lopped into segments by a lawnmower. But we really weren't worried about a frontal attack in that third week of November in 1950. We had killed Communists by the thousands all the way across North Korea, bulldozing their bodies into trenches and packing the fill down with tanks, until they fled into the hills under a gray sky and hid like bandits. Then the winter swept down out of China across the Yalu, and the hills cracked clear and sharp, and our F-80s and B-25s bombed them twelve hours a day with napalm and phosphorous and incendiaries that generated so much heat in the soil that the barren slopes were still smoking the next morning.

Jason Bradford was seated with his back against the ditch, looking at a picture on the front page of *The Stars and Stripes*. He had a blanket pulled up to his chin, and his mittened hands stuck out from under the blanket. The mitten on his right hand was cut away around the trigger finger. During the night his patrol had run into a North Korean listening post and had lost one marine to a potato masher that the Koreans had got away before the sergeant stitched them all over the hole. Jace's eyes were red around the rims, and he kept fingering his cheek as though he had a toothache.

'Give me another hit of gin, Doc,' he said. 'I'm going to get warm if I have to let the stuff eat down to my toenails.'

I took a bottle of codeine out of my pack and handed it to him.

'Cheers,' he said, and drank from the bottle's lip, washing the codeine over his teeth and swallowing it with the pleasure a martini would give him. 'Now, look at that picture. A picture like that is not an accident.'

A reporter from *The Stars and Stripes* had been photographing an airborne squadron of B-25s, but when the picture was developed, the planes appeared only in the right-hand corner and the frame was filled with the head and shoulders of Jesus Christ.

'You see, I took a course in meteorology at Amherst, and those kinds of clouds don't make a formation like that,' Jace said.

'That's what they call an optical delusion,' the corporal sitting across from us said. He was a tall hillbilly boy from north Alabama named Willard Posey. He hated the Marine Corps for a different reason than the rest of us: the corps had sent him to Korea to fight for gooks, whom he considered inferior even to blacks.

'There's a preacher on a radio station in Memphis that sells them things,' he said.

'Willard, my friend, the whole world is not like the hill country of north Alabama. You have to understand that one of these days,' Jace said.

'I ain't got your education,' Willard said, 'but I know that feller in Memphis is a crook and that ain't no picture of Jesus. You reckon he'd be looking down on a country full of heathens that tie up men with wire and machine-gun them?'

A week earlier we had found the bodies of sixteen marines frozen in the snow by the side of a railway track. We guessed that they had been captured in the south and for some reason taken off a prisoner train and executed. The bailing wire was so tight on their wrists that we couldn't snip through it without tearing the bloated skin.

Jace fingered his cheek again, pushing ice crystals from his mitten into his beard as though his jaw had no feeling.

'You remember that bunch of gooks we took prisoner about two months ago?' he said. 'The lieutenant sent them to the rear with the ROKs. Do you think those guys made it beyond the first hill?'

'That's monkeys killing monkeys. They been doing that to each other on this shit pile for hundreds of years. That don't have nothing to do with us.'

'It has everything to do with the lieutenant, and with us, too, Willard,' Jace said.

'You better lay off that gin,' Willard said, and picked up his M-1 and walked farther down the ditch.

Jace took another drink out of the bottle and rested his head back in his helmet. He had turned down officer's school at Quantico, which his education and good looks and career as a college lacrosse player should have made a natural extension of his life.

'Willard is not educable,' I said.

'Ah, but that's it. He has been taught.'

'Don't make a mystery out of a simple man.'

'You southerners hang together, don't you? When it comes down to that choice between reason and blathering with a mouthful of collard greens, there's something atavistic in you that makes you home in on the latter like a fly on a pig flop.'

'What is it, Jace?'

'That kid last night.'

'It was just bad luck.'

'My ass. He was only on the line one day. He shouldn't

have been put on patrol. I could hear him breathing in the dark behind me, the kind of breathing you hear when a guy's heart is coming out his mouth. He must have wanted to prove something, because he worked himself up right behind the point. When we walked into the gooks, a potato masher came flying out of the hole. He just stared at it and poked at it with his foot, like it was something he didn't want to touch but couldn't run away from at the same time.'

In the rear someone was trying to start a cold engine in a tank. The starter ground away like Coke-bottle glass in the still air.

'I must have been looking at him, yelling at him, because I saw him light up like fire was painted on one side of him.'

'Give me the codeine and go to sleep.'

'No sleep today, Doc. We're going to be stringing mines. Somebody said the First Division captured some Chinese at a reservoir up the road.'

'Chinese?'

'They probably grabbed some Korean mountain people who speak a dialect, and some dumbass translator didn't know how to classify them.'

'You better sleep, anyway.'

Jace turned his face at me and squinted in the sunlight. His helmet cut a diagonal shadow across his eyes and made his face look as though it were sewn together from mismatched parts.

'What you got to understand is that I'm a practical man,' he said. 'I have one foot solidly in this world. That's because I come from a family that never got lost in the next world. We knew how to hold on to a big chunk of this one and deal with it.'

I didn't know what introspection was taking him through a maze inside of himself or even if introspection was the word for it. His voice had a wired edge to it, and fatigue was an explanation that only civilians used. I had seen craziness come in many forms since I had been in Korea, but it usually got men when they first went on the firing line or after an artillery barrage when they became hysterical and had to be sedated with morphine. But Jace had been on the line since Inchon and had had his ticket punched at every stop across North Korea.

'Let me explain it this way,' he said. 'The first Bradford in Massachusetts was a ship's carpenter, and the Puritans were building churches all over the place. But it takes a lot of time to build a church out of squared logs, especially when you got to stop and kill off all the Indians and press witches to death. The first Bradford, the carpenter, was a religious man, and he had an idea that would take care of the problem for everybody. He hired a bunch of guys like himself and built the church on contract. He paid the other guys out of his pocket, and all he asked from the community was a small piece of land set aside in his name. He built churches in Salem, Cambridge, Haverhill, anywhere he found Puritans and wood. This went on for thirty years, until some farmers figured out that he probably owned more land than anyone else in the commonwealth. So these manure slingers got together and had him tried as a witch, and they had some good evidence to use against him. He was as strong as a draft horse, and he could poke one finger in the end of a musket and hold it out at arm's length. So the manure slingers said he was in league with Old Nick, and they tried to make him confess by ordeal. They staked him out in a field and put an oak door over his body and then added one stone to it at a time. You see, the deal was that if a witch confessed, all his property went back into the public domain. They crushed his chest and snapped his ribs like sticks, but he never let a word of guilt pass his lips.

'His sons inherited his property and they figured a way to protect it against the manure slingers. They incorporated under the name We Build Churches, Inc. You can't try a corporation for witchery, can you? Those

Puritans would deep fry the balls of an individual, but they knew a business company was sacred.

'And my family has been building churches ever since, and we still own some of the land that was given to the carpenter. There's a bank in Cambridge built right on top of where he used to keep a smithy.

'Does that make sense to you? Do you know what I mean now by having a vision of both worlds?'

One eye seemed pulled down on his cheek, as though he were aiming along the sights of his M-1.

I didn't want to answer. I simply wanted the codeine back and to talk with the lieutenant about rotating Jace early. As a corpsman I could do it by saying that I thought he had walking pneumonia.

I heard a truck with snow chains on crunching up the road through the frozen rice field behind us. One of the chains was broken and swinging under the fender.

'That looks like the foot warmers now,' I said. 'Give me the codeine so you don't blow your face off.'

I walked down the ditch past Willard, who was standing against the embankment with his hands in his armpits, smoking a cigarette without taking it from his mouth. The lieutenant was farther on with his back turned to me and his face bent down over an engineer's compass placed on a mess kit that he had flattened into the snow for a level. He turned an angle on the compass gingerly with one finger and then drew the angle on his note pad.

'Could I speak with you a minute, Lieutenant?'

'Go ahead,' he said, his blue eyes still preoccupied with the mine pattern we were going to lay. He was an Annapolis graduate and a good officer, but he was single-minded sometimes and irritated by what he considered a complaint.

'Bradford's been spitting up phlegm for two weeks. I think he might have pneumonia.'

'What's his temperature?'

'He won't let me take it.'

98

The lieutenant's eyes swept into mine.

'What kind of bullshit are you handing me, Doc?'

'I thought he ought to ride back with the mine truck to the aid station.'

'What you thought is you'd slip me a candyass con. You've been a corpsman too long for that, Doc.'

'I'm supposed to make my recommendation to you, Lieutenant.'

'You'd better listen to me and never do something like this again.'

'Yes sir.'

I walked back down the ditch feeling stupid and humiliated. Up ahead, I saw that Jace had climbed over the embankment and was headed toward the truck. As I passed Willard he caught my sleeve and pulled me to him.

'Don't wrinkle my threads,' I said.

'Stay cool and have a smoke. I want to tell you something.' He lit a Camel from the one he was smoking and handed it to me. 'I heard what you said to the lieutenant, and I also heard what Bradford told you about that kid that got blowed up last night. You done the right thing trying to get him out of here. He ain't seeing things good in his head, and that gets people knocked off.'

'What do you mean?'

'That kid wasn't behind the point. He was in the rear all the time. Them three gooks was in a hole at the top of an arroyo, and we didn't see them till the potato masher come end over end at us. We all went flying down the hill with it rolling down after us, but the kid stood there like his feet was locked in ice. Bradford was the last one down. Maybe he could have knocked the kid back. Maybe any of us could. It ain't nobody's fault. But I wanted you to know it didn't happen the way Bradford said. I tell you what. I'm going to stay so close on his butt he'll think he's got piles. If he starts talking crazy again or if I think he's going to screw up, I'm telling the lieutenant the same thing you did.'

'You're all right, Willard.'

'Shit. I got thirteen days to rotation and I ain't getting knocked off because of a crazy man.'

When the sun went down over the hills, a red light spilled across the land and we felt the temperature drop in minutes. The wind blew down out of the hills, and the snow that had fallen that morning was polished into a thin, frozen cake that you could punch your finger through. Beyond the concertina wire the depressions where the mines had been set looked like slick dimples on a piece of moonscape. My feet and ears ached in the cold as though they had been beaten with boards.

In the purple gloom of the ditch Jace was looking around the edges of his pack for something. When he couldn't find it, he flipped the pack over, then unsnapped the canvas flap and rooted in it with an increasing urgency.

'Who took my newspaper?' he said.

Willard and I looked at his anxious face without replying.

'I want to know who took it. It was tucked inside the strap.'

'The Indian was trying to start a fire,' Willard said.

'You lying son of a bitch.'

'You say that to me again and I'm going to break every bone in your face.'

'You just try it. I'm not one of your darkies on the plantation. You took it, didn't you? Say it. You had to destroy what didn't fit into that ignorant southern mind of yours?'

'What?'

'You heard me. You can't think past what you hear on a hillbilly radio station or a bunch of captured gooks that get marched off behind a hill.'

'I saw the Indian with it,' I said.

'You tend to your own business, Doc,' Willard said.

In the distance we heard the popping of small arms like a

string of firecrackers, followed by two long bursts from a BAR on our right flank.

'What's that asshole doing?' Willard said, his face wooden in the red twilight.

Then we saw the Chinese moving out of the hills toward us. They appeared on the crests in silhouette, like ants swarming to the top of a sinking log, and poured down the slopes and arroyos onto the rice field. They marched a mortar barrage ahead of them across the field, blowing up the mines we had set earlier and sending geysers of snow and yellow earth high into the air. We shrank into fetal positions in the bottom of the ditch, each man white-faced and alone in his terror, as the reverberations through the ground grew in intensity. Then when they had bracketed our line, they turned it on in earnest. The explosions were like locomotive engines blowing apart. The ditch danced with light, flame rippled along the strands of concertina wire, and a long round hit the gasoline dump behind us and blew a balloon of fire over us that scalded our skin.

When the barrage lifted, the snow in the craters around us was still hissing from the heat of the buried shrapnel, and the rice field and the horizon of the hills were covered with small, dark men in quilted uniforms. They came at us in waves and walked over their own dead while we killed them by the thousands. The long stretch of field was streaked with tracers, and occasionally one of our mines went off and blew men into the air likes piles of rags. We packed snow on our .30-caliber machine guns and fired them until the rifling went and the barrels melted. When somebody down the line yelled that they were pushing civilians ahead of them, the firing never let up. If anything, the machine gunners kept the trigger frozen back against the guard to get at the men who carried those murderous burp guns with the fifty-round drum clips.

The bottom of the ditch was strewn with spent shell casings and empty ammunition boxes. Willard was next to me, firing his M-1 over the edge of the embankment, his unused clips set in a neat line in the snow. I heard a shell whang dead center into his helmet and ricochet inside. He pirouetted around in slow motion, his helmet rolled off his shoulder, and the blood ran in red strings from under his stocking cap. There was a surgical cut along the crown of the skull that exposed his brain. He slid down against the ditch wall with one leg folded under him, his jaw distended as though he were about to yawn.

'Get the wounded ready to move, Doc,' the lieutenant said. 'We're going to get artillery in forty-five minutes and pull.'

'In forty-five minutes we're going to be spaghetti.'

'They got a priority in another sector. Get those men ready to move.'

Five minutes later the lieutenant got it through the throat, and the artillery never came. Before we were overrun, we put a flamethrower in their faces and cooked them alive at thirty yards. Their uniforms were burnt away, and their blackened bodies piled up in a stack like people caught in a fire exit. Farther down the ditch I saw Jacé with his back propped against the embankment, his face white with concussion and his coat singed and blown open.

I hadn't heard a grenade in the roar of burp guns, but when I pulled back his jacket, I saw the blood welling through the half-dozen tears in his sweater. His eyes were crossed, and he kept opening his mouth as though he were trying to clear his ears. I laid him down on a stretcher and buckled only the leg strap and made a marine pick up the other end.

'There ain't no place to go,' the marine said.

'Over the top. There's an ambulance behind the tank.'

'Oh shit, they're in the ditch.'

The flank had gone, and then suddenly they were everywhere. They held their burp guns sideways on their shoulder slings and shot the living and the dead alike. Marines with empty rifles huddled in the bottom of the ditch and held their hands out against the bullets that raked across their bodies. The very brave stood up with bayonets and entrenching tools and were cut down in seconds. For the first and only time in my life I ran from an enemy. I dropped the stretcher and ran toward the right flank, where I heard a BAR man still hammering away. But I didn't have far to go, because I saw one of the small dark men on the embankment above me, his Mongolian face pinched in the cold, his quilted uniform and tennis shoes caked with snow. He had just pulled back the spring on the magazine and reset the sling, and I knew that those brass-cased armor-piercing rounds manufactured in Czechoslovakia had finally found their home.

Luke the Gook. How do you do. Punch my transfer ticket neatly, sir. Please do not disturb the dogtags. They have a practical value for reasons that you do not understand. Later they must be untaped and inserted between the teeth because the boxes get mixed up in the baggage car, and I do have to get off at San Antone tonight. Oh sorry, I see you must be about your business.

But he was a bad shot. He depressed the barrel too low on the sling, and his angle of fire cut across my calves like shafts of ice and knocked me headlong on the body of the lieutenant as though a bad comic had kicked my legs out from under me. In the seconds that I waited for the next burst to rip through my back, I could hear the lieutenant's wristwatch ticking in my face. But when the burp gun roared again, it was aimed at a more worthy target, the BAR man who stood erect in the ditch, the tripod flopping under the barrel, firing until the breech locked empty and he was cut down by a half-dozen Chinese.

I spent the next thirty-two months in three POW camps. I was in the Bean Camp, which had been used by the Japanese for British prisoners during W.W.II, Pak's Palace outside of Pyong-yang, and Camp Five in No Name Valley just south of the Yalu. I learned how political lunatics could turn men into self-hating loathsome creatures who would live with the guilt of Judas the rest of their lives. I spent six weeks in a filthy hole under a sewer grate, with an encrusted G.I. helmet for a honey bucket, until I became the eighth man of eleven from our shack to inform on an escape attempt. But sometimes when I lay in the bottom of the hole and looked up through the iron squares at the clouds turning across the sky, I thought of Jace and Willard and Puritans knocking their axes into wood. Then at some moment between vision and the crush of the dirt walls upon me, between drifting light and the weight of witches' stones upon my chest, I knew that I would plane and bevel wood and build churches. I would build one at my home in Yoakum, in Goliad and Gonzales and San Antonio, any place there were pine trees and cottonwoods and water oaks to be felled. Then I saw the sky re-form as a photograph and the ice clouds turn soft and porous as a eucharist.

When It's Decoration Day

Through the darkness and the tangle of hackberry trees he could still see the burning glow of Atlanta against the sky, like red heat lightning that trembled and then faded on the edge of the horizon. He hadn't believed that a city built of stone and mortar and scrolled iron could burn (or that anything so large and fiercely determined to resist defeat and occupation could be vulnerable against an army that brought war on defenseless people and gave Negroes weapons to fire upon white men). But that afternoon, when they had mired the gun carriage in a slough bottom and the lieutenant had forced the two freed convicts to push against the wheels at revolver point, he heard the armory by the railroad depot explode, a roar that split the hard, blue sky apart like an angry rip that peeled away from the earth's surface, and before he could release the spokes of the wheel in his hand or feel the weight of the cannon crushing back into the mud bottom or even leap backward from his own preoccupation with the pain in his back and the sweat bees that swarmed around his head in the heat, he already felt the first tremors roll through the ground under him like a displaced piece of thunder. He saw the geyser of dirt and powdered brick rise in the air above the city and flatten off in the wind, then there was a second explosion, muffled, a contained thump that rippled the black water in the bottom of the slough, and he guessed that Sherman's artillery had hit one of the powder dumps they had buried yesterday on Peachtree Creek.

Now, under the moon, the smoke drifted through the trees and hung in the shallow depressions, and the cannon and its carriage, coated with dried mud, creaked through the soft dirt of the forest floor behind the two mules. The lieutenant had called a rest only once since they whipped the mules out of the slough bottom, and the boy's sun-faded, butternut brown uniform was heavy with perspiration, and the weight of his Springfield rifle, which he held with one arm crooked over the inverted barrel, cut into the shoulder bone like a dull headache. His face was drawn in the moonlight, and his long, blond hair stuck out damply from under his gray cap. There was a thin, red-brown scar under his eye, like a burn, where a Minié ball had flicked across his face at Kennesaw Mountain (where, for the first and only time, he had seen Negroes in Yankee uniforms break through the fog, kneel in a ragged line, and shoot at him – a vision so unbelievable to him in the turning mist and the scream of grape and cannister that he lowered his rifle and stared again until the Minié ball ticked across his face like a hot finger).

The lieutenant bent under a hackberry branch and turned his horse in a circle, and automatically the column, even the mules, stopped at the same moment. They could see a yellow clay road in the moonlight at the edge of the forest, and in the distance the country opened up on rolling green pasture, rick fences, clumps of oak trees, and unplowed cotton acreage. The lieutenant raised himself in the stirrups, pulled off his flop hat, and pushed his long, wet hair back over his head with his fingers.

'Let's rest it here, boys, then we're going to turn off by that church house yonder and get into Alabama,' he said.

'You want to let the mules out of harness, sir?' the

sergeant said.

The other men remained motionless and watched the officer fix the hard lump of tobacco in the back of his jaw.

'Leave them as they are,' he said.

'Do we have fires, Lieutenant?' the sergeant said.

'We have to chew it cold tonight, Sergeant.'

The soldiers leaned their rifles against the tree branches and sat in clumsy, flat positions on the ground, their knees drawn up before them, their faces bent down into their own exhaustion, the haversack of molded biscuits and dried corn lying like an obscene weight between their thighs. The sweat and heat in their uniforms steamed in the air, and their unshaved faces and uncut hair gave them the look of neglected dead men or collapsed scarecrows under an angry, whalebone moon.

The boy, Wesley Buford, who was sixteen and one of the few from the South Carolina Home Guard who hadn't been killed or captured at Kennesaw Mountain, had the same quiet anger toward the officer as the other men, not only for the quivering in the backs of his thighs and the dead piece of biscuit in his mouth, but because the very fact of a man's birth could guarantee him a horse, a saber, an English side arm, and an inapproachable distance and command over other men's lives, even in the last few weeks of a country's defeat. The sergeant, who was also from South Carolina (a hard, squat timber cutter with a discolored eye like a broken egg yolk and a thumb clipped off at the palm), was the only one who ever spoke directly to the lieutenant, and then it was only to request the next order. The other enlisted men, landless crackers with burnt-out faces, sometimes stared hard at the officer's back, but their eyes never met his and their conversation always stopped whenever he sawed back the bit on his horse to wait for the column to pass him.

Then there were the two convicts, freed from the city prison just before Sherman advanced north of Peachtree Creek, who still wore their striped black-and-white cotton jumpers and the blue trousers they had stripped off two dead Union soldiers. They had received a pardon that had been given collectively in less than one minute by a justice of the peace to seventy-five inmates who raised their hands together in the gloo of a cell block to affirm that they would defend the Confederacy, the Sacred Cause, and Jefferson Davis, and two hours later they had tried to desert. Their teeth were black and rotted to the gums from chewing tobacco, their skin was jaundiced from months spent in a dark cell, and their eyes were rheumy and filled with a mean mixture of hatred toward the officer and the sergeant and disdain for the enlisted men who were fools enough to fight in a war that had already been lost.

The taller of the two finished his biscuits, the dry crumbs dropping from his mouth, and pulled the wood plug from his canteen. His tight, gray cap made a deep line in his wet hair. He flicked his boot against the boy's foot.

'Hey, give me a twist,' he said.

'I ain't got none,' the boy, Wesley Buford, said.

'What's that sticking out your pocket?'

'I ain't got none for you.'

'Well, goddamn, Merle. Listen to this one.'

Merle, the second convict, snuffed down in his nose and spit between his thighs.

'I was listening to him back there on the cannon,' he said. '"Push them spokes. Hit them mules." I thought maybe I joined the nigger army.'

'Well, sho,' the taller man said. 'They give him a Yankee Springfield. That lets him give orders.'

The boy's eyes watched them both with the caution that now came instinctively to him, with a great deal of accuracy, after two months in the infantry.

'I didn't give you no orders. You wasn't laying into the wheel,' he said.

'Yes sir, that's what we got. A soldier that knows how to do it,' the tall convict said. 'What if I reach over there and take that tobacco?'

The boy's hand moved up the stock of his rifle. His calloused thumb touched the heavy hammer on the loading breech.

'You ain't going to cock that on us,' Merle, the second convict, said. 'We got the Indian sign on you, boy. Tomorrow you're going to tote for us.'

'That's right,' the other man said. 'When them mules shit, you wipe their ass. And when I turn around, you bring me my water can.'

'Come with me, Buford.' It was the sergeant's voice. He stood in the darkness behind the two convicts, a rain slicker draped over his shoulders. His bad eye looked like a luminous piece of fish scale in the moonlight. The tall convict took a twisted leaf of dried tobacco from his pocket and cut off a thick piece between his thumb and knife blade.

Wesley walked silently with the sergeant through the wet hackberry branches to the main clearing, where the cannon stood at a tilted angle in the mud. The grease bucket and brush for the hubs were suspended from the carriage axle by a strand of baling wire.

'I was going to get it after I ate,' Wesley said.

'I ain't worried about that gun. We're probably going to be in a prison camp before it gets fired again,' the sergeant said. 'You be careful with them convicts. They'll cut your throat for your biscuits, and half these men won't do nothing to stop it.'

'What do you mean prison camp? The lieutenant said there wasn't no Federals south of Atlanta and we'll be in Alabama in another day.'

'You ain't listening to me.' For just a moment the boy caught the raw smell of corn whiskey on the sergeant's breath. 'You ain't got to get killed in this war. You keep yourself alive a few more days and you'll be on your way back to your family. Don't you know that, boy? We got beat.'

'We whupped them every time till Kennesaw. We –'

'You walk at the head tomorrow with me. I don't want to see you near them convicts. Now get on them hubs till they're slick as spit.'

The boy leaned his Springfield against the cannon barrel, pulled off his shirt, and crawled under the carriage to unfasten the grease bucket from the baling wire. There was a V-line of sunburn around his neck, and his spine and ribs stood out hard and pale against his skin when he bent over the axle hubs with the grease brush. He heard the sergeant breathing deeply behind him, then the sound of the wood plug being pulled from the canteen and once again the rank odor of corn liquor that had been taken too early from the still.

Later, he spread his rain slicker under a dry overhang on the edge of the clearing and slept with his shirt over his face. As he began the several levels of sleep that he always had to go through before he reached that moment of blue-black unconsciousness just before dawn or the cock of a picket's rifle, he heard first the distant cough of thunder out of a piney woods and yellow sky where there should have been no thunder, the black smoke rising in a haze above the treetops, and then the scream of Whistling Dick tearing with its blunt, iron edges through the air into the middle of their line. The earth exploded out of the trench, and muskets, cannon wheels, haversacks, and parts of men were left strewn on the yellowed edge of a huge crater. Then he heard the cavalry on the flank break toward the woods, the sabers drawn and glinting in the sun, and he knew the Federals would be engaged long enough for them to withdraw and regroup beyond the range of their artillery.

The last level of his sleep was usually a short-lived one, and it came only after the spatter of pistol and carbine fire assured him that the Confederate cavalry had held the Federals in check momentarily, but this time he was back at his father's sawmill in South Carolina by the edge of a black swamp, and he and his brother were snaking logs across a sand basin to a loading wagon. He could smell the swamp and its fetid odor of stagnant water, quicksand, dead garfish on the banks, and the mushrooms that burst into bloom off rotting tree trunks. The sunlight turned green through the trees and broke on the water in a tarnished yellow cast, and he could see the giant bullfrogs and alligators frozen like pieces of dark brown stone in the dead current. His brother Cole was stripped to the waist, the sweat running in rivulets down his freckled shoulders and dusty back. His face was hot and bright with his work, the exhausted piece of chewing tobacco stiff against one cheek, and when he doubled the reins around his blond fist and flicked them in a swift crack, the mules strained against the harness and pulled the chained logs over the embankment in a shower of sand. He could talk to the mules in a way that only Negroes could, and he could fall and plane timber better than any man at the mill (his square hands seemed almost shaped for the resilient swing of the ax into the wood). He released the mules and walked into the shallows to pick up the rattlesnake watermelon where it had been left to cool and the dinner bucket of fried rabbit. His face was happy and beaded with sweat when he broke the ripe melon across a rock in a bright red explosion of pulp and seeds and picked the meat out with his thick fingers.

'Daddy don't want us quitting this early,' Wesley said.

'It's Saturday afternoon, ain't it? You and me is going to town, and when we get done drinking beer I'm taking you over to Billy Sue's. Get on down here, boy, and eat your dinner. I ain't going to be waiting on you.'

Wesley looked at his brother's happy green eyes and the smear of melon juice on his mouth, and he knew then that neither of them would ever die.

The false dawn had already touched the eastern horizon beyond the woods and filled the trees with a smoky, green light when the sergeant tapped the toe of his boot into his shoulder. He could smell fatback and biscuits cooking in the gravy over a wet fire, and after the dream had slipped back into a private place inside him, he saw the two convicts hunched by the fire with their dinner pails, the mules still standing with one foot rested in front of the gun carriage, and the long clay road that wound through the trees and the dim fields toward a small, white-washed church house, a fragile board building with mist rising off the yard. He raised himself on his slicker and looked at it again, and it bothered him in the same way the convicts had when they first joined the column.

'Fill your pan and eat it later,' the sergeant said. His good eye was watery and red, and his words were deep in his throat.

'Is there something wrong with me eating with every-body else?'

'Just do what I tell you. The lieutenant wants me and you up ahead a half mile. A couple of them Louisiana Frenchies come in last night and said the Yankees got around behind us. They might drop a whole shithouse on our head if they catch us out in the open.'

Wesley walked to the fire and squatted in the smoke while the cook, an old man with his trousers partly buttoned, poured a mixture of hot water, boiled corn, and honey into his pan. The boy sipped at the scalding edge of the pan and looked through the trees at the long stretch of clay road and the white church building.

'Get some meat and biscuit. They won't be no more hot food today,' the old man said.

'I ain't hungry.'

'He don't like to eat near the likes of us,' one of the convicts said.

'Don't get in front of me today,' Wesley said. He picked up his Springfield, laid it over his shoulder, and walked off with the sergeant into the mist while the two convicts stared blankly after him.

The low clouds on the eastern horizon were pink now

with the sun's first hard light, and the white circle of moon was fading as though it were being gathered into the blueness of the day. Sparrow hawks floated over the wet fields, and somewhere beyond the church he could hear a dog barking, an ugly, relentless sound sustained by its own violation of the quiet air. He opened the breech of his rifle, snapped it shut again, and pulled back the hammer to half cock.

'Don't go seeing Federals where they ain't none,' the sergeant said. 'You pop one cap and that bunch back there is scared enough to throw their damn Minié balls all over this road.'

'Look at them wheel tracks. They wasn't cut that deep by no wagon.'

The sergeant looked at the heavy, curled ruts in the clay with his watery eye and unconsciously moved the cartridge box on his belt from its position on his side to the center of his stomach.

'You're durn near blind, ain't you?' Wesley said.

'The only blind I got is what come out of my canteen last night. You just watch the edge of that woods up yonder and don't blow your toes off in the meantime.'

'What are we supposed to do if we get hit out here? There ain't a hole big enough for a whistle pig to hide in.'

'That's what it's all about, son.'

'How come the lieutenant don't get on point except when we're in the woods?' he said angrily, and instantly felt stupid for his question, but the fear had already started to grow and quicken around his heart as they neared the church, and the white lines of the building against the green fields beyond made the skin in his face pinch tight against the bone.

'You didn't see him when we pulled off Kennesaw. He might look like he was born with a mammy's pink finger up his ass, but he walked a horse trailing its guts down the hill with two wounded on its back while their whole line let off on him. I seen his tunic jump twice when a Minié cut through it, and his face never even turned.' The sergeant was talking too fast now, and the knuckles in his hand were white around the hammer and trigger guard of his carbine. He sucked in his cheeks to gather the moisture in his mouth and spit a thin stream of tobacco juice in front of him. 'You don't worry about him on point. He's only got one trouble. He don't quit, and that's going to get us all in a hard place in the next few days.'

Wesley stared hard at the church building, and then his heart clicked inside him.

'Something moved in the window,' he said, his breath tight in his throat.

'Keep walking.'

'I seen it. I knowed there was Federals in there.'

'Keep that goddamn rifle where it is.' The sergeant's voice was low and his gray face was pointed straight ahead. 'They're probably skirmishers, and they'll let us pass to get to the column. When we hit the timber, we'll move right around and behind them.'

'They're going to cut us up right here on the road.'

'You shut, you hear?'

The boy could feel the blood draining out of his face, and sweat dripped from his hair and ran down his neck into his collar. His heart was clicking rapidly now, like a bad watch, and his breathing swelled inside his chest as though there were no oxygen in the humid air. He wished he had taken some shells from his cartridge box and stuck them inside his belt, because the half-second's difference in loading could keep the Yankees on the floor of the church until he had a chance to make for the woods. He wanted to wipe the sweat from his eyes, but his hands felt wooden and locked onto the rifle, and he knew that if he moved in any irregular fashion, a gray storm of Minié balls would leave him and the sergeant ripped apart on the road like piles of rags.

'A hundred more feet, son, and then we'll be coming up their ass,' the sergeant said. The strands of chewing tobacco were like dry burns on his lips.

Wesley looked at the dark green of the pines and the mist burning away in the sunlight. Then in the time that his eyes could throb with the knowledge that it was too late, that they were caught forever in a rain-washed piece of farmland between two thick woods, a window in the church filled with a man and the long barrel of his rifle thrown hurriedly against the jamb.

Wesley whirled the Springfield toward the window and fired before the stock touched his shoulder. The man's face flattened in an oval pie of disbelief, the back of his head roared upward into the sash, and his rifle balanced once on the window's edge, then toppled out on the ground. Wesley knocked the swollen cartridge out of the breech with the flat of his hand and pushed another flush into the chamber. Every window in the church exploded with puffs of dirty smoke, the sergeant's carbine went off close to his ear, and he swung his sight on an officer who was cocking and firing his revolver through a dark opening between the front doors. The ball tore the door's edge away in a shower of white splinters, he saw the officer's hands go to his face as though he had been scalded, and then he and the sergeant were running down the clay road toward the hackberry trees and the cannon that the lieutenant was already turning into position. Wesley pulled his haversack strap and canteen string off his shoulder and tried to get another cartridge out of his box without spilling the rest. He heard a Minié whine away behind him, then two more that thropped with a hollow rush of air close to his head.

'Don't go in a straight line! They'll hit you sure!' the sergeant yelled.

The men ramming the powder bag down the mouth of the cannon seemed miniature in the distance, their motions stiff and muted in the shimmering heat. The lieutenant was jacking the elevation screw on the carriage, and then Wesley saw one of the convicts carry a heavy bucket to the front of the cannon and loop the bail over the barrel.

'Goddamn, they're loading with grape.'

'Shut up. Just go down when I do.'

'They can't reach the church house with grape. They're going to tear us in half.'

'Watch the lieutenant's arm.'

The convict finished loading the handfuls of iron balls out of the bucket, a private shot the ramming rod once down the barrel, and the lieutenant raised his hand high above his head and kept it there several seconds.

'Bury your pecker,' the sergeant said.

They fell forward on their elbows in the middle of the road, and Wesley clenched his fists and wrapped his arms around his head just as the cannon thundered in a roar of black smoke and pitched upward on its carriage. He felt the ground shake under his loins, and the wide pattern of grapeshot sucked by overhead in a diminishing scream. It was quiet for less than a second, then he heard the iron balls rain on the church house like dozens of hammers clattering into wood. He turned and saw the walls covered with small, black holes, powdered bricks from the chimney scattered across the roof, and a wisp of smoke rising from one eave.

'Some of them balls must have still been glowing,' Wesley said.

'Get it moving, son. We ain't home yet.'

They started running again, but this time Wesley knew that they had an aura of magic around them, and the two or three Yankees who were still firing couldn't place a Minié closer than a few feet from them. The breech and barrel of his Springfield were coated with clay, he had lost his haversack, canteen, bayonet, and half of his cartridges on the road, but the trees were only fifty yards away, and the private was already reaming out the cannon barrel with water so they could stuff in the next powder bag. The rest of the men had formed a bent line through the trees, their butternut brown uniforms almost indistinguishable from the trunks in the deep shade of the woods, and each time a rifle recoiled among the leaves, he heard the lead shot flatten out an instant later against the side of the church house.

Then he saw the sergeant jerk forward and his carbine fly into the air. The muscles in his face collapsed, the mouth hung open, and his legs, still running, folded under him as though all the bone had been removed. Then he simply sat down. The Minié had almost been spent when it embedded in the base of his scalp, and the lead protruded in a gray lump from the proud flesh.

'Drop him and run for the cannon,' he heard the lieutenant yell above the rifle fire. Then a moment later, after the cannon roared again and covered him with its heat, 'Can't you hear me, Private? He's dead.'

The battle lasted through the morning until the Federals were burned out of the church house and forced to run across the open fields to the opposite woods. But later Wesley could remember little of it in any sequence. There had been the terrible thirst and the white sun boiling out of a cloudless sky, the green horse-flies humming over the sergeant's body, the acrid smoke that floated in the trees and burned the inside of his lungs, the wounded who were carried deeper into the woods and left their thick, scarlet drops on the dead leaves. The only detail that remained etched in time, like a clock suddenly ticking upon the twelfth hour, was the church roof bursting into pockets of flame. He stopped firing and watched the shingles curl and snap in the heat while great holes caved open in the roof and showers of sparks shot into the sky. The flames leaped out the windows and raced up the building's sides, and then the Federals were in the middle of an unplowed field, their weapons abandoned, some of them limping and holding on to each other in a foolish dance toward the woods. They crumpled silently like stick figures in the distance, and Wesley loaded again and felt the same awful surge of blood and victory in his head as every man firing next to him.

They buried the sergeant and three enlisted men in the woods, pulled the cannon from its carriage and drove a cold chisel into the priming hole, and made a litter of tree limbs and blankets on the stripped gun mount for the two wounded who couldn't walk. One man had been shot through both jaws and had a filthy gray shirt tied around his mouth to hold his chin and teeth in place. The old cook had been hit in the stomach while pouring water down the cannon barrel, and the dressing he held to the swollen, black hole above his navel was already sticking to his fingers. They moved across the fields past the scorched brick foundation of the church house, past the bodies of the Federals, which had started to swell in the heat, and Wesley had to look away when he saw the magpies picking like chickens after corn at the crusted wounds. The two convicts began to walk on the edge of the fields when they saw the first dead, slowing gradually while the column moved ahead of them. The lieutenant turned his horse in a half circle and slipped the leather loop off the hammer of his pistol.

'I want you men in front of the mules.'

'They got ammunition, Lieutenant. That officer yonder probably has a Colt's.'

'You'll move back on the road or be shot.'

Their dirty, cotton prison jumpers stuck to their chests. They squinted up at the lieutenant in the sun, their sallow faces filmed with sweat, then walked onto the road ahead of him.

In the few moments that the column was stopped, Wesley had watched the other men rather than the convicts, and he had sensed, in the way he would the hidden brightening of color in a man's eyes, a bitter wish inside all of them that the convicts would push it to the edge. It wasn't any one thing that he could look at clearly in the center of his mind, but instead something that was collectively wrong and displaced for that moment on a yellow clay road between two steaming fields: the immobility of the man in front of him, the thick lump of tobacco frozen in his cheek, the silence along the column and the fact that no one unstrung his canteen, or maybe the smell of their bodies and the sweat running down their necks now that they had stopped. Yes, that was it, he thought. *They had stopped.* They were in the open where they could be hit again if more Federals had moved up through the woods, and this time they were without their cannon and carrying wounded, but not one man had shown a flick or quiver in his face at the possibility that a skirmish line was already being formed behind that violent green border of trees.

They moved down the road, and the man on the carriage litter with the shirt tied around his mouth began to chew on his tongue and froth blood and saliva. There were no Federals in the woods, only three dead Negro children. They lay in a row among the leaves, as though they had gone to sleep, and the pine trunks around them were scoured in white strips from a rain of grapeshot.

'What the hell was they doing there? Why wasn't they home with their people?' the man behind Wesley said.

But he had already quickened his step past the lieutenant, who was trying to saw up the bridle on his horse and keep him from spooking sideways into the tree limbs.

That night, after the moon had risen with a rain ring around it in the green twilight, the mist started to gather in the woods, and the first drops of rain clicked flatly on the high spread of branches overhead. They shaved willow poles from a creek bed, slanted them into the ground, and stretched their slickers over the notched ends and weighted the bottoms with rocks to make dry lean-tos. The cook, whose intestine was bulging against the dressing that he still held to his stomach, and the man who had been shot through both jaws were placed under the cannon carriage with a canvas tarpaulin across the four wheels. The cook's face already had the iridescent shine of the dead, and he had urinated several times in his trousers. The other man had tried to pull his teeth loose with his fingers, and pieces of bone had dried in the crust of blood along his cheek.

Wesley used his bowie, which his father had given him when he was twelve, to hack the pine saplings away from the base of a limestone boulder and make a shelter that would be as dry and comfortable as anything the Cherokees had made in South Carolina. The knife was forged from a heavy wood rasp, hammered and sharpened and honed to a blue edge, and it sliced through the saplings with one easy downward movement of the arm. He pitched handfuls of dry pine needles inside the shelter, took off his shirt and spread it evenly over the needles, and put the barrel of his Springfield on the edge of the cloth. He sat in the opening and ate the two biscuits and soda crackers that he had saved in his pocket, and looked through the wavering tree trunks at the bright fire close by the cannon carriage. The light rain had started to drip off the overhead leaves and hiss in the burning pine gum.

Beyond the fire the lieutenant was seated over a small folding table inside the open flap of his tent. The light from a candle that he had melted to the table flickered on his pale, handsome face while he wrote in a steady motion with an ink quill across a piece of paper. Wesley watched him as he would someone who moved about in a strange world that he would never fully understand, one that existed above all the common struggles that most men knew. He wondered if the lieutenant had also sensed that electric moment back on the clay road or if he had caught it and dismissed it with the same indifference he had shown toward the hot-eyed stares of the convicts after he had drawn his revolver on them. And he wondered if those endless pages that he filled with a flowing calligraphy every night they were allowed fires contained some plan or explanation about the miles they marched each day, the trenches they dug and then abandoned, the whole mystery of an army's movement that stopped and started on a whimsical command.

But even if Wesley had read those letters written to a wife in Alabama, he would not have understood the language in them, as it belonged to a vision of the world that had the same bright, clear shape as a medieval romance: 'We have lost many of our bravest young soldiers, whom God in His great Mercy will surely reward for their sacrifice in our Cause. Sherman has burned Atlanta and released his troops upon an unprotected and innocent population in vengeance for the battles that they could not win honorably. But I do not think that Lee will ever surrender to such men and open our land to occupation by the Federals. Should he do so, there are many contingents of our Army already forming in Texas to continue the war from Mexico. Regardless, we are proud to have fought for the South, and our honor has never been stained by inhumanity or reprisal towards those who have been so cruel in their invasion of our country. I only pray that you will remain well and in strong spirit until we are home again –'

Wesley saw the lieutenant place the quill by the paper's edge, pinch his eyelids with his fingers, and motion a private to the opening of the tent. The private nodded, the shadow and firelight wavering on his back, then walked toward Wesley's lean-to. He had an empty tin plate and wooden spoon in his hand, and he was irritated at being given an order before he could fill his plate with the gruel that was cooking on the fire. His coat was spotted with dark drops of rain.

'He wants to see you,' he said.

'What for?'

'He don't exactly give me written notes.'

Wesley propped the barrel of the Springfield on a small

rock inside the lean-to and put on his shirt and cap. As he walked toward the lieutenant's tent, the wind blew through the high limbs overhead and shook a cold spray of rain across the clearing. The fire had burned into ash and red coals, with the sweet smell of pine rosin steaming off into the rain, and the other men were shoving in pine-cones and twigs to build the flame again under the blackened pot of gruel.

He had never spoken directly to the lieutenant before, and he stood in front of the open tent flap with the candlelight touching both of their faces while the heat thunder rolled somewhere beyond the woods.

'Combs said you wanted to see me, sir.'

The lieutenant pinched his eyelids again, and for the first time Wesley noticed how long and thin his fingers were.

'Yes. Pull the flap and sit down.'

There was a sawed-off pine stump on the far side of the table, and after Wesley had closed the flap and tied the thongs to the tent pole, he felt the sudden enclosure of warmth and light against the rain that ticked on top of the canvas.

'Do you know what those men are thinking about out there tonight, Buford?'

He was surprised that the lieutenant knew his name, and even more so at the question, but he kept his expression flat and looked somewhere between the candle's flame and the lieutenant's face.

'No sir.'

'You have no idea?'

'I go my own way, Lieutenant.'

'They want to quit. Each one of them tonight sees himself as one of the men dying under the gun carriage. They're not ready to talk among themselves yet about desertion, but they will be in a few more days.'

Wesley's eyes looked for a moment at the lieutenant's, then back at the candle flame again.

'You know all that, don't you? You saw it on the road this afternoon.'

The pine stump felt hard under Wesley, and he began to perspire inside his shirt.

'I didn't pay no mind to the others, sir. I was worried about them setting up on us in the woods again.'

'No one else was.'

'That's them, Lieutenant. It ain't me. I been hit before.' Then he felt foolish at the mention of the red-brown scar under his eye.

'Why did you join the army?'

'They killed my brother at Cold Harbor.'

'I see.' The lieutenant drew his thumbnail back and forth on the letter in front of him and left a deep indention on the edge. The heat thunder rumbled dully again beyond the woods, and the rain streaked in dark spots down the sides of the tent.

'Do you believe we have a chance of winning this war?'

'Maybe we ain't going to win, but Lee ain't ever going to give up, either. We whupped them every time with Hood till Johnston made us cut and run. Maybe if Hood was still general we'd –'

He had seen the attention begin to fade in the lieutenant's eyes. He pressed his palms damply against his thighs and looked at the shadows from the candle moving on the canvas.

'Did you know the sergeant well?'

'We was together through Carolina till we joined up with you at Kennesaw.'

'Do you think you could do his job if you were promoted to corporal?'

'Sir?'

'By noon tomorrow we should be at a field hospital in Alabama where we can leave our wounded. Then we're supposed to re-form on the Tallapoosa River with several thousand troops who are as lost as we are. Between here and there we'll probably encounter advance cavalry and skirmishers, and if Sherman's flank has moved south, we'll have the choice of fighting that gentleman's entire army or surrendering to them.' The lieutenant rubbed the corner of his eye with two fingers, and Wesley saw the redness along the rim.

'Sir, I wouldn't be no good at ordering people around. There's others out there that's been in the army a lot longer than me.'

'Yes, and most of them would run the first time they were put on the point.'

'I tell you, Lieutenant, I just wouldn't be no good at it.'

'There's a bayou about four miles ahead of us, and there should be a railroad bridge across it if the Federals haven't burned it. I want you to take one man with you on point before dawn and wait for us there. If you see any Federals, don't fire on them. Just get back to us.'

Already Wesley's mind was back on the clay road in the early morning with the white church house framed in the mist. For an instant he thought he could smell the fear again in his body.

'How far out you want us?'

'Within sound of any firing.'

'Yes sir.' He brushed the back of his fingers across his mouth. He felt inside that in some way he had been tricked, but he didn't know how.

'You'd better go back to your lean-to now.'

Wesley rose from the pine stump and started to untie the canvas flap from the tent pole.

'How long we got to keep them two convicts with us, Lieutenant?'

'Until I can turn them over to a provost. Good night.'

Wesley walked through the rain toward his shelter. The fire had burned down to a red glow under the blackened logs, and the crumbled white ash was dented with raindrops. Inside the lean-to, he lay back on the pine needles with his cap under his head and pulled his slicker over him. He started to think about tomorrow, then stopped and tried to hold an empty, clear space in the center of his mind. He had learned that from the sergeant: never think about what you had to do tomorrow and never think about it afterward. Later, after he began to sink into the first level of sleep, with the rain falling on the cut saplings overhead, he thought he heard the cook cry out like a man's murderous face appearing suddenly in a church-house window.

The air was wet and gray in the trees when he awoke just before dawn. The other men were still sleeping, their muddy boots sticking out the ends of their lean-tos. He shook the water off his slicker, rolled it tightly and tied it with two leather thongs, then unlocked the breech of his Springfield and knocked out the damp cartridge and replaced it with another. He walked to the closest lean-to and pulled hard on the man's ankle.

'What the hell's the matter with you?' The soldier's unshaved face was thick with sleep in the gloom of his shelter. His damp blanket was twisted around his neck.

'The lieutenant wants me and you on point today.'

'Shit on that, Buford. He didn't tell me nothing about it last night.'

'You can go argue with him about it. He's up in his tent right now.'

'Well, shit.'

'Get some biscuits off the wagon. We ain't going to stop till we hit a bayou about four miles up from here.'

The man stripped the blanket back from his body, pulled his cap on his head, and crawled out of the lean-to with his rifle held up before him.

'All I can say is somebody around here has got his goddamn ass on upside down,' he said, and walked to the wagon, where he began stuffing handfuls of biscuits into his haversack.

Wesley watched him, then glanced at the lieutenant's darkened tent and wondered at how easy it had been to be a corporal after all.

They moved off into the trees and the mist that floated in pools around the trunks. The woods glistened dimly from the rain, and the wet undergrowth streaked his trousers. There were sharply etched tracks of deer in the soft earth, fresh droppings that still steamed in the pine needles, and the faint and delicate imprint of grouse that had been feeding by a slough. Farther on, after the tip of the early sun had broken the horizon and slanted its light through the treetops, he began to see other signs on the forest floor: the heavy boot marks of stragglers, cartridge papers scattered behind a rotten oak stump, a dead campfire with a half-burned dressing in it, and finally a distinct trail of broken branches where a column must have passed.

'You reckon they're ours?' the other soldier said. The bill of his cap was on sideways, and his black hair hung over his ears.

'Somebody was pinned behind that oak, and he wasn't shooting at his own people,' Wesley said.

'Well, I ain't going to get shot walking into a Yankee camp. Let's set till them others catch up. Shit, we don't even know where we're at.'

'It opens up down yonder. If we see anything there we can pull out. Set here and they might just come right up your ass.'

There was no breeze in the woods, and as the sun climbed higher they felt the heat gather in the trees with the wet smell of the pine needles. The haversack strap around Wesley's shoulder left a wide stain across his shirt, and he had to wipe the sweat out of his eyes to see clearly through the dappled light. Then the woods began to thin, the forest floor became more even and easy for walking, and he saw a flash of sunlit green meadow in the distance. There were outcroppings of limestone, covered with lichen, between the trees, and as they approached the meadow the wind came up and bent the branches over their heads.

They rested against the lee side of a large boulder and ate the biscuits and dried corn from the other soldier's haversack. Wesley looked out across the meadow at the red clay bayou and the miniature railway bridge that crossed it and the burnished span of track that arched out of sight into another woods. There was a squat water tower before the bridge, and several cords of pitch wood stacked under it, but there was no picket.

'Just look at the shit in that field,' the other soldier said.

The meadow, which had been cultivated in the spring for hay, was rutted with deep wheel tracks and strewn with the equipment of a retreating army: molded boots, wet barrels of salt that had burst at the staves, the splintered spokes of cannon wheels, rotted clothing and blankets, sacks of parched corn that crawled with slugs, halters, crushed canteens, buckets of twisted horseshoes and nails, and the dressings raked out the back of a surgeon's wagon.

They crossed through the meadow and made the railway bridge before noon. The pilings were thick with brush in the slow, red current, and the dorsal fins of garfish turned in lazy circles in the shadow of the bridge. The track was banked high with yellow dirt and cinders, and as he leaned back in the shade against the first stanchion of the bridge, he felt the tremble of the train far down the track. He climbed up the embankment, pushing the stock of his Springfield into the shaling dirt, and then he saw it curving out of the woods with the long stream of smoke blowing back flatly over the tops of the cars.

Wesley heard the other soldier breathing hard beside him. 'That's our goddamn luck, ain't it? A hospital train,' he said.

The engine's wheels locked to a stop under the water tower, and a Negro fireman climbed up on the roof to pull down the tin spout. The windows in the hospital cars were open, and Wesley could see the wounded lying in the tiers of wooden bunks. Their unshaved faces were ashen in the heat, and within minutes green flies had started to drone around the windows.

'Can you smell it?' the other soldier said.

'Be quiet.' Wesley's eyes focused on the captain who was walking toward them from the last car. He wore a surgeon's insignia on his coat, and his rolled sleeves were spotted with blood.

'What's ahead of us, soldier?' he said, looking past Wesley as he spoke.

'We ain't been no further than the bridge, sir. We got some wounded behind us that's real bad, if you got room for them.'

'Where's your commanding officer?' His eyes were still fixed on a distant spot across the bayou.

'With the column. They ought to be coming through them trees any minute.'

'I'll give him until we finish loading wood. There's Yankees tearing up track all the way down the line behind us. If your officer isn't here when we leave, you can ride with us up on the spine or sit here and wait for the Federals.' The captain turned and started to walk back toward the last car.

'Sir, a couple of our wounded ain't going to make that field hospital if they got to go much further,' Wesley said.

'What field hospital?'

'The one the lieutenant says is in Alabama.'

'You're in Alabama now, son.'

'Captain, we got hit hard yesterday, and them men ain't going to make it.'

The surgeon sucked in on his lip, his face shaded in the brim of his hat, and spit into the piled yellow dirt of the embankment.

'All right,' he said. 'Get up on that water tower, and if you see anything blue down the line, fire one shot. Then jump for the top of the car.'

A half hour later, with his body flattened on the hot

boards of the tower's roof, he saw the column move out of the trees and start across the meadow. Only one man was tied prone on the cannon carriage now as it swayed in the ruts, and two other men sat on the back end with their knees pulled up before them. The lieutenant had already whipped his horse ahead of the column at the first sight of the hospital train, and Wesley held his Springfield in one hand and climbed down backward off the tower into the tender. They unstrapped the cook's litter from the carriage and carried him inside one of the cars. There were spittoons at the bottom of each tier of bunks and slop jars that had spilled over on the floors. When Wesley left him, the cook's eyes were yellow and wide, the two pupils black as cinders, as though he had jaundice, and his wooden identification tag and leather thong were clenched tightly in his palm.

A mile past the bayou they began to pick up stragglers, and by midafternoon they had overtaken a company of Mississippi infantry. Each time they crossed a rise, more men emerged out of the woods and formed into the lengthening column. Ahead, Wesley could see an ambulance wagon stopped in the middle of the road, with one mule down in its harness, while the column divided in two and swelled out into the muddy fields past it. The ground became more churned and littered with equipment as they neared the Tallapoosa River, then the officers' horses caught the smell of water in the wind and began to rear and pitch their heads against the bit. The country was open and rolling now, the clay road was as scarlet as blood in the late sun, and he saw the green line of trees along the river and knew that they would be in a safe camp by that evening with artillery and reserves set up behind them.

Then he saw the hospital train backing down the burnished tracks. Steam rolled out from under the wheels, and the engineer was leaning far out the window to see past the last car. Three soldiers with muskets were up on the spine, and the surgeon stood in the vestibule steps with his hand on the passenger rail and one boot already skipping across the rocks of the embankment. The lieutenant turned his horse out of the column and kicked him in a shower of clay toward the surgeon.

'You can bet that's our fried ass tonight,' a soldier in front of Wesley said.

'That's General Hood camped on the river, mister,' a Texas soldier next to him said. His face looked like the edge of a hatchet. 'The only frying that's going to get done is that pair of Yankee balls we put in our skillet.'

The lieutenant trotted his horse along the edge of the column and stopped abreast of Wesley. His horse was frothing green and white saliva from its bit.

'Pull our men out of the line and get them behind the railway grade, Corporal,' he said.

'Sir?'

'The Yankees have already cut the track ahead of us, and we're probably going to be attacked in the next hour. Send the wounded behind the train and keep the men in position until I get back with an ammunition carrier.'

'Lieutenant, I can't –'

But the lieutenant had already galloped his horse down the road's edge through the soldiers who were spreading across the railroad embankment and digging shallow holes in the cinders and dirt.

The sun was red over the trees on the river's bank, and Wesley saw the two convicts walk toward him in silhouette against the sky. Their striped jumpers were stained with red clay and sweat, and the tall man had a pinfire revolver stuck in the top of his trousers.

'We're caught, ain't we?' he said.

'You ask the lieutenant about that.'

'You're the corporal, ain't you?'

'Just dig a hole with them others. If we get hit with Whistling Dick tonight, you'll wish you dug plumb down to China.'

'I tell you what, butch. Before we leave out of here, we're going to take a little piece of you with us,' the tall convict said.

'Neither one of you is going to run nowheres, unless into a provost or a Minié, and I might be the one that puts it there.'

'What you mean provost?'

Wesley saw the lieutenant cantering his horse in front of an ammunition wagon, and he walked across the railroad embankment and slid down into the shallow trench that the other men were scooping out with barrel staves and tin plates.

He lay flat against the slope and looked across the trampled meadows at the sun burning into the horizon. The low strips of cloud were aflame with light, and the water oaks along the river bank threw long shadows across the dead current. In the distance he heard a solitary rifle crack, then the irregular spatter of more rifles firing deep in the opposite woods, and that old, blood-draining fear out of a dream started to tighten again in his stomach. He stared hard at the edge of the trees until the trunks began to recede and grow large again in the fading light. Every man on the line had his rifle cocked and pointed across the embankment, with the point of his bayonet stuck in the dirt beside him.

'Where the hell they at?' the man next to Wesley said. The stock of his musket was dark with the perspiration from his hands.

Then Wesley saw the branches of the trees begin to move unnaturally and the dark shapes of men walking in a crouch through the shadows.

'Oh, goddamn, look at them sons of bitches,' the soldier next to him said.

The Federals were coming out of the woods as far as Wesley could see. Three cannon drawn by mules crashed out of the underbrush, followed by a mortar mounted on a huge four-wheel carriage. The gun crews turned the cannon into position, unhitched the mules, and whipped them into the woods, while three men loaded an iron ball into the mortar. Their officers galloped their horses up and down the line, forming their men into ranks for the advance across the meadow. Then their ambulance wagons moved up on the rear, and Wesley pulled back the hammer on his Springfield and wrapped his fingers tightly in the trigger guard.

We won't have no chance, he thought. They got enough artillery to blow us all over this track. That mortar can take twenty yards out of our line in a lick. We should have set up in the woods. There ain't no sense in trying to hold against artillery when you ain't got none to back you up.

He heard the lieutenant's horse behind him and turned in the dirt on his elbow. The lieutenant had the reins knotted around his fist and held a carbine propped against his thigh with the other hand. The clean features of his face were covered with the sun's last red light.

'They're coming right up the middle, gentlemen,' he said. 'They have reserves all the way back through those woods, and they're going to try to crack us before dark. If we can hold until then, Hood will be on their flank by morning.'

Wesley slid backward on his elbows down the railway embankment and walked in a bent position to the lieutenant's horse. His head felt suddenly cold in the breeze.

'Lieutenant, half of them is going to run when they start throwing it in on us.' His voice was empty and dry in his throat.

'They're behind us, too, Corporal. It's either here or a prison camp at Johnson's Island.'

'Sir, them men ain't going to care when it starts to come in, and I ain't going to be able to hold them.'

'We'll each do what we should. You had better get back into the line.'

The lieutenant turned his horse away from Wesley and

broke into a canter toward the ammunition wagon, his face as sculptured and cool and impossible to read as marble.

The first cannon lurched backward on its wheels in an explosion of smoke and dirt. Wesley pressed his face flat into the hard cinders with his arms over his head as the shell screamed through the air and burst in front of the railway embankment thirty yards down from him. Then the other two cannon roared almost in unison, and his heart pounded against the earth while he waited for that sudden ripping sound, like tin tearing apart, that meant it was coming in on his position. But they had elevated too high, and both shells exploded in the trees somewhere behind the hospital train.

The crew on the cannon were swabbing out the barrel with water when the mortar went off. The carriage seemed to crush into the earth from the recoil, and he heard the huge iron ball begin to arch out of its trajectory and slip downward through the air like a peal of thunder. The heat and the vacuum from the explosion made his head ring and his skin burn, as though someone had opened a furnace door next to him. He looked up, his eyes filled with sweat and dirt, and saw a deep crater where there had been twenty feet of embankment and track. The wounded and the dead were half buried in the dirt and splintered ties, and one soldier sat on the edge of the hole with both palms pressed against his ears.

'Here they come!' someone behind him yelled.

The Federals began advancing in broken lines across the fields, their bayonets fixed, while their artillery fired over them. Their line seemed to waver in the smoke that drifted ahead of them in the wind, and then it would re-form again in a brilliant wash of twilight. One of the hospital cars was hit, and the dry, wooden frame burned into a collapsed, blackened pile on the wheels within minutes. Then an odd, long round from a cannon burst next to the ammunition wagon by the edge of the woods, and blew it, the mules, and driver into one flame that scorched the tops of the pines. Wesley rolled onto his back and slipped his bayonet into the groove on the end of his Springfield.

'That pig sticker won't do you no good now, boy,' the Texas soldier said, his head just below the level of the track. 'Wait another minute, and give them a rose petal between the eyes.'

He didn't hear the soldier or even the cannister crossing through the air and thumping into the wooden sides of the train. The lieutenant was still mounted, the carbine held at a right angle to his body, the bit sawed back against the horse's teeth, and there was a rip in the dirty cloth of his sleeve and a wide area of blood that ran to the elbow. The horse's eyes were wide with fright, and he twisted his head against the bridle and tried to turn in a circle.

'Get down, Lieutenant! Get off him!' Wesley yelled.

The weight of the Springfield rested across his stomach, and he had to raise his head on the incline to speak.

'Lieutenant, they're going to cut you out of the saddle.'

The two convicts, who had been crouched behind the wheels of the locomotive, broke for the trees with their shoulders bent low. The lieutenant aimed his carbine across his forearm and fired, and one of the tall convict's legs jerked violently under him, and he went down on his buttocks in the grass. The other convict kept running for the timber.

'You better stop worrying about that crazy man up there and start shooting,' the Texas soldier said.

Wesley turned on his stomach again and slid his rifle over the edge of the grade. The first line of the Federal advance was much closer now, and there were hundreds more in the swirling smoke behind them. The line seemed to bend and break apart momentarily with each hard volley, then other Federals filled their ranks and stepped over the dead. Wesley balanced his rifle on the track, cupped his left hand over the stock, and sighted on a white flash of undershirt below a man's throat. The shot dropped and hit the man full in the chest, knocking him backward in the field with his arms stretched out by his sides. He pulled back from the track to reload and looked into the dead face of the Texas soldier. There was a small hole in the crown of his skull, and his wooden teeth had fallen in the dirt.

Wesley slammed the breech shut and squeezed off the trigger into the Federal line without aiming. The hammer snapped dryly, and he had to pry loose the bad cartridge with his knife. Far down the line he saw men rising to their feet with their rifles in front of them while Yankees leaped across the tracks.

His fingers were thick and shaking when he put another cartridge in the breech, then he heard the lieutenant shout behind him: 'This is it, gentlemen. Hurrah for Jefferson Davis. Let's put them in hell tonight.'

The lieutenant cut his spurs into the horse's flanks and thundered over the embankment with his carbine raised in the air. His flop hat flew back off his head, and his hand on the reins was scarlet and shining with blood.

They followed him into the field, screaming out of some memory from Chickamauga or New Hope Church or Chancellorsville, their faded brown-and-gray uniforms almost lost in the haze of smoke and vanishing light. Wesley felt them fall on each side of him, then he saw the lieutenant sit straight in the saddle, as though he had remembered a forgotten thought, and the carbine drop loosely from his hand onto the ground. The horse shook his head against the collapsed reins and bolted out of the smoke toward the railway grade. The lieutenant fell backward off his rump and remained motionless in the field with one boot twisted under his thigh.

Wesley fired straight into a man's face three feet in front of him and pushed his bayonet into the breastbone of a sergeant who was already hit and falling. Then he heard the distant cough of a cannon in the pines, a peeling rip across the sky, and the blunt edges of the shell breaking out of its trajectory. Whistling Dick, he thought. Why are they throwing it in with their own people here?

The shell burst in front of him, and in that second's roar of light and earth he thought he felt a finger reach up and annoint him casually on the brow.

Lower Me Down with
a Golden Chain

The American priest and two nuns who ran the
orphanage in the Guatemalan village of San Luis
said they had never actually seen the rebels. Sometimes at night they thought they could hear a firefight in
the mountains, a distant popping like strings of fire-
crackers, and two labor contractors had been shot to death
in their truck by the rebels on a nearby coffee plantation.
But the most direct contact that Father Larry and the nuns
had with the war was the occasional visit to the village by
the army – steel-helmeted Indians in camouflage fatigues
– and the overhead flights of American-made helicopters
that caused the children to scream in terror because their
villages had been strafed from the air.

'Sometimes after I've fallen asleep I think I hear people
out there in the banana trees,' Father Larry said. He
pointed across the red, dusty road to the thick stands of
banana trees and the jungle that climbed gradually toward
low, blue mountains and a dead volcano. The volcano
looked black against the cobalt sky. 'But maybe it's only
animals. Anyway, they don't come here. At least, not in a
way that we recognize them.'

He was a kindly man, still somehow more gentleman
than priest, an exile from Boston money, a quietly

fanatical Red Sox fan with a taste for Jack Daniels rather than local rum. I supposed that his reluctance to speak of unpleasant things was more a matter of breeding with him than fear of the possible.

'Why do they always kill them in their underwear?' I said.

'I haven't seen that here.' His face was round and Irish with light liver spots under the skin. His black horn-rims made his bald head look larger than it was.

'You saw it in El Salvador.'

'I don't know why they make them undress. Maybe to humiliate them. I think you're probably a good journalist, but don't try to find these things out. Spend a few days with us, write a story about the children or the gunships or whatever you want, and then go back home. The rebels won't harm us and we have nothing the army wants. But you –' He pointed his finger at me. 'They're not getting the guns they want and they blame the American press.'

We were sitting on the porch of his small white stucco house with a bottle of Jack Daniels between us. The sun was blazing on the bougainvillea and the tangle of red and yellow roses that grew along the porch rail.

'I'm a Catholic, too, Father. Maybe I want to be here for other reasons.'

He lit a filter-tipped cigar to hide the irritation in his face.

'This is not a place where you play with ideas. If you're interested in discovering your identity, join an encounter group in the United States. You are presently surrounded by people who are morally insane. They kill their victims in their underwear because they often burn and mutilate them first.'

In Wichita, Kansas, where I taught creative writing at WSU, people worried about the spread of humanism. The city was surrounded by eighteen Titan missile silos. No one ever mentioned them. Daniel Berrigan, the Jesuit ex-con who did three years for splashing chicken blood on draft files, came to town while he was out on appeals bond after vandalizing some missile components in a General Electric plant. He was a serious man, maybe the best speaker I had ever heard, jailhouse tough but with eyes that seemed to see darkly into a terrifying prospect. He said our monstrous inventions might impose a suffering on the children of the earth that even St. John's Revelation did not describe adequately. He was obviously a reasonable, compassionate, and sane man. There was no television coverage of his talk. Half of the audience was made up of the 150 people whom we could assemble at a maximum at one of our antinuke rallies. Our small coalition of nuns, Mennonites, socialists, and Catholic Worker lefties was looked upon tolerantly.

North of Wichita a religious group burned rock-and-roll records and copies of *Playboy* magazine. Local businessmen voiced their concern when the Defense Department announced the Titans might be removed from Sedgwick County by 1985. The city voted down the gay-rights ordinance and banned musical concerts in the parks, and a group complained when a local high school chose the name Blue Devils for its football team. The sunsets in Kansas were like blood across the western sky. The countryside was so green in the spring, so soaked with melted snow and bursting with new wheat, that I gave up talking about Titan missiles, too, and drank 3.2 beer in happy bars with the people who worked at Boeing.

Three days later and fifty kilometers down the road from Father Larry's orphanage, Captain Ramos told me he liked Americans, that he had lived two years in Miami and would like to go back again when this war was over, but that we Americans were too critical about human rights in other countries.

'You should understand our problems. You had them in Viet Nam,' he said. We were parked in his jeep on a dusty, red road that bordered a long meadow that ended at the base of a mountain. The grass was tall and green and waving in the breeze, and in the center of the meadow was a crooked irrigation ditch that gaped like a ragged surgical incision in the earth. Divots of grass had been blown loose from the ditch's lip. Two dozen enlisted men in camouflage fatigues were in a kneeling position by the road. On each flank an M-60 machine gun formed part of a floating, mobile X that could tear apart anything that tried to raise up out of the ditch.

'You see what we have to deal with?' he said. 'They won't surrender. They're Marxist fanatics and they understand nothing but the gun.'

'What would happen to them if they surrendered?' I said.

'That's a matter up to the prisoners.'

Behind his back Captain Ramos' men called him Huachi-nango, or Redfish, because he was a big, dark man whose face turned a coarse red when he drank rum. He wore prescription blue sunglasses and a moustache and smelled of cigars and hair tonic. He looked impatiently over his shoulder for the 105 that was being towed on the back of a truck from the army barracks in town. To pass the time he asked me if his name would be in *Playboy* or *Esquire* magazine. I answered that I would probably end up publishing an article or two in a Catholic publication.

'The Catholic press in the United States is leftist. Like the Maryknolls,' he said.

I felt uncomfortable.

'I don't think that's true,' I said.

'They claim to be missionaries but they give sanctuary to the rebels. Your priest friend at the orphanage, what does he tell you?'

'He doesn't talk politics. His only interest is in caring for the children.' My words were too quick.

'I suspect otherwise. But as long as we get no reports, he's of no interest to us. We do not interfere with innocent

140

people.'

'Will those guys out there surrender when they know you've got a 105?'

'At a certain point options pass,' he said.

Later, the enlisted men unhooked the howitzer from the U.S. Marine Corps six-by, clanked a gleaming artillery shell into the breach, and fired. When a young Indian soldier jerked the lanyard, the gun roared forward on its wheels, lifting a small cloud of dust into the bright air, and a moment later the round exploded in a black geyser of dirt on the far side of the ditch. Blackbirds rose in a frenzy from the tall grass. The gunners were good, and with two more rounds they had the ditch registered. The soldiers waited on Captain Ramos' order. He lit a fresh cigar and puffed reflectively as though a deep philosophical consideration were working in his mind.

'Captain, I'm a neutral. I could walk out there with a white flag,' I said quietly.

But he wasn't listening. I had thought he was weighing the lives of the people in the ditch. He called a private over to the jeep and told him to put all the spent shell casings in the truck. I was told later that the captain owned half of a scrap-metal business in Puerto Barrios.

For fifteen minutes they blew parts of people out of the ditch. A soldier with an asbestos mitten threw the smoking shell casings behind the gun; a barechested soldier whose bronze skin was covered with pinpoints of dirt and sweat slammed another shell into the breech, locked down the handle, and the gun roared with a force that left us opening and closing our mouths. There was coral under the loamy earth, and when a round burst on the ditch's edge, shrapnel sang across the field and a pink cloud of powered rock drifted out over the grass.

The rebels tried to respond with some bolt-action Enfield junk. Through my binoculars I saw their heads and shoulders shred in the M-60 crossfire from the flanks. A barefoot man in a T-shirt and blue jeans leaped from the

The Convict and Other Stories

ditch and ran through the tall grass toward the mountain. His spinal column was arched inward as though he expected an invisible and deathly finger to touch his skin at any moment. There was a terror on his face that I had seen only on the faces of those who had been tortured by death squads before they were executed. One of the machine gunners turned his sights casually on the running man and blew the T-shirt off his back.

When it was over Captain Ramos offered me a sip of white rum from his flask.

'Do you want to take pictures?' he said. 'We are not ashamed of what we have done. Nothing dishonorable happened here today.'

I told him I didn't.

'This is a sad business,' he said. 'Do you remember what Adolf Eichmann said before he was hanged by the Jews? A man must serve his prince, and an unfortunate man must sometimes serve a bad prince. I think there's great wisdom in that.'

'I think it's Nazi bullshit,' I said.

'Ah, my friend, you can afford to be a moralist because you are not a participant.'

I drive my rented car to a village outside of Quezaltenango to interview some distributors of American powdered-milk formula. Baby formula gets the hard sell down here. The people who push it wear white jackets like nurses or medical technicians wear, although none of them are medical people. The missionaries try to encourage the Indians to continue breast-feeding their infants rather than use the formula, since they often mix the formula with contaminated water and the children get sick and die.

On this bright morning the baby-formula people have packed their van and blown town. A death squad was working the area last night, and it was time to get out of Dodge and look for new horizons. For various reasons no one likes to find the victims of the death squad. The bodies are usually mutilated; the tropical heat accelerates the decomposition process rapidly, and the rancid smell hangs in the underbrush like an invisible fist; and often the victim's body has a note fastened to it that threatens the same fate to anyone who buries the remains.

Five sugar-cane cutters were shot at close range on the river bank. They all wear purple-and-orange jockey under-shorts, and their thumbs are tied behind them with baling wire. My guess is that they were shot with .45-caliber dum-dums, probably from a grease gun. Large greenbottle flies hum thickly in the hot shade of the canebreak where their bodies lie, and the blood from their torn wounds has leaked into the stream. The local police will not come to the riverbank. Instead, a tear-streaked man backs a truck through the broken stalks, and he and a group of women snip the wire on the victims' blackened thumbs, wash their faces and chests with wet rags, and lift their bodies onto the pickup.

Nobody can understand why the five cane cutters were killed. The youngest of them is sixteen. His mother is hysterical and will not let the village carpenter measure him with his yardstick. I use a wide-angle lens to photograph the bodies and the weeping women under the colonnade in front of the empty police building.

Maybe the baby-formula pushers retained a measure of decency by blowing Dodge. I feel like a voyeur in search of misery with camera and pen. I hear on the news from Guatemala City that the marines are kicking butt and taking names in Grenada. It seems that on this morning the world is dividing itself more distinctly into observers and participants. Provide, provide, Robert Frost said, or somebody will provide for you. I convince myself he meant two glasses of white rum before attempting lunch in the village's only café, which is within earshot of the burial procession to the village cemetery.

*

I was raised in New Orleans by a gentle aunt who lived in the Garden District. I never knew any black people who were not servants or yardmen. There were none in our parish church or in our schools and neighborhoods. Along the moss-shaded and brick-paved streets where I grew up, people of color were servile visitors who showed up at back doors early in the morning and disappeared across Magazine Street by suppertime. They had only first names unless they had reached a sufficient age to be called 'Auntie' or 'Cap.' Even at mass I never questioned the presence of only one race in the cathedral. William Faulkner once said that for southerners segregation was simply a fact, it was simply *there*. It had always existed, it always would. We gave it no more thought than we would the warm, magnolia-scented climate in which we lived.

But wonderful gentleman and writer that he was, Mr Faulkner was wrong about this one. There were southerners who questioned the laws of segregation and found them odious (as he himself did), an insult to reason, a collective sin that jaded the entirety of the Jeffersonian dream. I remember some of those southern people – members of the Catholic Worker movement, the Congress of Racial Equality, the Southern Christian Leadership Conference. Bull Connor turned German police dogs on them and blew them skittering down sidewalks with firehoses; George Wallace's state troopers trampled them under horses at the Selma bridge; the Ku Klux Klan lynched them in Neshoba County, Mississippi.

Against our protest they reconstructed Golgotha before our eyes and forced us to drive the nails or to stand by in guilty witness. Their rent flesh, their bones exhumed from an earthen dam, would not leave our television sets. The barking dogs, the frightened hymn of Negro clergy surrounded by a mob, followed us into the kitchen where we tried to fix a drink. We asked patience and understanding in them that we didn't require of ourselves.

I visited a Catholic Worker friend in the Baton Rouge

jail. He and the elderly black man in the cell with him had been tear-gassed. Their eyes were swollen and red in the gloom. During the demonstration state police had killed two black students on the steps of Southern University; the old man was confused and thought white people had been killed, and he was sure he was going to be sent to die in Angola penitentiary. He was singing

> Lower me down with a golden chain
> And see that my grave is kept clean.

My friend hadn't been arraigned yet, but a priest and I paid the old man's bail. The hack waited by the cell door for him to walk out into the corridor. I looked at the old man's red eyes in the dim light. He was still convinced white people were dead and Negroes would pay for it. But he said, 'No sirs, I cain't leave this white boy by hisself.'

In approximately five years they changed what we had let stand for 350.

The guerilla leader was dressed in a pair of blue jeans, tennis shoes, a faded print shirt covered with blue-and-yellow parrots, and a John Deere tractor cap. He looked like someone who sold peanuts at an American baseball game. He sat in the open door of a bullet-pocked Huey helicopter, which had crashed through the canopy of ficus trees and was now rusted and cob-webbed with vines and wispy air roots from the ficus. He was in a contemplative mood, and he smoked an enormous hand-rolled cigarette while he balanced his warm bottle of Dos X's on his knee. His parents, who were laborers on a coffee plantation, had named him Francisco for a great saint, but he was not a religious man himself, he said. His problem was of this world: the acquisition of more and better guns.

'We shot this helicopter down with rifles that are forty years old,' he said. 'But we were lucky. If we had the equipment the government has, we could be in

Guatemala City in six weeks.'

The men eating their lunch under the trees were armed with W.W. II M-1 and Enfield rifles and a few captured M-16s. Most of the men were young and dressed in dark, ragged clothes. Some of them had laced leaves and jungle vine through the straw of their hats.

'Mortars would be a stupendous thing to have. Our Uzi machine guns like the Israelis sell to the government in Chili,' Francisco said. 'We have to deal with black marketeers in the United States who always cheat us if they can.'

I'd had four hot beers and I broached a more difficult subject. Yesterday the rebels had burned the transportation bus that ran between San Luis and the next town. It seemed to me a pointless and stupid act.

'What did your country do in Viet Nam?' he said. His Indian eyes were black and unblinking, as though his eyelids were stitched to his forehead. 'You bombed their trains, their bridges, their electric plants, and finally their cities. Why do you object to a bus?'

'I don't agree with what my government did in Viet Nam.'

'I think Americans don't agree with losing.'

'After the bus, you were in a firefight with some soldiers. You called out their officer under a white flag.'

'Yes?'

'You shot him.'

'One of the young ones did. One whose parents were tortured. Do you want to know what they did to his mother?'

I looked away from his face.

'I'd like to photograph the Huey. I won't photograph any of your men,' I said.

'This light isn't good for your camera. You can take pictures at another time.'

'All right.'

'You're angry. But why? You have everything you want

— a story for your magazine, the ability to see the war in safety from both sides. I saw you through field glasses when Captain Ramos killed all those in the ditch. But I hold no grudge toward you. You should not be angry over a small denial.'

I could feel the blood in my face.

'I have only small desires and cannot satisfy those,' he said. 'I would like some Pepsi Cola to drink. I don't like beer. i gives me diarrhea.'

'Why don't you go into San Luis and buy some like everybody else? They have stacks of it there.'

He was thoughtful a moment.

'Does the American missionary there also have medicine? We would pay for it.'

'No.'

'You are sure?'

'He's not a doctor. He and the nuns only take care of the children.'

'What do they give them when they're sick? Pepsi Cola? You are a very entertaining journalist.'

I found Father Larry with two Indians by the new clinic, mixing mortar in a wood box. He was a thick-chested man, and white hair grew out of his T-shirt and his face was dusty and hot with his work.

'I need to talk to you,' I said.

'It looks like you made a couple of early bar stops today.' He looked up and smiled behind his black horn-rims.

'I drink too much. It's one of my problems.'

'Everybody drinks too much down here,' he said.

'I think I've said stupid things and provoked some people, Father. I think you should leave.'

'Go to my house and fix all of us drinks.'

'No. This country is an open-air mental asylum. You should be in Boston teaching at a Jesuit college and taking in the games at Fenway.'

'Nothing you said to anybody is going to have any effect

on my life. Try to learn some humility while you're down here.'

'Father, I watched an army captain blow a ditch full of people into lasagna. He gave it as much importance as paring his fingernails. Then I interviewed a guerilla leader who gets high sniffing cordite. Both of them have you on their minds. Good God, give me credit for some perception. These guys have you right in the middle.'

'You're wrong about that, my friend. There's no middle in this world. You remember when they used to sing "Which Side Are You On?" down in Mississippi? That's what it's all about.'

I drove to the coast and stayed in an expensive hotel on a magnificent stretch of white beach. Charter boats out for kingfish drifted through the emerald and inky blue patches of the Pacific, and the late sun seemed like a red planet slipping beyond the earth's watery rim. I ate lobster in a dining room with linen-covered tables and French doors that gave onto palm trees and yellow hibiscus, drank two bottles of Madeira wine, and paid for everything with my Diner's Card. Father Larry haunted me.

In 1942 I was frightened by the stories that I heard adults tell about Nazi submarines that waited in the mouth of the Mississippi for the oil tankers that sailed unescorted from the refineries in Baton Rouge. People said you could see the fires at night burning low on the southern horizon. In my mind the Nazis were dark-uniformed, evil men with slit eyes who lived under the water and could reach out and murder innocent people in a defenseless world whenever they wished. At night I prayed that the Nazis would not come to New Orleans, that I would always be safe in my bed in my aunt's house.

Then one Sunday night when we were visiting my cousins in Pointe a la Hache, the priest called and said the Germans had torpedoed two freighters and the survivors were going to be brought to the Catholic elementary school. We packed blankets and canned goods and drove in a rainstorm to the small school building, where the coast guardsmen were unloading people on stretchers off of a canvas-covered truck. The cafeteria was brightly lit and crowded with cots and tables pushed together, and the oil-streaked, fire-blackened people on them filled me with horror. They vomited sea water and oil, cried out for morphine, stared wild-eyed out of poached faces that had no eyebrows or hair. My aunt wept silently for them and told me to go into the kitchen with the old nun who was fixing soup.

But I couldn't move. I felt as though I were looking into hell itself. I couldn't accept that the war, the Nazis, had reached into my world and filled a school building like my own with so much unrelieved suffering. I was drowning in the thought that truly wicked men could do whatever they wished to us.

A coast guardsman in a T-shirt and bell-bottom dungarees with a white sailor's hat on the back of his head saw the expression in my face and squatted down in front of me. Every muscle in his lean body seemed to ripple when he moved. His eyes were clear blue and there wasn't a doubt or fear anywhere in them. On one brown arm was a tattoo of an enormous American flag surrounded with a circle of blue stars.

'Don't you worry, boy. Uncle Sam is going back out there and blow them sons of bitches plumb back to Krautland,' he said.

I never knew my father, but I was sure he could have been no finer a man that this one. I also knew now what people meant when they said that one day the lights would go on again all over the world.

But that sailor wasn't with Father Larry in San Luis, Guatemala. Instead, Francisco came with his guerillas to the village, asking for medicine and bandages. The nuns told me they believed that he simply wanted to show the

Indians he could come into the village in daylight without fear of the army. He smiled and bowed courteously when Father Larry explained that they had little medicine to spare, and then he invited the clergy and the children to a dinner of tripe, baked bread, and goat's milk. Francisco would never become an important figure in the revolution and in all probability would be killed and buried in an anonymous jungle grave, but he had a flair for the romantic among his people and a clumsy Guevara-like disregard for his fate.

But on the late afternoon that he and his men left the village with cases of Pepsi Cola on their shoulders, he presented to Captain Ramos the invitation and sanction that an idle, heavily armed, rut-filled contingent of troops lusts for – reason to occupy or attack a village that has no means to defend itself.

The soldiers killed sixteen Indians in San Luis the following day. The people they killed had no weapons, no politics, no knowledge of the world outside their village. A terrified peasant man tried to hide in the church. The soldiers dragged him outside squealing like a pig, shoved him on the floor of a jeep, and drove him out into a field, where they murdered him. There was no more rationality in concealing his execution than there was in anything else they did that day. They took away the bodies of the dead Indians on a U.S. Army truck, then off-loaded them into a helicopter and threw them out at high altitudes over the countryside.

That night three men in civilian clothes with bandannas on their faces tried to kidnap Father Larry from his house. When he refused to go with them, they stabbed him to death with a bayonet.

I'm back in Wichita, Kansas. Out there under those frozen, snowy wheat fields are eighteen Titan missiles that sleep in gleaming silos manned by crews of technicians who look like my sons. The man who can send them ripping across the skies to destroy the Soviet Union, or all of Europe, is an ex-sportscaster. My aunt, with her genteel and kind Old South innocence, has passed into history. I imagine that time has had its way with that coast guardsman, too (he who could reach below the oil-flaming water with that tattooed arm and pull men back from eternity). But sometimes when I think of spring, then of baseball and Beantown and Fenway Park, I'm sure Father Larry would tell me it's always the first inning. Like that elderly black man in the Baton Rouge jail, he knew that courage and faith are their own justification and that heaven's prisoners don't worry about historical place.

Water People

Our drill barge was moored out in the middle of this long flat bay, like a big rectangle of gray iron welded onto a cookie sheet, I mean it was so hot anything you touched scalded your hands and the sun was a red ball when it rose up out of the water and you could smell dead things on the wind out in the marsh, amongst all those flooded willows and cypress and gum trees. That was right before Hurricane Audrey hit the Louisiana coast in 1957. The thunder showers we got in the afternoon weren't anything more than hot steam, and when lightning hit on the sandbars you could see it dancing under the chop, flickering, like yellow snakes flipping around in a barrel full of dark water.

Skeeter was our shooter, or dynamite man, and was about forty years old and thought to be weird by everybody on board, partly because he was a preacher over in Wiggins, Mississippi, but also because he had a way of coming up behind you and running his hands down your hips. In other words, he wasn't apt to make a skivvy run to Morgan City, although that could have been because he was a religious man. The truth is doodle-buggers did the dirtiest work in the oil field and it was no accident other people referred to us as white niggers.

I watched Bobby Joe, our driller, drop the last six-can stick of explosives down the pipe and feed the cap wire off his palms. Bobby Joe's chest looked like it was carved from a tree stump, it was lean and hard and tapered, swollen with muscle under the arms, tanned the gold-brown color of worn saddle leather. He had a BCD from the Crotch for busting up a couple of S.P.'s. He told me once his little boy drowned in a public swimming pool that was full of colored people and Puerto Ricans in Chicago. The next day he told me he'd lied because he was drunk and I'd better not tell anybody what he'd said. Like I'm on board to write the history of Bobby Joe Guidry.

I wrapped the cap wire around the terminals on Skeeter's detonator and screwed down the wingnuts and said 'You're lit, pappy,' and everybody went aft or got on the jugboat that was tied to the stern, and when Skeeter gave it the juice those eighteen cans of hot stuff went off with a big *thrummmmmp* deep down in the earth and fish jumped all over the bay like they'd been shocked with an electric current; the force of the explosion kicked the drill barge's bow up in the air and slapped it back against the surface, then a second later brown water and sand and cap wire came geysering out of the pipe the way wildcat wells used to come in years ago and a yellow cloud of smoke drifted back across the jugboat and filled the inside of your head with a smell like a freshly tarred gravel road.

Skeeter wore a long-sleeve denim shirt and a cork sun-helmet and steel-rim glasses that caused him to crinkle his nose all the time. His face was round, puffed with the humidity, always pink with fresh sunburn, and his eyes blue and watery and red along the rims, like they were irritated from the smoke that seeped out of the water after he'd zapped the juice into the hole and given things down below a real headache. Bobby Joe was wiping the drilling mud off his chest with a nasty towel he'd gotten out of the engine room. His hair was the color of dry straw under his tin hat and there was a green and red Marine Corps tattoo on his upper arm that was slick and bright with sweat.

'Y'all put too many cans down, Bobby Joe,' Skeeter said.

Bobby Joe went on wiping at his hands with that rag and didn't even look up.

'I tell you how to do your job, Skeet?' he said.

'We're killing fish we ain't got to. You can blow the casing out the hole, too,' Skeeter said.

'You study on things too much.' Bobby Joe still hadn't looked up, he just kept on wiping at those big, flat hands of his that had scars like white worms on the backs of his fingers.

'Hit don't say nowhere we got to blow half the damn bay into the next parish,' Skeeter said.

'Skeet, you put me in mind of an egg-sucking dog sniffing around a brooder house,' Bobby Joe said. 'I declare if you don't.'

We knew it was a matter of time before one of those two ran the other off. The party chief would abide any kind of behavior that didn't hurt the job; that's why he'd let a liberty boat head for the hot pillow joints in Morgan City the fifth night out on the hitch, about the time some guys would start messing around in the shower and pretend it was just grab-assing; but he wouldn't put up with guys hiding vodka in their seabags or fighting over cards or carrying a personal grief out on the drill barge, it got people hurt or killed, like the time this Mexican boy I'm fixing to tell you about fell off the bow and got sucked under the barge just when the skipper kicked over the screws, and not to be overlooked it cost the company a shitload of money.

His nickname was Magpie because he was missing two teeth up front and he had black hair with a patch like white paint in it. He weighed about three-hundred pounds and traveled around the country eating light bulbs and blowing fire in a carnival act when he wasn't doodle-bugging. Bobby Joe said he saw him cheating in the bouree game and told him to his face. Magpie might have looked like a pile of whale shit but I saw him pick up a six-foot gator by its tail once, whip it around in the air, and heave it plumb across the barge's deck and leave two or three drillers with wee-wee in their socks. Magpie told Bobby Joe they were going to have a beer and learn some helpful hints about behavior when they got off the hitch, and Bobby Joe replied he knew just the spot because the dispenser for toilet seat covers in the can had a sign on it that said *Pepperbelly Place Mats*.

A week later we were way down at the mouth of the Atchafalaya, with storm winds capping the surface, and Magpie fell off the drill into the current and was swept down under the hull just as I was running at the bridge, waving my arms and yelling at the skipper who was looking back over his shoulder at the jugboat with a cigarette in his mouth. This retarded kid on the jugboat was the first to see Magpie surface downstream. He vomited over the rail, then started screaming and running up and down on the deck till his father put him in the pilot house and wiped his face and held his head against his chest. Think of water that runs by the discharge chute on a slaughter house. The thunder and wind were shrieking like the sky was being ripped loose from the earth. I don't care to revisit moments like that.

The quarterboat was moored with ropes to a willow island and at sunset Skeeter would stand out on the bow in the mosquitoes by himself, where all the sacks of drilling mud were stacked, or sometimes get a pirogue and paddle back through the flooded trees. I used to think he was running a trot-line but I found out different when he didn't think anybody was watching him. He had a paper bag full of these little plastic statues of Jesus, the kind people puts on their dashboard, and he'd tie fish twine around the feet with a machinist's bolt on the other end and hold it to his head with his eyes squinted shut, then sink it in the water and paddle on to the next spot.

'You been out here long, W.J.?' he said when he was tying the pirogue back up.

'Not really.'

'I felt sorry for him; it wasn't right the way some guys made fun of him behind his back. He was at Saipan during the war. That was a lot more than most of us had done.

'You got something fretting you, Skeet?'

'A Mexican boy gets shredded up in the propellor and don't nobody seem bothered.'

'Bobby Joe says Magpie was fooling around and hanging off the rail taking a whiz. It's just one of them things.'

'Nobody else seen hit.'

'Them ain't good thoughts, Skeet.'

'Bobby Joe wasn't watching his little boy when he drowned in that swimming pool. He blames them other people for not saving him. I was in that bouree game. That Mexican boy wasn't cheating.'

At breakfast on the quarterboat we got anything we wanted; you just had to pass through the galley and tell the cook; pancakes, eggs, stacks of bacon and fried ham, grits, coffee, cereal, white bread and butter and jam. Dinner was even better: steaks, fried chicken, meatloaf, gumbo and catfish on Fridays, mashed potatoes, rice and milk gravy, sweating pitchers of Kool-Aid and iced tea, cake or ice cream for dessert.

Lunchtimes though we were out on the drill barge and usually cooked up something pretty putrid, like Viennas and rice, in the small galley behind the bridge and ate it in the lee of the pilot house. The sky was the color of scorched brass when Bobby Joe sniffed at the air and said to Skeeter, 'Is there something dead out where you keep your dynamite at?'

'Could be,' Skeeter said.

'It's mighty strong. You ought to do something about it, Skeet, wash it off in the shallows, slap some deodorant on it.'

'I might have hit on my clothes. I ain't got hit on my conscience.'

Bobby Joe puffed on a filter-tipped cigar without missing a beat.

'I wish I was smart,' he said. He leaned forwards and tipped ashes off the side of the deck. 'Then I could figure out how come I like girls and I didn't turn out to be a faggot. I'm here to tell you, boys, it's a pure mystery.'

Skeeter stared at Bobby Joe and rolled a wood match back and forth across his false teeth. You could flat hear that match clicking it was so quiet.

At quitting time that day the party chief said anybody who wanted could go into the levee on the crewboat as long as they were back in the galley sober at 0600 the next morning. The upper deck of the quarterboat was divided into two rows of tiny one-man cabins, with the showers and a can at one end of the gangway and a recreation room with a big window fan, where we played cards, at the other. The rain had just stopped and the air was cool and smelled like fish and wet trees, with yellow and purple clouds piled out on the Gulf, wind blowing through the willow islands and mullet jumping where the sunlight still shone above the dead cypress; everybody was in a good mood, whistling, combing their hair with Lucky Tiger and butch wax, putting on starched khakis, skin-tight jeans, snap-button shirts, and hand-tooled belts with chrome buckles as big as Cadillac bumpers and Indian stitching along the edges.

Bobby Joe was sitting on the edge of his bunk, buffing the points of his black cowboy boots till the leather was full of little lights. Skeeter leaned against the hatchway with his arms folded across his chest, crinkling his nose under his glasses.

'What you want, Skeeter?'

'You ain't got to carry hit.'

'Carry what? What the fuck are you talking about?'

'What happened to your little boy.'

'I hate guys like you. You're always feeding off some-body's grief. You quit pestering me.'

'I don't mean you no harm.'

You could hear Bobby Joe breathing. Another guy had just cut his hair for him out on deck, and there was a white stretch of skin half-mooned under the hairline on his neck. His hands opened and closed into rocks, his knuckles swelling up the size of quarters. Then he just about knocked Skeeter down tearing out the door into Skeeter's cabin. He ripped the mattress back off Skeeter's bunk and grabbed the paper bag with all the little statues of Jesus in it, wadded it up in his hands, and pushed the screen out on the stick and flung the bag straight out into the willow and cypress trees. You could see it spinning in an eddy just before the paper turned dark with water and went under.

'Now you leave me alone,' Bobby Joe said, his hands trembling at his sides, the veins in his forearms purple and thick as soda straws.

'All right, Bobby Joe. I promise I won't bother you no more,' Skeeter said.

He wasn't expecting that.

I'd been to Claudette's before and always thought the girls were pretty nice, no worse or better than us, anyway, people don't always get to choose what they are, that's the way I figured it. Most of them came from mill or farm towns in Texas and Louisiana and Mississippi, the kind of towns where people worked in ammunition or roach paste factories, places where hanging out at the Dairy Queen or down at the filling station was the biggest thing going on Saturday night, which wasn't the reason they got in the life, I think, although that's what they tried to tell you when you asked how they ended up in a hundred-year-old two-story house next to colored town with a blue light over the door and the paint eaten off the wood by the salt and a pimp in the front room who once knocked the glass eye out of a girl for sassing him.

You want to get one of them mad? Ask her about her father, what kind of guy was he, did he ever take her to a kid's show or a county fair, did he know what happened to her, did he *care* what happened to her, something like that, and tell me about it.

I never thought they were bad girls, though. As long as you bought a beer, it was six-bits for a little-bitty Schlitz, you could talk to them, or listen to the jukebox and you didn't have to take one of them upstairs, nobody'd bother you, really.

But I saw something that changed my thinking. It was a weekday afternoon and business was slow except for a roughneck who'd just been paid off his rig and three kids with boogies, flat-tops with ducktails on the sides, and black jeans and boots with steel taps and chains dripping off the leather, the kind of stomp-ass stuff juvenile delinquents wore back in those days. The roughneck was juiced to the eyes, by himself, no crew to take care of him, and kept splitting open his billfold and showing off his money to the girls, like this would have them lining up to glome his twanger.

One of the three kids said something about rolling the guy. Then a girl pulled the kid over by the jukebox, you could see them wreathed in cigarette smoke against the orange and purple light from the plastic casing, their heads bent together like two question marks, her hair like white gold, her mouth glossy and red, she was pretty enough to make you hurt, I'll never forget what she said to him because it wasn't just the words, it was the smile on the kid's face when she said it, like a twisted slit across bread dough. 'Y'all take him somewhere else and do it, okay? Then come back and spend the money here.'

It was pretty depressing.

After most of the others took off for the levee, I went out on the jugboat with Skeeter to move his dynamite caps and primers to a new sandbar. The caps and primers were a lot more sensitive than the actual dynamite, and he kept them in a big steel lockbox on a sandbar and he had to move the box every week or so to keep up with the drill barge.

'I wouldn't let it bother me, Skeet,' I said. 'Bobby Joe's got a two-by-four up his butt sometimes.'

'Hit ain't him.'

'So what's got you down?'

'My ministry ain't gone no where. Same back in Wiggins. I might as well be out talking in a vacant lot.'

We unloaded the box, then heaved it empty up on the deck. The water was capping in the south and you could smell salt in the wind and see birds flying everywhere.

'Maybe if you went about it a little different,' I said. 'Sinking those little dashboard statues is a mite unusual.'

'I done something I never could make up for,' he said. 'A bunch of Japs was down in a cave, maybe seventy or eighty of them. I blew the mountain in on top of them. You could hear a hum through the coral at night, like thousands of bees singing. It was all them men moaning down there.'

He scratched a mosquito bite on his face and looked at the willow island and the leaves that were starting to shred in the wind.

'Sometimes people have to do bad things in a war,' I said.

'I almost had myself convinced they wasn't human. Then I seen them people going off the cliffs at Saipan. Women threw their babies first, then jumped after them, right on top of the rocks, they was so scared of us.'

I pulled the anchor and we drifted out into the current. The sun's afterglow made a dark red light in the water.

'What's that got to do with statues?' I said.

'I bring Jesus to them people who jumped into the sea. The same water is wrapped all the way around the earth, ain't hit? Hit ain't that way with land. You could drive this boat from here to Saipan if you had a mind.'

'I say don't grieve on it. I say let the church roll on, Skeeter.'

But there was no consoling him. He sat on the deck rail, his face like an empty pie plate, and I kicked the engines over and hit it hard across the bay. The sky in the south had gone white as a bone, the way it does when the barometer drops and no birds or other living things want to be out there.

Hurricane Audrey flat tore south Louisiana up. It killed maybe five hundred people in Cameron Parish, just south of Lake Charles, and left drowned people hanging in trees out in the marsh. We rode it out though, with the wind screaming outside, houseboats spinning around upside down in the current, and coons climbing up the mooring ropes to hide from the rain on the lee side of the deck.

Then the third day the sun rose up out of the steam like a yellow balloon over the cypress trees and we were climbing back on the crewboat and headed for the drill barge again. The night before I'd been out looking for a bunch of recording jugs that got washed overboard, and till we picked up the dynamite caps and primers at the lockbox out on the sandbar, I didn't even notice Skeeter was gone and we had a new shooter on board, a man with a steel-gray military haircut and skin the color of chewing tobacco who didn't have much to say to anybody and worked a crossword puzzle. Everybody was enjoying the ride out to the barge, smoking hand-rolls, drinking coffee, relaxing on the cushions while the bow slapped across the waves and the spray blew back over the windows, when I asked, 'Where's Skeeter at?'

Suddenly nobody had diddily-squat on a rock to say.

'Where's he at?' I said.

'He drug up last night,' one fellow finally said.

'That don't make sense. He would have told me,' I said.

'He got run off, W.J.,' another guy said.

'The hell he was,' I said. Then I said it again, 'The hell he *was*.'

All I could see were the backs of people's heads staring at the windows. The engines were throbbing through the deck like an electric saw grinding on a nail.

At first I thought the party chief decided it was either Bobby Joe or Skeeter and it was easier to hire a new shooter than a driller who had to keep a half dozen other men who hated authority in line and make them like him for it at the same time.

But that evening, when I talked to Ray, the party chief, he cut right to it. So did I, just as soon as I found Bobby Joe up in his cabin, playing solitaire on his bunk, biting a white place on the corner of his lip.

'You sorry sonofabitch.'

'I don't let a whole lot of people talk to me like that, W.J.'

'He won't be able to work anywhere. That was a lousy thing to do, Bobby Joe.'

'A man oughtn't have to work with a queer.'

'You told Ray Skeeter came on to you.'

'How do you know he didn't?'

''Cause I know you're a damn liar, Bobby Joe. I know you lied about Magpie cheating, too.'

'You're in my light.'

'Too bad. You're going to hear this,' I said, and sat down on his bunk, right on top of his cards. His face twitched, like a rubber band snapping under the skin. Then I told him everything I knew about Skeeter, the coral rocks humming with the voices of Jap soldiers trapped down below, women with their babies dropping off the cliffs into the sea, all the guilt he was carrying around twelve years after we set fire to the air over their cities and had parades and got back down to making money.

'I ain't got nothing to say to you, W.J.'

'I bet you ain't.'

I was too hard on Bobby Joe, though. Two nights later he started acting weird, almost like Skeeter, paddling the pirogue out in the swamp, raking a pile of silt up on the paddle and staring at it, walking along the edge of a sandbar like he'd lost something while cicadas droned in the sky and the sun's last light looked like electric blood painted on the trees.

'The hurricane blew them sloughs slick as spit,' I said to Bobby Joe.

'Where you figure Skeeter headed to?' he asked. He bit on his thumbnail and looked at it.

'Back to Wiggins, I expect.'

'You think?'

'They'd know where he's at.'

Bobby Joe drug up the next day, told Ray to mail his check general delivery, New Iberia, Louisiana. I never saw him or Skeeter again. But I sure heard about them; they must have been looking for each other all over the oil patch, one man trying to forgive the other so he could lay his own burden down.

Sometimes when it's hot and the barometer starts falling and the bottom of the sky turns green in the south, the way it does right before a storm, I start to think about Bobby Joe and Skeeter, or the girls in the hot pillow joint who'd set up a drunk to get rolled, or the guys who didn't speak up when the party chief ran Skeeter off, and I commence to get a terrible headache, just like when you'd breathe that awful cloud of yellow smoke boiling off the water when we'd zap the juice into the hole and blow carp and catfish belly-up to the surface, never worrying about it or asking a question, like it was all a natural part of our old war with the earth and whatever was down there.

Texas City, 1947

Right after W.W. II everybody in southern Louisiana thought he was going to get rich in the oil business. My father convinced himself that all his marginal jobs in the oil fields would one day give him the capital to become an independent wildcatter, perhaps even a legendary figure like Houston's Glenn McCarthy, and he would successfully hammer together a drilling operation out of wooden towers and rusted junk, punch through the top of a geological dome, and blow salt water, sand, chains, pipe casing, and oil into the next parish.

So he worked on as a roughneck on drilling rigs and as a jug-hustler with a seismograph outfit, then began contracting to build board roads in the marsh for the Texaco Company. By mid-1946 he was actually leasing land in the Atchafalaya Basin and over in east Texas. But that was also the year that I developed rheumatic fever and he drove my mother off and brought Mattie home to live with us.

I remember the terrible fight they had the day she left. My mother had come home angry from her waitress job in a beer garden on that burning July afternoon, and without changing out of her pink dress with the white piping on the collar and pockets, she had begun butchering chickens on the stump in the backyard and shucking off their feathers in a big iron caldron of scalding water. My father came home later than he should have, parked his pickup truck by the barn, and walked naked to the waist through the gate with his wadded-up shirt hanging out the back pocket of his Levis. He was a dark Cajun, and his shoulders, chest, and back were streaked with black hair. He wore cowboy boots, a red sweat-handkerchief tied around his neck, and a rakish straw hat that had an imitation snakeskin band around the crown.

Headless chickens were flopping all over the grass, and my mother's forearms were covered with wet chicken feathers.

'I know you been with her. They were talking at the beer joint,' she said, without looking up from where she sat with her knees apart on a wood chair in front of the steaming caldron.

'I ain't been with nobody,' he said, 'except with them mosquitoes I been slapping out in that marsh.'

'You said you'd leave her alone.'

'You children go inside,' my father said.

'That gonna make your conscience right 'cause you send them kids off, you? She gonna cut your throat one day. She been in the crazy house in Mandeville. You gonna see, Verise.'

'I ain't seen her.'

'You sonofabitch, I smell her on you,' my mother said, and she swung a headless chicken by its feet and whipped a diagonal line of blood across my father's chest and Levis.

'You ain't gonna act like that in front of my children, you,' he said, and started toward her. Then he stopped. 'You all get inside. You ain't got no business listening to this. This is between me and her.'

My two older brothers, Weldon and Lyle, were used to our parents' quarrels, and they went inside sullenly and let the back screen slam behind them. But my little sister Drew, whom my mother nicknamed 'Little Britches,' stood mute and fearful and alone under the pecan tree, her cat pressed flat against her chest.

'Come on, Drew. Come see inside. We're gonna play with the Monopoly game,' I said, and tried to pull her by the arm. But her body was rigid, her bare feet immobile in the dust.

Then I saw my father's large, square hand go up in the air, saw it come down hard against the side of my mother's face, heard the sound of her weeping, as I tried to step into Drew's line of vision and hold her and her cat against my body, hold the three of us tightly together outside the unrelieved sound of my mother's weeping.

Three hours later her car went through the railing on the bridge over the Atchafalaya River. I dreamed that night that an enormous brown bubble arose from the submerged wreck, and when it burst on the surface her drowned breath stuck against my face as wet and rank as gas released from a grave.

That fall I began to feel sick all the time, as though a gray cloud of mosquitoes were feeding at my heart. During recess at school I didn't play with the other children and instead hung about on the edges of the dusty playground or, when Brother Daniel wasn't looking, slipped around the side of the old red-brick cathedral and sat by myself on a stone bench in a bamboo-enclosed, oak-shaded garden where a statue of Mary rested in a grotto and camellia petals floated in a big goldfish pond. Sometimes Sister Roberta was there saying her rosary.

She was built like a fire hydrant. Were it not for the additional size that the swirl of her black habit and the wings of her veil gave her, she would not have been much larger than the students in her fifth-grade class. She didn't yell at us or hit our knuckles with rulers like the other nuns did, and in fact she always called us 'little people' rather than children. But sometimes her round face would flare with anger below her white, starched wimple at issues which to us in our small parochial world seemed of little importance. She told our class once that criminals and corrupt local politicians were responsible for the slot and racehorse machines that were in every drugstore, bar, and hotel lobby in New Iberia, and another time she flung an apple core at a carload of teenagers who were baiting the Negro janitor out by the school incinerator.

She heard my feet on the dead oak leaves when I walked through the opening in the bamboo into the garden. She was seated on the stone bench, her back absolutely erect, the scarlet beads of her rosary stretched across the back of her pale hand like drops of blood. She stopped her prayer and turned her head toward me. Fine white hair grew on her upper lip.

'Do you feel sick again, Billy Bob?' she asked.

'Yes, Sister.'

'Come here.'

'What?'

'I said come here.' Her hand reached out and held my forehead. Then she wiped the moisture off her palm with her fingers. 'Have you been playing or running?'

'No, Sister.'

'Has your father taken you to a doctor?'

I didn't answer.

'Look at me and answer my question,' she said.

'He don't, he doesn't have any money right now. He says it's because I had the flu. He boiled some honey and onions for me to eat. It made me feel better. It's true, Sister.'

'I need to talk to your father.'

She saw me swallow.

'Would he mind my calling him?' she asked.

'He's not home now. He works all the time.'

'Will he be home tonight?'

'I'm not sure.'

'Who takes care of you at night when he's not home?'

'A lady, a friend of his.'

'I see. Come back to the classroom with me. It's too windy out here for you,' she said.

'Sister, you don't need to call, do you? I feel okay now.

168

My father's got a lot on his mind now. He really works hard.'

'What's wrong in your house, Billy Bob?'

'Nothing. I promise, Sister.' I tried to smile. I could taste bile in my throat.

'Don't lie.'

'I'm not. I promise I'm not.'

'Yes, I can see that clearly. Come with me.'

The rest of the recess period she and I sharpened crayons in the empty room with tiny pencil sharpeners, stringing long curlicues of colored wax in the waste basket. She was as silent and as seemingly self-absorbed as a statue. Just before the bell rang she walked down to the convent and came back with a tube of toothpaste.

'Your breath is bad. Go down to the lavatory and wash your mouth out with this,' she said.

Mattie wore shorts and sleeveless blouses with sweat rings under the arms, and in the daytime she always seemed to have curlers in her hair. When she walked from room to room she carried an ashtray with her into which she constantly flicked her lipstick-stained Chesterfields. She had a hard, muscular body, and she didn't close the bathroom door all the way when she bathed, and once I saw her kneeling in the tub, scrubbing her big shoulders and chest with a large, flat brush. The area above her head was crisscrossed with improvised clotheslines from which dripped her wet underthings. Her eyes fastened on mine; I thought she was about to reprimand me for staring at her, but instead her hardboned, shiny face continued to look back at me with a vacuous indifference that made me feel obscene.

If my father was out of town on a Friday or Saturday night, she fixed our supper (sometimes meat on Friday, the fear in our eyes not worthy of her recognition), put on her blue suit, and sat by herself in the living room, listening to the Grand Ole Opry or the Louisiana Hayride, while she drank apricot brandy from a coffee cup. She always dropped cigarette ashes on her suit and had to spot-clean the cloth with dry cleaning fluid before she drove off for the evening in her old Ford coupe. I don't know where she went on those Friday or Saturday nights, but a boy down the road told me that Mattie used to work in Broussard's Bar on Railroad Avenue, an infamous area in New Iberia where the women sat on the galleries of the cribs, dipping their beer out of buckets and yelling at the railroad and oil field workers in the street.

Then one morning when my father was in Morgan City a man in a new silver Chevrolet sedan came out to see her. It was hot, and he parked his car partly on our grass to keep it in the shade. He wore sideburns, striped brown zoot slacks, two-tone shoes, suspenders, a pink shirt without a coat, and a fedora that shadowed his narrow face. While he talked to her he put one shoe on the car bumper and wiped the dust off it with a rag. Then their voices grew louder and he said, 'You like the life. Admit it, you. He ain't given you no wedding ring, has he? You don't buy the cow, no, when you can milk through the fence.'

'I am currently involved with a gentleman. I do not know what you are talking about. I am not interested in anything you are talking about,' she said.

He threw the rag back inside the car and opened the car door.

'It's always trick, trade, or travel, darlin',' he said. 'Same rules here as down on Railroad. He done made you a nigger woman for them children, Mattie.'

'Are you calling me a nigra?' she said quietly.

'No, I'm calling you crazy, just like everybody say you are. No, I take that back, me. I ain't calling you nothing. I ain't got to, 'cause you gonna be back. You in the life, Mattie. You be phoning me to come out here, bring you to the crib, rub your back, put some of that warm stuff in your arm again. Ain't nobody else do that for you, huh?'

When she came back into the house she made us take all

the dishes out of the cabinets, even though they were clean, and wash them over again.

It was the following Friday that Sister Roberta called. Mattie was already dressed to go out. She didn't bother to turn down the radio when she answered the phone, and in order to compete with Red Foley's voice she had to almost shout into the receiver.

'Mr. Sonnier is not here,' she said. 'Mr. Sonnier is away on business in Texas City. . . . No, ma'am, I'm not the housekeeper. I'm a friend of the family who is caring for these children. . . . There's nothing wrong with that boy that I can see. . . . Are you calling to tell me that there's something wrong, that I'm doing something wrong? What is it that I'm doing wrong? I would like to know that. What is your name?'

I stood transfixed with terror in the hall as she bent angrily into the mouthpiece and her knuckles ridged on the receiver. A storm was blowing in from the Gulf, the air smelled of ozone, and the southern horizon was black with thunderclouds that pulsated with white veins of lightning. I heard the wind ripping through the trees in the yard and pecans rattling down on the gallery roof like grapeshot.

When Mattie hung up the phone the skin on her face was stretched as tight as a lampshade and one liquid eye was narrowed at me like someone aiming down a rifle barrel.

The next week, when I was cutting through the neighbor's sugarcane field on the way home from school, my heart started to race for no reason, my spit tasted like pecans, my face filmed with perspiration even though the wind was cool through the stalks of cane; then I saw the oaks and cypress trees along Bayou Teche tilt at an angle, and I dropped my books and fell forward in the dirt as though someone had wrapped a chain around my chest and snapped my breastbone.

I lay with the side of my face pressed against the dirt, my mouth gasping like a fish's, until Weldon found me and went crashing through the cane for help. A doctor came out to the house that night, examined me and gave me a shot, then talked with my father out in the hall. My father didn't understand the doctor's vocabulary, and he said, 'What *kind* of fever that is?'

'Rheumatic, Mr. Sonnier. It attacks the heart. I could be wrong, but I think that's what your boy's got. I'll be back tomorrow.'

'How much this gonna cost?'

'It's three dollars a visit, but you can pay me when you're able.'

'We never had nothing like this in our family. You sure about this?'

'No, I'm not. That's why I'll be back. Good night to you, sir.'

I knew he didn't like my father, but he came to see me one afternoon a week for a month, brought me bottles of medicine, and always looked into my face with genuine concern after he listened to my heart. Then one night he and my father argued and he didn't come back.

'What good he do, huh?' my father said. 'You still sick, ain't you? A doctor don't make money off well people. I think maybe you got malaria, son. There ain't nothing for that, either. It just goes away. You gonna see, you. You stay in bed, you eat *cush-cush* Mattie and me make for you, you drink that Hadacol vitamin tonic, you wear this dime I'm tying on you, you gonna get well and go back to school.'

He tied a perforated dime on a piece of red twine around my neck. His face was lean and unshaved, and his turquoise eyes were as intense as a butane flame when he looked into mine.

'You blame me for your mama?' he asked.

'No, sir,' I lied.

'I didn't mean to hit her. But she made me look bad in

172

front of y'all. A woman can't be doing that to a man in front of his kids.'

'Make Mattie go away, Daddy.'

'Don't be saying that.'

'She hit Weldon with the belt. She made Drew kneel in the bathroom corner because she didn't flush the toilet.'

'She's just trying to be a mother, that's all. Don't talk no more. Go to sleep. I got to drive back to Texas City tonight. You gonna be all right.'

He closed my door and the inside of my room was absolutely black. Through the wall I heard him and Mattie talking, then the weight of their bodies creaking rhythmically on the bedsprings.

When Sister Roberta knew that I would not be back to school that semester she began bringing my lessons to the house. She came three afternoons a week, and she had to walk two miles each way between the convent and our house. Each time I successfully completed a lesson she rewarded me with a holy card. Each holy card had a prayer on one side and a beautiful picture on the other, usually of angels and saints glowing with light or ethereal paintings of Mary with the Infant Jesus. On the day after my father had tied the dime around my neck Sister Roberta had to walk past our neighbor's field right after he had cut his cane and burned off the stubble, and a wet wind had streaked her black habit with ashes. As soon as she came through my bedroom door her face tightened inside her wimple, and her brown eyes, which had flecks of red in them, grew round and hot, and she dropped her book bag on the foot of my bed and leaned within six inches of my face as though she were looking down at a horrid presence in the bottom of a well. The hair on her upper lip looked like pieces of silver thread.

'Who put that around your neck?' she asked.

'My father says it keeps the *gris-gris* away.'

'My suffering God,' she said, and went back out the door

in a swirl of cloth. Then I heard her speak to Mattie: 'That's right, madam. Scissors. So I can remove that cord from his neck before he strangles to death in his sleep. Thank you kindly.'

She came back into my bedroom, pulled the twine out from my throat with one finger, and snipped it in two.

'Do you believe in this nonsense, Billy Bob?' she said.

'No, Sister.'

'That's good. You're a good Catholic boy, and you mustn't believe in superstition. Do you love the church?'

'I think so.'

'Hmmmm. That doesn't sound entirely convincing. Do you love your father?'

'I don't know.'

'I see. Do you love your sister and your brothers?'

'Yes. Most of the time I do.'

'That's good. Because if you love somebody, or if you love the church, like I do, then you don't ever have to be afraid. People are only superstitious when they're afraid. That's an important lesson for little people to learn. Now, let's take a look at our math test for this week.'

Over her shoulder I saw Mattie looking at us from the living room, her hair in foam-rubber curlers, her face contorted as though a piece of barbed wire were twisting behind her eyes.

That winter my father started working regular hours, what he called 'an indoor job,' at the Monsanto Chemical Company in Texas City, and we saw him only on weekends. Mattie cooked only the evening meal and made us responsible for the care of the house and the other two meals. Weldon started to get into trouble at school. His eighth-grade teacher, a lay woman, called and said he had thumbtacked a girl's dress to the desk during class, causing her to almost tear it off her body when the bell rang, and he would either pay for the dress or be suspended. Mattie hung up the phone on her, and two days later the girl's father, a sheriff's deputy, came out to the house and made Mattie give him four dollars on the gallery.

She came back inside, slamming the door, her face burning, grabbed Weldon by the collar of his T-shirt and walked him into the backyard, where she made him stand for two hours on an upended apple crate until he wet his pants.

Later, after she had let him come back inside and he had changed his underwear and blue jeans, he went outside into the dark by himself, without eating supper, and sat on the butcher stump, striking kitchen matches on the side of the box and throwing them at the chickens. Before we went to sleep he sat for a long time on the side of his bed, next to mine, in a square of moonlight with his hands balled into fists on his thighs. There were knots of muscle in the backs of his arms and behind his ears. Mattie had given him a burr haircut, and his head looked as hard and scalped as a baseball.

'Tomorrow's Saturday. We're going to listen to the LSU-Rice game,' I said.

'Some colored kids saw me from the road and laughed.'

'I don't care what they did. You're brave, Weldon. You're braver than any of us.'

'I'm gonna fix her.'

His voice made me afraid. The branches of the pecan trees were skeletal, like gnarled fingers against the moon.

'Don't be thinking like that,' I said. 'It'll just make her do worse things. She takes it out on Drew when you and Lyle aren't here.'

'Go to sleep, Billy Bob,' he said. His eyes were wet. 'She hurts us because we let her. We ax for it. You get hurt when you don't stand up. Just like Momma did.' I heard him snuffling in the dark. Then he lay down with his face turned toward the opposite wall. His head looked carved out of gray wood in the moonlight.

I went back to school for the spring semester, and because

of the warmth of the season, the balmy winds off the Gulf, the flaming azaleas in people's yards, the heavy, fecund smell of magnolia and wisteria on the night air, I wanted to believe that a new season was beginning in my heart as well. I couldn't control what happened at home, but the school was a safe place, one where Sister Roberta ruled her little fifth-grade world like an affectionate despot.

I was always fascinated by her hands. They were like toy hands, small as a child's, as pink as an early rose, the nails not much bigger than pearls. She was wonderful at sketching and drawing with crayons and colored chalk. In minutes she could create a beautiful religious scene on the blackboard to fit the church's season, but she also drew pictures for us of Easter rabbits and talking Easter eggs. Sometimes she would draw only the outline of a figure – an archangel with enormous wings, a Roman soldier about to be dazzled by a blinding light – and she would let us take turns coloring in the solid areas. She told us the secret to great classroom art was to always keep your chalk and crayons pointy.

Then we began to hear rumors about Sister Roberta, of a kind that we had never heard about any of the nuns, who all seemed to have no lives other than the ones that were immediately visible to us. She had been heard weeping in the confessional, she had left the convent for three days without permission, two detectives from Baton Rouge had questioned her in the mother superior's office.

She missed a week of school, and a lay teacher took her place. She returned for two weeks, then was gone again. When she came back the second time she was soft-spoken and removed, and sometimes she didn't even bother to answer simple questions that we asked her. She would gaze out the window for long periods, as though her attention were fixed on a distant object, then a noise – a creaking desk, an eraser flung from the cloakroom – would disturb her, and her eyes would return to the room, absolutely empty of thought or meaning.

I stayed after school on a Friday to help her wash the blackboards and pound erasers.

'You don't need to, Billy Bob. The janitor will take care of it,' she said.

She was putting paper clips one by one in a box on top of her desk.

'All the kids like you, Sister,' I said.

'What?' she said.

'You're the only one who plays with us at recess. You don't ever get mad at us, either. Not for real, anyway.'

'It's nice of you to say that, but the other sisters are good to you, too.'

'Not like you are.'

'You shouldn't talk to me like that, Billy Bob.' She had lost weight, and there was a solitary crease, like a line drawn by a thumbnail, in each of her cheeks.

'It's wrong for you to be sad,' I said.

'You must run along home now. Don't say anything more.'

I wish you were my mother, I thought I heard myself say inside my head.

'What did you say?' she asked.

'Nothing.'

'Tell me what you said.'

'I don't think I said anything. I really don't think I did.'

My heart was beating against my rib cage, the same way it had the day I fell unconscious in the sugarcane field.

'Billy Bob, don't try to understand the world. It's not ours to understand,' she said. 'You must give up the things you can't change. You mustn't talk to me like this anymore. You –'

But I was already racing from the room, my soul painted with an unrelieved shame that knew no words.

The next week I found out the source of Sister Roberta's grief. A strange and seedy man by the name of Mr. Trajan, who always had an American flag pin in his lapel when you saw him inside the wire-cage office of the grocery and package store he operated by the Negro district, cut an article from copies of the Baton Rouge *Morning Advocate* and the Lafayette *Daily Advertiser* and mailed it to other Catholic businessmen in town. An eighth-grader who had been held back twice, once by Sister Roberta, brought it to school one day, and after the three o'clock bell Lyle, Weldon, and I heard him reading it to a group of dumbfounded boys on the playground. The words hung in the air like our first exposure to God's name being deliberately used in vain.

Her brother had killed a child, and Sister Roberta had helped him to hide in a fishing camp in West Baton Rouge Parish.

'Give me that,' Weldon said, and tore the news article out of the boy's hand. He stared at it, then wadded it up and threw it on the ground. 'Get the fuck out of here. You go around talking about this again and I'll kick your ass.'

'That's right, you dumb fuck,' Lyle said, putting his new baseball cap in his back pocket and setting his book satchel down by his foot.

'That's right, butt face,' I added, incredulous at the boldness of my own words.

'Yeah?' the boy said, but the resolve in his voice was already breaking.

'Yeah!' Weldon said, and shoved him off balance. Then he picked up a rock and chased the boy and three of his friends toward the street. Lyle and I followed, picking up dirt clots in our hands. When the boy was almost to his father's waiting pickup truck, he turned and shot us the finger. Weldon nailed him right above the eye with the rock.

One of the brothers marched us down to Father Higgins' office and left us there to wait for Father Higgins, whose razor strop and black-Irish, crimson-faced tirades were legendary in the school. The office smelled of the cigar butts in the wastebasket and the cracked leather in the chairs. A walnut pendulum clock ticked loudly on the wall. It was overcast outside, and we sat in the gloom and silence until four o'clock.

'I ain't waiting any more. Y'all coming?' Weldon said, and put one leg out the open window.

'You'll get expelled,' I said.

'Too bad. I ain't going to wait around just to have somebody whip me,' he said, and dropped out the window.

Five minutes later Lyle followed him.

The sound of the clock was like a spoon knocking on a hollow wood box. When Father Higgins finally entered the room, he wore his horn-rimmed glasses and was thumbing through a sheaf of papers attached to a clipboard. The hairline on the back of his neck was shaved neatly with a razor. At first he seemed distracted by my presence, then he flipped the sheets of paper to a particular page, almost as an afterthought, and studied it. He put an unlit cigar stub in his mouth, looked at me, then back at the page.

'You threw a rock at somebody?' he said.

'No, Father.'

'Somebody threw a rock at you?'

'I wouldn't say that.'

'You *wouldn't* say that? Then what are you doing here?'

'I don't know.'

'That's interesting. All right, since you don't know why you're here, how about going somewhere else?'

'I'll take him, Father,' I heard Sister Roberta say in the doorway. She put her hand on my arm, walked me down the darkly polished corridor to the breeze-way outside, then sat me down on the stone bench inside the bamboo-enclosed garden where she often said her rosary.

She sat next to me, her small white hands curved on the edges of the bench, and looked down at the goldfish pond while she talked. A crushed paper cup floated among the hyacinth leaves.

'You meant well, Billy Bob,' she said, 'but I don't want

179

you to defend me anymore. It's not the job of little people to defend adults.'

'Sister, it said –'

'It said what?'

'You were in trouble with the police. Can they put you in jail?'

She put her hand on top of mine. Her fingernails looked like tiny pink seashells. 'They're not really interested in me, Billy Bob. My brother is an alcoholic, and he killed a little boy with his car, then he ran away. But they probably won't send my brother to prison because the child was a Negro.' Her hand was hot and damp on top of mine. Her voice clicked wetly in her throat. 'He'll be spared, not because he's a sick man, but because it was a colored child he killed.'

When I looked at her again her long eyelashes were bright with tears.

She stood up with her face turned away from me. The sun had broken through the gray seal of clouds, and the live oak tree overhead was filled with the clattering of mockingbirds and bluejays. I felt her tiny fingernails rake gently through my hair, as though she were combing a cat.

'Oh you poor child, there're lice eggs in your hair,' she said.

Then she pressed my head against her breast, and I felt her tears strike hotly on the back of my neck.

Three days later Sister Roberta saw the cigarette burn on Drew's leg in the lunchroom and reported it to the social welfare agency in town. A consumptive rail of a man in a dandruff-flecked blue suit drove out to the house and questioned Mattie on the gallery, then questioned us in front of Mattie. Drew told him she had been burned by an ember that had popped out of a trash fire in the backyard.

He raised her chin with his knuckle. His black hair was stiff with grease.

'Is that what happened?' he asked.

'Yes, sir.' Drew's face was dull, her mouth downturned at the corners. The burn was scabbed now and looked like a tightly coiled gray worm on her skin.

He smiled and took his knuckle away from her chin. 'Then you shouldn't play next to the fire,' he said.

'I would like to know who sent you out here,' Mattie said.

'That's confidential.' He coughed on the back of his hand. His shirt cuff was frayed on his thin wrist. 'And to tell you the truth, I don't really know. My supervisor didn't tell me.' He coughed again, this time loud and hard, and I could smell his deep-lung nicotine odor. 'But everything here looks all right.'

Weldon's eyes were as hard as marbles, but he didn't speak.

The man walked with Mattie to his car, and I felt like doors were slamming all around us. She put her foot on his running board and propped one arm on his car roof while she talked, so that her breasts were uplifted against her blouse and her dress made a loop between her legs.

'Let's tell him,' Lyle said.

'Are you kidding? Look at him. She could make him eat her shit with a spoon,' Weldon said.

It was right after first period the next morning that we heard about the disaster at Texas City. Somebody shouted something about it in the playground, then suddenly the whole school was abuzz with rumors. Cars on the street pulled to the curb with their radios tuned to news stations, and we could even hear the principal's old wood-cased radio from the open window upstairs. A ship loaded with fertilizer had been burning in the harbor, and while people on the docks had watched fire-fighting boats pumping geysers of water onto the ship's decks, the fire had dripped into the hold. The explosion filled the sky with rockets of smoke and rained an umbrella of flame down on the Monsanto chemical plant. The force of the secondary explosion was so great that it blew out windows in

Houston, fifty miles away. But it wasn't over yet. The fireball mushroomed laterally out into an adjacent oil field, and rows of storage tanks and wellheads went like strings of Chinese firecrackers. People said the water in the harbor boiled from the heat, the spars on steel derricks melted like licorice.

We heard nothing about the fate of my father either that afternoon or evening. Mattie got drunk that night and fell asleep in the living-room chair by the radio. I felt nothing about my father's possible death, and I wondered at my own callousness. We went to school the next morning, and when we returned home in the afternoon Mattie was waiting on the gallery to tell us that a man from the Monsanto company had telephoned and said that my father was listed as missing. Her eyes were pink with either hangover or crying, and her face was puffy and round, like a white balloon.

When we didn't respond, she said, 'Your father may be dead. Do you understand what I'm saying? That was an important man from his company who called. He would not call unless he was gravely concerned. Do you children understand what is being said to you?'

Weldon brushed at the dirt with his tennis shoe, and Lyle looked into a place about six inches in front of his eyes. Drew's face was frightened, not because of the news about our father, but instead because of the strange whirring of wheels we could almost hear from inside Mattie's head. I put my arm over her shoulders and felt her skin jump.

'He's worked like a nigra for you, maybe lost his life for you, and you have nothing to say?' she asked.

'Maybe we ought to start cleaning up our rooms. You wanted us to clean up our rooms, Mattie,' I said.

But it was a poor attempt to placate her.

'You stay outside. Don't even come in this house,' she said.

'I have to go to the bathroom,' Lyle said.

'Then you can just do it in the dirt like a darky,' she said, and went inside the house and latched the screen behind her.

By the next afternoon my father was still unaccounted for. Mattie had an argument on the phone with somebody, I think the man in zoot pants and two-tone shoes who had probably been her pimp at one time, because she told him he owed her money and she wouldn't come back and work at Broussard's Bar again until he paid her. After she hung up she breathed hard at the kitchen sink, smoking her cigarette and staring out into the yard. She snapped the cap off a bottle of Jax and drank it half-empty, her throat working in one long, wet swallow, one eye cocked at me.

'Come here,' she said.

'What?'

'You tracked up the kitchen. You didn't flush the toilet after you used it either.'

'I did.'

'You did what?'

'I flushed the toilet.'

'Then one of the others didn't flush it. Every one of you come out here. Now!'

'What is it, Mattie? We didn't do anything,' I said.

'I changed my mind. Every one of you outside. All of you outside. Weldon and Lyle, you get out there right now. Where's Drew?'

'She's playing in the yard. What's wrong, Mattie?' I made no attempt to hide the fear in my voice. I could see the web of blue veins in the top of her muscular chest.

Outside the wind was blowing through the trees in the yard, flattening the purple clumps of wisteria that grew against the barn wall.

'Each of you go to the hedge and cut the switch you want me to use on you,' she said.

It was her favorite form of punishment for us. If we broke off a large switch, she hit us fewer times with it. If we came back with a thin or small switch, we would get whipped until she felt she had struck some kind of balance between size and number.

We remained motionless. Drew had been playing with her cat. She had tied a piece of twine around the cat's neck, and she held the twine in her hand like a leash. Her knees and white socks were dusty from play.

'I told you not to tie that around the kitten's neck again,' Mattie said.

'It doesn't hurt anything. It's not your cat, anyway,' Weldon said.

'Don't sass me,' she said. 'You will not sass me. None of you will sass me.'

'I ain't cutting no switch,' Weldon said. 'You're crazy. My mama said so. You ought to be in the crazy house.'

She looked hard into Weldon's eyes, and there was a moment of recognition in her colorless face, as though she had seen a growing meanness of spirit in Weldon that was the equal of her own. Then she wet her lips, crimped them together, and rubbed her hands on her thighs.

'We shall see who does what around here,' she said. She broke off a big switch from the myrtle hedge and raked it free of flowers and leaves, except for one green sprig on the tip.

I saw the look in Drew's face, saw her drop the piece of twine from her palm as she looked up into Mattie's shadow.

Mattie jerked her by the wrist and whipped her a half-dozen times across her bare legs. Drew twisted impotently in Mattie's balled hand, her feet dancing with each blow. The switch raised welts on her skin as thick and red as centipedes.

Then suddenly Weldon ran with all his weight into Mattie's back, stiff-arming her between the shoulder blades, and sent her tripping sideways over a bucket of chicken slops. She righted herself and stared at him open-mouthed, the switch limp in her hand. Then her eyes grew hot and bright with a painful intention, and I could see the bones flex along her jaws.

Weldon burst out the back gate and ran down the dirt road between the sugarcane fields, the soles of his dirty tennis shoes powdering dust in the air.

She waited for him a long time, watching through the screen as the mauve-colored dusk gathered in the trees and the sun's afterglow lit the clouds on the western horizon with flame. Then she took a bottle of apricot brandy into the bathroom and sat in the tub for almost an hour, turning the hot-water tap on and off until the tank was empty. When we needed to go to the bathroom, she told us to take our problem outside. Finally she emerged in the hall, wearing only her panties and bra, her hair wrapped in a towel, the dark outline of her sex plainly visible to us.

'I'm going to dress now and go into town with a gentleman friend,' she said. 'Tomorrow we're going to start a new regime around here. Believe me, there will never be a reoccurrence of what happened here today. You can pass that on to young Mr. Weldon for me.'

But she didn't go into town. Instead, she put on her blue suit, a flower-print blouse, her nylon stockings, and walked up and down on the gallery, her cigarette poised in the air like a movie actress.

'Why not just drive your car, Mattie?' I said quietly through the screen.

'It has no gas. Besides, a gentleman caller will be passing for me anytime now,' she answered.

'Oh.'

She blew smoke at an upward angle, her face aloof and flat-sided in the shadows.

'Mattie?'

'Yes?'

'Weldon's out back. Can he come in the house?'

'Little mice always return where the cheese is,' she said.

I hated her. I wanted something terrible to happen to her. I could feel my fingernails kniving into my palms.

She turned on one high heel, her palm supporting one elbow, her cigarette an inch from her mouth, her hair wreathed in smoke.

'Do you have a reason for staring through the screen at me?' she asked.

'No,' I said.

'When you're bigger you'll get to do what's on your mind. In the meantime, don't let your thoughts show on your face. You're a lewd little boy.'

Her suggestion repelled me and made water well up in my eyes. I backed away from the screen, then turned and ran through the rear of the house and out into the backyard where Weldon, Lyle, and Drew sat against the barn wall, fireflies lighting in the wisteria over their heads.

No one came for Mattie that evening. She sat in the stuffed chair in her room, putting on layers of lipstick until her mouth had the crooked, bright-red shape of a clown's. She smoked a whole package of Chesterfields, constantly wiping the ashes off her dark-blue skirt with a hand towel soaked in dry-cleaning fluid; then she drank herself unconscious.

It was hot that night, and dry lightning leaped from the horizon to the top of the blue-black vault of sky over the Gulf. Weldon sat on the side of his bed in the dark, his shoulders hunched, his fists between his white thighs. His burr haircut looked like duck down on his head in the flicker of the lightning through the window. When I was almost asleep he shook both me and Lyle awake and said, 'We got to get rid of her. You know we got to do it.'

I put my pillow over my head and rolled away from him, as though I could drop away into sleep and rise in the morning into a sun-spangled and different world.

But in the false dawn I woke to both Lyle and Weldon's faces close to mine. Weldon's eyes were hollow, his breath rank with funk. The mist was heavy and wet in the pecan trees outside the window.

'She's not gonna hurt Drew again. Are you gonna help or not?' Weldon said.

I followed them into the hallway, my heart sinking at the realization of what I was willing to participate in, my body as numb as if I had been stunned with Novocaine. Mattie slept in the stuffed chair, her hose rolled down over her knees, an overturned jelly glass on the rug next to the can of spot cleaner.

Weldon walked quietly across the rug, unscrewed the cap on the can, laid the can on its side in front of Mattie's feet, then backed away from her. The cleaning fluid spread in a dark circle around her chair, the odor as bright and sharp as a slap across the face.

Weldon slid open a box of kitchen matches and we each took one, raked it across the striker, and, with the sense that our lives at that moment had changed forever, threw them at Mattie's feet. But the burning matches fell outside the wet area. The blood veins in my head dilated with fear, my ears hummed with a sound like the roar of the ocean in a seashell, and I jerked the box from Weldon's hand, clutched a half-dozen matches in my fist, dragged them across the striker, and flung them right on Mattie's feet.

The chair was enveloped in a cone of flame, and she burst out of it with her arms extended, as though she were pushing blindly through a curtain, her mouth and eyes wide with terror. We could smell her hair burning as she raced past us and crashed through the screen door out onto the gallery and into the yard. She beat at her flaming clothes and raked at her hair as though it were swarming with yellow jackets.

I stood transfixed in mortal dread at what I had done.

A Negro man walking to work came out of the mist on the road and knocked her to the ground, slapping the fire out of her dress, pinning her under his spread knees as though he were assaulting her. Smoke rose from her scorched clothes and hair as in a depiction of a damned figure on one of my holy cards.

The Negro rose to his feet and walked toward the gallery, a solitary line of blood running down his black cheek where Mattie had scratched him.

'Yo' mama ain't hurt bad. Get some butter or some bacon grease. She gonna be all right, you gonna see. You children don't be worried, no,' he said.

He smiled with his snuff-stained gums to assure us that everything would be all right.

The volunteer firemen bounced across the cattle-guard in an old firetruck whose obsolete hand-crank starter still dangled from under the radiator. They coated Mattie's room with foam from a fire extinguisher and packed Mattie off in an ambulance to the charity hospital in Lafayette. Two sheriff's deputies arrived, and before he left, one of the volunteers took them aside in the yard and talked with them, looking over his shoulder at us children, then walked over to us and said, 'The fire chief gonna come out here and check it out. Y'all stay out of that bedroom.'

His face was narrow and dark with shadow under the brim of his big rubber fireman's hat.

I felt a fist squeeze my heart.

But suddenly Sister Roberta was in the midst of everything. Someone had carried word to the school about the fire, and she'd had one of the brothers drive her out to the house. She talked with the deputies, helped us fix cereal at the kitchen table, made telephone calls to find a place for us to stay besides the welfare shelter. Then she looked in Mattie's bedroom door and studied the interior for what seemed a long time. When she came back in the kitchen her eyes peeled the skin off our faces. I looked straight down into my cereal bowl.

She placed her small hand on my shoulder. I could feel her fingers tapping on the bone, as though she were processing her own thoughts. Then she said, 'Well, what should we do here today? I think we should clean up first. Where's the broom?'

Without waiting for an answer she pulled the broom out of the closet and went to work in Mattie's room, sweeping the spilled and unstruck matches as well as the burned ones in a pile by a side door that gave onto the yard. The soot and blackened threads from the rug swirled up in a cloud around her veils and wings and smudged her starched wimple.

One of the deputies put his hand on the broomstick.

'There ain't been an investigation yet. You can't do that till the fire chief come out and see, Sister,' he said.

'You always talked like a fool, Gaspard,' she said. 'Now that you have a uniform, you talk like a bigger one. The house smells like an incinerator. Now get out of the way.'

With one sweep of the broom she raked all the matches out into the yard.

We were placed in foster homes, and over the years I lost contact with Sister Roberta. But later I went to work in the oil fields, and I think perhaps I talked with my father in a nightclub outside of Morgan City. An enormous live oak tree grew through the floor and roof, and he was leaning against the bar that had been built in a circle around the tree. His face was puckered with white scar tissue, his ears burnt into stubs, his right hand atrophied and frozen against his chest like a broken bird's foot. But beyond the layers of mutilated skin I could see my father's face, like the image in a photographic negative held up against a light.

'Is your name Sonnier?' I asked.

He looked at me curiously.

'Maybe. You want to buy me a drink?' he said.

'All right,' I said.

He ordered a shot of Beam with a frosted schooner of Jax on the side.

'Are you Verise Sonnier from New Iberia?' I asked.

He grinned stiffly when he took the schooner of beer away from his mouth.

'Why you want to know?' he said.

'I think I'm your son. I'm Billy Bob.'

His turquoise eyes wandered over my face, then they lost interest.

'I had a son. But you ain't him,' he said. 'Buy me another shot?'

'Sure. Why not?' I said.

Sometimes he comes to me in my dreams, and I wonder if ironically all our stories were written on his skin back there in Texas City in 1947. Or maybe that's just a poetic illusion purchased by time. But even in the middle of an Indian summer's day, when the sugarcane is beaten with purple and gold light in the fields and the sun is both warm and cool on your skin at the same time, when I know that the earth is a fine place after all, I have to mourn just a moment for those people of years ago who lived lives they did not choose, who carried burdens that were not their own, whose invisible scars were as private as the scarlet beads of Sister Roberta's rosary wrapped across the back of her small hand, as bright as drops of blood ringed round the souls of litttle people.

Winter Light

He lived alone at the head of the canyon in a two-story log house that controlled the access to the National Forest area behind his property. His house was built up on a slope above a creek that flowed down from a chain of lakes high up on the plateau, and from his writing desk at his second story window he could look out over the wide sweep of valley below and see the snow blowing out of the ponderosa on the crests of the hills and the sharply etched tracks of deer that had gone down to drink in the stream during the night. He could also see the long black scar of a road that wound its way up from the interstate, past the one working ranch left in the valley, to the foot of his property and finally to the public woods behind his house.

The sunlight was red on the snow, the shadows already purple in the trees, the wind colder and flecked with ice crystals against the window glass, and he knew the hunters would be there soon. They almost always came in the late afternoon, because it was only a ten-mile drive from town and with a little luck they could get in a few shots before the official close of the hunter's day thirty minutes after sunset.

He was fifty-eight and he had taken early retirement

from his position as a literature professor at the university, but he had no interest in the activities of retirement or people his own age. Most of his friends were college students, and in one way or another his property always seemed marked more by their presence than his: tipi poles stacked against his tool shed, the willow-stick outline of a sweat lodge by the creek, a communal vegetable garden whose rows were now frozen into iron ridges.

A red Toyota jeep, as bright against the snow as a fire engine, ground in four-wheel-drive up the road, then slowed as the driver and his passenger peered through their ice-streaked windows at the signs fastened to the trunks of larch pines at the foot of the professor's property:

THIS IS A PRIVATE ROAD
NO HUNTING
NO SHOOTING
NO TRESPASSING

But they drove on anyway, and he met them outside his door, with a cup of coffee in his hand, in his worn corduroy pants, lace-on boots, and flannel shirt. He had played basketball for L.S.U., and he was tall and angular, bareheaded in the wind, his skin red and coarse with the cold.

He was not unkind to them. He never was. Sometimes he invited them inside; usually they simply went away, confused or mildly irritated. But these two were different. The passenger had a dark light in his face and wore an untrimmed beard and spit regularly in the snow. His hands were square and big and seamed with dirt, and he opened and closed them impatiently. The driver was a fat man who wore three shirts that hung outside his pants, galoshes, a neon-orange hunter's vest, a narrow skinning knife in a scabbard on his side. He smiled while he talked, but his eyes did not go with his face.

The professor, whose name was Roger Guidry, listened to the driver talk, his slender fingers wrapped around his coffee cup, his head nodding absently as he scraped at the snow with the tip of his boot. Then when the overweight man had finished, he said, 'You can walk in from the other side and hunt, if you want.'

'The other side?' the driver said.

'Yes.'

'How far a walk is that?'

'Fifteen miles.'

'Fifteen miles,' the driver said, nodding his head up and down. 'Fifteen miles in snow, you're saying?'

'That's right.'

'I told you we're bow hunters. We're not going to put a bullet into somebody's house or shoot somebody's cows.'

'I know that.'

'Listen –' the driver said.

The passenger hit him on the arm and said, 'Forget it. Let's go.'

'Just a minute,' the driver said. 'You're telling me to walk fifteen fucking miles through snow?'

'It's your choice.'

'My choice?'

'That's right.'

'I've heard about you.'

'Oh?' Roger said.

'Yeah. I just didn't know it was this canyon.'

'I see.'

'We've still got time to go up the Blackfoot. Forget this guy,' the passenger said.

The driver put an unlit cigarette in his mouth and looked around the yard as though he were deciding something. Then he laughed, lit his cigarette, and looked off down the valley.

'Too much,' he said, then they both got in the jeep, backed it around in the snow, cracking an old tomato stake in the vegetable garden, and crunched down the road over their own long lines of stenciled tire tracks.

The coffee cup was cold in the professor's hand. He

looked down at the creek that flowed out of the dark stands of pine and fir in the National Forest. In the center the riffle was a deep blue-green between sheets of ice that looked like teeth. Through the willow frame of the sweat lodge he could see two smooth, round boulders that always reminded him of a woman's breasts, and behind them a barkless and polished cottonwood that beavers had toppled into the stream to form an eddying pool whose pebbled bottom was always marbled with the shapes of cutthroat and brookie trout. In the spring and summer he and the students would fish the pool, have community dinners among the ferns on the bank, pack far up into the canyon, where the cinnamon bears and white-tailed deer were never hunted and bighorn sheep grazed through the saddles high up on the peaks.

The frozen trunks of the ponderosas creaked in the wind, powdering the snow in the twilight.

In the spring, he thought.

He didn't remember at which particular stage of his dissatisfaction with university life that he had decided to take early retirement. Others had tried to dissuade him – he was a wonderful teacher, he would be hurt financially, he would be missed by his students. And there was truth in what they said, but he had reached the age, he told himself, when he no longer had to apologize or defend.

Maybe it had been the interminable department and committee meetings, the jealousies and hatreds that his colleagues kept alive like green wounds for decades, the self-anointed liberals whose pension plans were invested in nuclear energy, South Africa, and the Boeing Company. He tried, at least in his own mind, not to be hard on them, but in reality they filled him with a visceral disgust. There was always a sneer in their laughter, an atmosphere of bitterness and personal failure in their meeting rooms that was as palpable as the smell of sweat. They denigrated anyone who accomplished anything and tried to sabotage any educational innovation that threatened their own meager positions.

No, he did remember when he made his decision to hang it up. A search committee had to meet during the Christmas holidays to choose from a huge file of applicants for a vacant position. The chair of the committee, Waldo Gates, and one of his allies, consistently gave low ratings to people with no publications and little experience. Waldo Gates, who lived across the creek from Roger, was also a hunter. He had even worn his mail-order camouflage fatigues and brown corduroy shooting vest to the meeting. His friend was dressed for the hunt, too, and both of them kept looking at their watches. After they had just sandbagged a Ph.D. from Stanford who had published two collections of critical essays, it was obvious to Roger that the department was about to hire an underqualified and frightened young woman who would be easily controlled by Waldo and his coterie, and Waldo and his committee ally would soon be duck hunting at the reservoir south of town.

Waldo sat at the desk at the front of the room. He wore a red chin beard and horn-rimmed glasses low on his nose. His eyes were lime-green, the size of dimes, and they never blinked when they looked over the top of his glasses at someone, which gave him the appearance of candor and directness and which always intimidated students and younger faculty members.

He held a file gingerly between his fingers and clicked it up and down on the desk.

'I think we've found the lady we need here,' he said. 'And it seems to me we have more or less a majority agreement on that, sooooooo' — his eyes roved over the five other faces in the room, and two junior faculty members glanced away — 'unless anyone else has anything to say, we can be on our way.'

'Going to make things fall down, are you?' Roger said.

'I beg your pardon,' Waldo said.

'Have you guys ever thought about an open season on people? You could establish these big reserve areas enclosed by electric fences where y'all could go inside and hunt each other for, say, three or four days at a time. Blow blood, brains, and hair all over the bushes and have a fine time. Except it'd be a genuine sport because the prey would have guns, too. What do you think, Waldo?'

'I think your cause is silly and your personal life needs some attention.' Waldo's lime-green eyes were as round and hard as tiny marbles in his soft face.

'Would you care to explain that?' Roger said.

'There's life after divorce. That's why people have divorces. You end a relationship and you go on with your life. You don't lay off your problems on your colleagues.'

'Maybe we could talk about that later, Waldo.' Roger cleared his throat slightly. 'Outside somewhere. I'll keep one hand in my pocket. In fact, I'll turn my back so the position will be more familiar for you.'

'I'm glad you've gotten that off your chest, Roger. I'll report your remarks to the dean. Then you can take it up with him. I believe our committee work is done, ladies and gentlemen. Sooooooo, unless Dr Guidry has any more threatening observations to make, let's be on our way.'

They left him alone in the room, feeling foolish and wrong. Did he always have to speak his mind, as a child would, he thought, then spend the rest of the day rationalizing his impetuosity? He looked wistfully out the window at the brown, grassy slope of the mountain behind the campus and the thick stands of ponderosa that grew along the crest and through the saddles. The trunks were orange in the sunlight, wet with melted snow, and the pine needles were as dark and shiny as clusters of splintered blue glass. High up on the windstream a hawk floated against the thin wafer of pink, winter sun. Then Roger heard the janitor knock his broom against one of the wood desks. He picked up his briefcase at his foot, smiled politely, and walked across the empty quadrangle to his pickup truck. His vehicle was the only one in the parking lot, and for some illogical reason that fact struck him as significant.

His son was away at Stanford, and his two daughters had started their own lives in Oregon and Minnesota. They came to see him in the summer, usually with friends, and their conversations were alive with subjects that seemed to exist just beyond the borders of his knowledge or his interest. After the divorce he had thought of his wife only with anger, and when the anger passed he could think of nothing except the ringing winter loneliness in his house.

The young women were available, certainly both out of affection as well as kindness. He woke hard in the morning, throbbing with desire, and he had to sit quietly on the side of his bed in his underwear and force his mind empty of their shapes, their bare thighs and breasts, their lips, their hands that wanted to stroke his sex. But he managed to live celibate, castigating himself in the silence for his prurient thoughts, on one occasion walking far up the canyon in knee-deep snow, beating his arms in the cold, saying, 'Bullshit, bullshit.' A white-tail doe criss-crossed the trail in front of him, staring back at him with brown, curious eyes.

The morning after the visit of the hunters in the Toyota jeep, he walked outside into the brilliant sunlight reflecting off the snow, the air that was as sharp and cold inside the lungs as ice water, and began stacking firewood in his wheelbarrow to take back to the house. His malamute, Boomer, who was as big and thick through the middle as a small cinnamon bear, frisked in the snow, snorting down in a badger hole by the garden, pulling a stick out of the snow and throwing it in the air.

Then Roger saw that it was not a stick, that it was made of aluminium and the flanged steel tip was the point of a hunter's arrow. He caught Boomer by the nape of skin on the back of his neck and forced him to release the shaft from his jaws. The point of the arrow felt as sharp as a razor against the ball of his thumb.

It could have come from Waldo's, across the creek, he thought. He looked through the leafless cottonwoods at the stacked hay bales that Waldo and his children used as an archery target. Yes yes yes, Waldo, he thought. Always Waldo. Last summer Waldo had been bothered by a skunk under his woodshed, and he had hired an out-of-work sawyer to tender-trap it inside a vinyl garbage bag; then the sawyer fitted the crimped end of the bag over his exhaust pipe, and while Waldo watched from his window, asphyxiated the animal to make a pair of gloves for Waldo's oldest son.

But Roger knew well the reason for his deliberate remembrance of a past grievance. The arrow didn't come from Waldo's property. Waldo was not a bow hunter, and also the trajectory of the arrow was almost straight down, which meant that it had not bounced off the top of a hay bale and flown across the creek but instead had been fired high into the air so that it would drop cleanly into Roger's yard.

It could have fallen out of their jeep when their doors were open, he told himself. It could have. Yes. But he felt his heart clicking against his ribs.

The next day was bright and clear and windless, and the valley looked white and dazzling under a blue-bird sky. By afternoon the sun was so warm that the snow had begun to pock in the fields and melt around the base of the ponderosa trunks. All day he waited for them to return. He knew it was only a matter of time. But when the sun finally dropped behind the pines on the valley's western rim and the snowfields turned as purple as a bruise, only one vehicle had come up the country road, Waldo's, carrying Waldo and a graduate teaching assistant, a statuesque blonde girl named Gretchen whom Waldo had requested as his grader.

But two days later, right at daybreak, he heard a four-wheel-drive transmission grinding up the road, and when he looked through his window, his breath clouding against the glass, he saw the red Toyota jeep stop at the foot of his property. The two hunters got out with shotguns and empty canvas backpacks, cut through the bare cottonwoods, stepped gingerly across the boulders in the creek, and threaded their way through fences, brush, trees, and an abandoned horse corral at the back of Waldo's property until they reached the trail that led into the National Forest.

In minutes he heard their shotguns booming. He put on his glasses and found Waldo's telephone number in the directory. The phone rang a dozen times before Waldo picked up the receiver, his voice full of sleep.

'Waldo, two guys just went through the back of your property,' Roger said.

'What guys? What are you talking about?'

'Two hunters. I wouldn't let them into the canyon, so they crossed the creek and climbed through your fences.'

'What do you want me to do about it?'

'You want guys with shotguns walking by your back-door without permission?'

'So when you see them, tell them to ask. In the meantime I don't appreciate your waking me up because of your personal problem with hunting. Get some help, Roger, because you're a public pain in the ass.'

The line went dead, and Roger looked out at the blueness of the morning, the black, leafless shapes of the cottonwoods along the creek bank, heard the deep booming echo of another shotgun blast up the canyon, and felt the cold ache through his naked feet like nails.

Two hours later the hunters walked out of the canyon in full sunlight, crunching through the sheath of ice and frozen snow along the creek's edge, their canvas packs fat with dead grouse. The driver, who still wore a skinning knife and galoshes that flopped on his feet, flipped a cigarette across the stream onto Roger's property, but neither he nor the other man, who had an untrimmed beard and a bitten look in his face, ever glanced in Roger's direction. Their tracks were jagged in the crusted snow. He heard one of the hunters laugh just before the driver started the jeep engine and ground the transmission into gear as sharply as Coke-bottle glass breaking.

That afternoon he drove into town and bought a forty-foot length of chain, a huge iron bolt and nut, and a Yale lock with two keys. A mile below his property, far down on the county road where he had no legal right to block access to the National Forest, he looped one end of the chain around a ponderosa trunk, bolted the links together against the bark, strung the rest of the chain across the road, and locked it to a steel eyelet on an old U.S. Forest Service signpost. Now the only other way to reach the National Forest was down Waldo's private road, and Waldo had a locked, electronic gate across his cattleguard.

The only neighbors who would be affected by the chain across the county road were a hippy carpenter and his girlfriend who lived just below Roger's place. Roger stopped by their log house, drank a cup of coffee with them, and gave them one of the keys to the padlock. While he explained the reason for the chain, the carpenter and his girlfriend smiled and nodded and rolled joints out of a bowl of reefer on top of a redwood table, and he realized that they were not really listening because they considered his behavior as conventional and expected as their own.

That night under a full moon that lighted the valley floor like a white flame, he walked down the road in the silence, the soles of his boots squeaking on the snow, and looked at the chain strung between the ponderosa trunk and the signpost. He lifted it up in his palm and bounced it against its tension. The links were heavy and cold and shiny with ice. They felt solid and good in his hand, the way the handle of a weapon probably did to some men. He let the chain slip off his fingers and rock clinking back and forth in the shadows. Far down the valley he could see the glow of headlights from the interstate highway against the clouds.

The season was almost over, he thought. Maybe they would not be back again this year. Maybe the birds had been enough for their pride.

But he knew it wasn't finished yet. They had found each other, right here, at the end of this valley, and they knew it and so did he.

Late in the afternoon he looked out his window and saw Gretchen, Waldo's grader, stepping carefully on the icy stones in the creek, her arms stretched out for balance, crossing onto his property. The wind was blowing, and her face was red with cold and there were ice crystals in her blonde hair. When he opened the door for her, her breath puffed up in a cloud of steam.

'The power went out, and I can't get the generator started,' she said.

Her eyes were blue and wide and the wind had made tears in them. He closed the door behind her. Her lug boots and the bottom of her blue jeans were caked with snow.

'Where's Waldo?' he said.

'He went up to the Cabin for a drink.'

'What are you doing at his house, Gretchen?'

'He just gave his midterms. He likes to grade them close by so I can ask him questions if I have to.'

Roger had known her since she had entered the English program five years ago. Her father had been a gypo logger who had been killed felling trees over in Idaho, and she lived with her mother in a clapboard house out by the pulp mill, where on a windless day the sweet-sour stench of processed pulp hung in the air like ripe sewage. She worked hard and did well in conventional classes in which the professor rewarded a student's ability to memorize, but she never took creative writing courses and one way or another she avoided studying with professors whose ideas were eccentric or unpredictable, except Roger, and he believed she enrolled in his courses only because he never gave anyone a grade lower than C.

'Where's Waldo's wife?' he said.

'She's out of town.'

'Are the kids by themselves?'

'They went with her.'

'I see. Well,' he said, veiling his eyes, 'let me turn off the stove and we'll get that generator started.'

'We don't have to. He'll be back pretty soon. I can just wait here, can't I?'

'Sure.'

'I mean, he won't be long.'

'Don't worry about it. Come on upstairs and have some soup with me.'

Her rear was tight against her blue jeans when she walked up the steps ahead of him. She took off her sheep-lined coat and hung it on a hook by the woodburning stove that Roger had made out of an oil drum. Her breasts rose up high against her sweater, and Roger had to look away from her.

'Waldo told his American lit class that Ronald Reagan will probably one day be considered a near-great president,' she said.

Roger was silent.

'Some of them put it in their exam papers,' she said.

'Ignore it.'

'What do you think, I mean about Reagan being near-great?'

'I'm retired, Gretchen. I try not to think anymore about what Waldo has to say. Let me get you some soup.'

'No, I can do it. I'll fix it for both of us. I'll make coffee, too, if that's all right.'

He watched her at the stove, the way her elbow tightened against the sleeve of her sweater, the thickness of her hair against her neck, her large farm-girl hands.

'What's a P-38?' she asked.

'A World War II airplane.'

'No. Waldo's little boy said his daddy wore a P-38 on a chain around his neck.'

'Oh. It's a GI can opener.'

'Was he in the war or something?' she said.

'No, and neither was Ronald Reagan. Listen, Gretchen, this is important to understand. These kind of men vicariously revise their lives through the suffering of others. Look, I don't want to tell you what to think or whom you should listen to . . .'

He stopped and looked down at the backs of his hands.

'I'm sorry,' he said.

'You don't like him because he hunts animals, do you? At least that's what he thinks.'

'What do you say we eat?'

Her eyes roamed over his face, and he felt himself swallow. She widened her eyes and the blue in them intensified, and for just a moment his vanity made him conclude that he was still attractive to a beautiful young woman and his heart raced in his chest in a way that it should not have.

Then he saw her cheeks color and her hand falter on the coffeepot.

'What is it?' he asked.

Her eyes reached out the window, out over the short pines and the frozen creek toward Waldo's house.

'He said he pulled a muscle carrying firewood. He said it throbbed all night and he couldn't sleep. He was standing behind me in the study while I was grading papers, and he had a tube of Ben-Gay in his hand.'

He looked away from her face and the shine in her eyes.

'He took off his shirt and sat down next to me. He said, "You won't mind putting just a little bit across my shoulders, will you?"'

'Gretchen, you don't have to confess anything to me –'

'While I put it on him, he kept saying I was a good girl.

He said it over and over.'

'I want you to forget this. You're a fine person. You don't have anything to be ashamed of. Just don't go out to Waldo's house again. Do your work at the office. If Waldo makes another overture toward you, report it to the dean. I'll back you up.'

'Am I a weak person? Is that why it was me instead of somebody else?'

'No, you're brave to work and go to school. You're brave to put up with the deviousness of older people,' he said, and folded his arms across her back. He could feel the wetness of her face against his throat. The thickness in his loins made him close his eyes and hold his breath so he would not see the gold down on the taper of her neck or smell the perfume in her hair.

The chain did not stop them the next morning. They simply drove around it, cracking over the ice, flattening the tree saplings along the creek bank. Then just before they reached Roger's property, they veered across the creek, scouring deep black tracks along the banks, and bounced over the rocks until they reached Waldo's horse lot and access to the National Forest. Roger watched them through the window as they unloaded a child's sled out of the Toyota's back. The snowfields danced with light, and the plumes from the hunters' mouths were thick and white in the windless air. Then Waldo came out of his back door in a nylon vest, with a battered cowboy hat on his head, and the three men talked like old friends, laughing at something funny, looking in the direction of Roger's house. The hunters had brought scoped rifles this time, and they wore them on shoulder straps and kept shifting the guns' weight on their backs as they talked, then they shook hands with Waldo and pulled their sled on a rope up into a heavy green stand of pines in the National Forest.

That afternoon the valley was sealed from rim to rim

with snow clouds, then a heavy white mist moved across the valley floor until the trees on the hills disappeared inside it, the rick fences and stone walls became as white as the fields, and the creek was recognizable only by a thin electric-blue riffle running through the ice. Thunder boomed through the valley, and when he heard an explosion echo off the cliff walls in the public woods, he tried to tell himself that it was only more thunder.

For some reason, that afternoon, for the first time in his life, he wondered what it would be like to kill someone. He remembered a graduate student he had had back in the 1960s, a studious but strange kid with myopic, close-set eyes who fried some element in his brain with LSD and once told Roger he had spent a morning in the shadows behind his second-floor apartment window, looking through the telescopic sights of an empty rifle at the passersby on the street. When Roger tried and failed to get the boy to see the campus psychologist, he wondered if the acid had inculcated such a sick urge in the boy's head or if it had simply liberated it.

Just before sunset the sky started to clear and a mauve-colored glow filled the trees on the valley's eastern rim. Roger let Boomer outside, then a few minutes later went outside himself with a propane torch to unfreeze the water line. He saw the hunters come out of the woods on the other side of the creek, dragging their sled across the glazed slickness of the snow. The doe lashed to the sled was so enormous and heavy that both men had to pull on the rope to get the sled up the incline to their jeep. They had already gutted her, and the slit from between her back legs to her throat looked like a long strip of red silk ribbon.

He moved the white-blue flame of the propane torch up and down the water pipe and tried not to look at them as they tied down the doe on the jeep's fender. But when enough time had passed for them to have closed their doors and started their engine and he had heard only silence, he looked up and saw them sharing a drink from a chrome flask, watching him.

He shut off the valve on the propane torch and went back inside, stamping the crust of mud and snow off his boots, the propane bottle hot in his clenched hand.

Their jeep ground across Waldo's property and along the frozen edges of the creek, and finally he could not hear it anymore. Then he heard a solitary rifle shot, a sharp, loud *crack* which meant that it was not an echo, that the muzzle had been pointed in the direction of his property.

He opened the front door, and it was so quiet outside that he could hear a lump of snow fall through the branches of a fir tree. Boomer lay on the creek bank, a pooling dark red hole in the side of his neck, his mouth opened stiffly against the ice. The wind blew patterns in the fur along the edge of his stomach.

Roger had bought the knife for eight dollars through a mail-order service that advertised in the family magazine in the Sunday newspaper. It was made in Taiwan and copied after the pattern of the Marine Corps K-Bar. It had a ball compass inserted in the end of the tooled grip, saw teeth and a blood groove on the blade, and a honed edge that could cut weightlessly through paper.

He knew that they would stop at the Cabin up on the highway. It was the hunters' place, it was Waldo's place, where they drank busthead boiler-makers at the bar, rolled the dice out of a leather cup for the drinks, and slammed the butt of their pool cues down on the floor after each shot. He didn't know why he was so sure they would be there (maybe it was the memory of the convict in an extension class at Deer Lodge who had told Roger, 'You see, Doc, right after a score you always go to a bar or a hot-pillow joint. A guy's got to share the feel of it, you know what I mean?'), and so when he came out on the highway and saw their jeep in the parking lot of the bar, the only unexpected moment of recognition was the fact that among all the pickups and cars in the lot they had parked one vehicle away from Waldo's Power Ram.

He stepped up on the wood porch and opened the door partway. A fire burned in a hearth beyond the pool table and a flat layer of cigarette smoke hung in the purple and orange neon haze over the long, railed bar. The two hunters were eating steaks at a table, their elbows pointed outward as they sliced meat away from the bone.

Roger's hand rested lightly on top of the big knife inside his coat pocket, the blade cold and hard under his fingers. He looked at the two hunters, and in his mind, for just a moment, he saw a series of images like blisters popping across the surface of the brain: his own shape moving quickly across the barroom floor, the backhanded slash of the blade across a cheekbone, across the back of a fat neck, the absolute horror in their eyes. But he felt both foolish and stupid now, and he closed the door and stepped back off the porch into the parking lot. The doe's head hung downward off the jeep's fender onto the front bumper, and her eyes were like brown glass in the starlight. He lifted on the tension of the nylon rope that bound her to the fender, sawed through it with the survival knife, and hefted her weight up on his shoulders. Her body had already stiffened in the cold, and her hair felt like bristles against his neck.

After he dropped her in the bed of his pickup truck, he walked back to the jeep, cut off the air stems of all four tires, then unscrewed the gas cap and systematically scooped up five handfuls of dirt and poured it into the tank.

As he pulled out onto the highway and skidded slightly on a strip of black ice, he heard an outraged voice behind him and saw in his rearview mirror the silhouettes of men filing quickly out the front door of the bar.

The vault of sky over the valley was bursting with constellations and the moon had risen high above the ponderosas and lighted the snowfields and the skeletal shapes of the cottonwoods along the creek as brightly as a phosophorous flare. He stopped his truck at the chain stretched across the road, unlocked it and let it drop clinking to the road, then drove across it and kept on going through his own property until he reached the wooden gate that gave onto the National Forest. From the tool box in the bed of his truck, he took a GI entrenching tool, screwed the adjustable blade into the position of a hoe, lifted the belly of the doe across his shoulders, and with her four legs gathered together across his chest, worked his way up the trail into the darkness of the forest, under the towering gray and pink cliffs that were filmed with ice in the moonlight.

He hadn't gone far when he heard the surge of a truck engine up his private road. He looked back down the trail and saw Waldo's Power Ram, with three men in the cab, stop in his yard, and behind them the headlights of cars and other pickups. He set the doe down in a tangle of huckleberry bushes and began chopping through the snow and frozen dirt with the shovel. There was no time to build a fire to thaw the ground, and with his bare hands he ripped away slabs of ice and frozen root systems that were meshed as hard as cable in the earth, felt his skin tear, a fingernail fold back on itself; then on his knees he chopped even harder into the dirt until he was down past the freeze-line and the blade of the shovel bit into the moist subsoil.

He hollowed out the hole deeper, flinging humus and dirt out to the sides, then pushed the doe into it and pressed the stiffness of her flat against the contours of the earth. As he scraped the snow and leaves back over her stomach and flanks, he saw blood on the wooden shaft of the entrenching tool, and in the heart-stopping urgency of the moment he did not know if it was the doe's or his own.

The wind blew down the canyon, and the ice crystals in the larch and ponderosa pine and fir trees glittered as though in a fantasy, rang almost as loudly as crystal. His face was white and shining with sweat in the moon's glow.

In Roger's front yard, Waldo and the hunters moved in a circle, massing their energies, their voices melding together with the sound of their truck and car engines, their shadows on the snow like simian figures moving about on a prehistoric savannah.

'We're here,' one of the hunters yelled to the others. 'We're here.'

The Convict

for Lyle Williams

My father was a popular man in New Iberia, even though his ideas were different from most people's and his attitudes were uncompromising. On Friday afternoon he and my mother and I would drive down the long, yellow, dirt road through the sugarcane fields until it became a blacktop and followed the Bayou Teche into town, where my father would drop my mother off at Musemeche's Produce Market and take me with him to the bar at the Frederic Hotel. The Frederic was a wonderful old place with slot machines and potted palms and marble columns in the lobby and a gleaming, mahogany-and-brass barroom that was cooled by long-bladed wooden fans. I always sat at a table with a Dr. Nut and a glass of ice and watched with fascination the drinking rituals of my father and his friends: the warm hand-shakes, the pats on the shoulder, the laughter that was genuine but never uncontrolled. In the summer, which seemed like the only season in south Louisiana, the men wore seersucker suits and straw hats, and the amber light in their glasses of whiskey and ice and their Havana cigars and Picayune cigarettes held between their ringed fingers made them seem everything gentlemen and my father's friends should be.

But sometimes I would suddenly realize that there was not only a fundamental difference between my father and other men but that his presence would eventually expose that difference, and a flaw, a deep one that existed in him or them, would surface like an aching wisdom tooth.

'Do you fellows really believe we should close the schools because of a few little Negro children?' my father said.

'My Lord, Will. We've lived one way here all our lives,' one man said. He owned a restaurant in town and a farm with oil on it near St. Martinville.

My father took the cigar out of his teeth, smiled, sipped out of his whiskey, and looked with his bright, green eyes at the restaurant owner. My father was a real farmer, not an absentee landlord, and his skin was brown and his body straight and hard. He could pick up a washtub full of bricks and throw it over a fence.

'That's the point,' he said. 'We've lived among Negroes all our lives. They work in our homes, take care of our children, drive our wives on errands. Where are you going to send our own children if you close the school? Did you think of that?'

The bartender looked at the Negro porter who ran the shoe-shine stand in the bar. He was bald and wore an apron and was quietly brushing a pair of shoes left him by a hotel guest.

'Alcide, go down to the corner and pick up the news-papers,' the bartender said.

'Yes suh.'

'It's not ever going to come to that,' another man said. 'Our darkies don't want it.'

'It's coming, all right,' my father said. His face was composed now, his eyes looking through the opened wood shutters at the oak tree in the courtyard outside. 'Harry Truman is integrating the army, and those Negro soldiers aren't going to come home and walk around to the back door anymore.'

'Charlie, give Mr. Broussard another manhattan,' the restaurant owner said. 'In fact, give everybody one. This conversation puts me in mind of the town council.'

Everyone laughed, including my father, who put his cigar in his teeth and smiled good-naturedly with his hands folded on the bar. But I knew that he wasn't laughing inside, that he would finish his drink quietly and then wink at me and we'd wave goodbye to everyone and leave their Friday-afternoon good humor intact.

On the way home he didn't talk and instead pretended that he was interested in mother's conversation about the New Iberia ladies' book club. The sun was red on the bayou, and the cypress and oaks along the bank were a dark green in the gathering dusk. Families of Negroes were cane fishing in the shallows for goggle-eye perch and bullheads.

'Why do you drink with them, Daddy? Y'all always have a argument,' I said.

His eyes flicked sideways at my mother.

'That's not an argument, just a gentleman's disagreement,' he said.

'I agree with him,' my mother said. 'Why provoke them?'

'They're good fellows. They just don't see things clearly sometimes.'

My mother looked at me in the back seat, her eyes smiling so he could see them. She was beautiful when she looked like that.

'You should be aware that your father is the foremost authority in Louisiana on the subject of colored people.'

'It isn't a joke, Margaret. We've kept them poor and uneducated and we're going to have to settle accounts for it one day.'

'Well, you haven't underpaid them,' she said. 'I don't believe there's a darkie in town you haven't lent money to.'

I wished I hadn't said anything. I knew he was feeling the same pain now that he had felt in the bar. Nobody understood him – not my mother, not me, none of the men he drank with.

The air suddenly became cool, the twilight turned a yellowish green, and it started to rain. Up the blacktop we saw a blockade and men in raincoats with flashlights in their hands. They wore flat campaign hats and water was dancing on the brims. My father stopped at the blockade and rolled down the window. A state policeman leaned his head down and moved his eyes around the inside of the car.

'We got a nigger and a white convict out on the ground. Don't pick up no hitchhikers,' he said.

'Where were they last seen?' my father said.

'They got loose from a prison truck just east of the four-corners,' he said.

We drove on in the rain. My father turned on the head-lights, and I saw the anxiety in my mother's face in the glow from the dashboard.

'Will, that's only a mile from us,' she said.

'They're probably gone by now or hid out under a bridge somewhere,' he said.

'They must be dangerous or they wouldn't have so many police officers out,' she said.

'If they were really dangerous, they'd be in Angola, not riding around in a truck. Besides, I bet when we get home and turn on the radio we'll find out they're back in jail.'

'I don't like it. It's like when all those Germans were here.'

During the war there was a POW camp outside New Iberia. We used to see them chopping in the sugar cane with a big white P on their backs. Mother kept the doors locked until they were sent back to Germany. My father always said they were harmless and they wouldn't escape from their camp if they were pushed out the front door at gunpoint.

The wind was blowing hard when we got home, and leaves from the pecan orchard were scattered across the lawn. My pirogue, which was tied to a small dock on the bayou behind the house, was knocking loudly against a piling. Mother waited for my father to open the front door, even though she had her own key, then she turned on all the lights in the house and closed the curtains. She began to peel crawfish in the sink for our supper, then turned on the radio in the window as though she were bored for something to listen to. Outside, the door on the tractor shed began to bang violently in the wind. My father went to the closet for his hat and raincoat.

'Let it go, Will. It's raining too hard,' she said.

'Turn on the outside light. You'll be able to see me from the window,' he said.

He ran through the rain, stopped at the barn for a hammer and a wood stob, then bent over in front of the tractor shed and drove the stob securely against the door.

He walked back into the kitchen, hitting his hat against his pants leg.

'I've got to get a new latch for that door. But at least the wind won't be banging it for a while,' he said.

'There was a news story on the radio about the convicts,' my mother said. 'They had been taken from Angola to Franklin for a trial. One of them is a murderer.'

'Angola?' For the first time my father's face looked concerned.

'The truck wrecked, and they got out the back and then made a man cut their handcuffs.'

He picked up a shelled crawfish, bit it in half, and looked out the window at the rain slanting in the light. His face was empty now.

'Well, if I was in Angola I'd try to get out, too,' he said. 'Do we have some beer? I can't eat crawfish without beer.'

'Call the sheriff's department and ask where they think they are.'

'I can't do that, Margaret. Now, let's put a stop to all

215

this.' He walked out of the kitchen, and I saw my mother's jawbone flex under the skin.

It was about three in the morning when I heard the shed door begin slamming in the wind again. A moment later I saw my father walk past my bedroom door buttoning his denim coat over his undershirt. I followed him halfway down the stairs and watched him take a flashlight from the kitchen drawer and lift the twelve-gauge pump out of the rack on the dining-room wall. He saw me, then paused for a moment as though he were caught between two thoughts.

Then he said, 'Come on down a minute, Son. I guess I didn't get that stob hammered in as well as I thought. But bolt the door behind me, will you?'

'Did you see something, Daddy?'

'No, no. I'm just taking this to satisfy your mother. Those men are probably all the way to New Orleans by now.'

He turned on the outside light and went out the back door. Through the kitchen window I watched him cross the lawn. He had the flashlight pointed in front of him, and as he approached the tractor shed, he raised the shotgun and held it with one hand against his waist. He pushed the swinging door all the way back against the wall with his foot, shined the light over the tractor and the rolls of chicken wire, then stepped inside the darkness.

I could hear my own breathing as I watched the flashlight beam bounce through the cracks in the shed. Then I saw the light steady in the far corner where we hung the tools and tack. I waited for something awful to happen – the shotgun to streak fire through the boards, a pick in murderous hands to rake downward in a tangle of harness. Instead, my father appeared in the doorway a moment later, waved the flashlight at me, then replaced the stob and pressed it into the wet earth with his boot. I unbolted the back door and went up to bed, relieved that the convicts were far away and that my father was my father, a truly brave man who kept my mother's and my world a secure place.

But he didn't go back to bed. I heard him first in the upstairs hall cabinet, then in the icebox, and finally on the back porch. I went to my window and looked down into the moonlit yard and saw him walking with the shotgun under one arm and a lunch pail and folded towels in the other.

Just at false dawn, when the mist from the marsh hung thick on the lawn and the gray light began to define the black trees along the bayou, I heard my parents arguing in the next room. Then my father snapped: 'Damn it, Margaret. The man's hurt.'

Mother didn't come out of her room that morning. My father banged out the back door, was gone a half hour, then returned and cooked a breakfast of *couche-couche* and sausages for us.

'You want to go to a picture show today?' he said.

'I was going fishing with Tee Batiste.' He was a little Negro boy whose father worked for us sometimes.

'It won't be any good after all that rain. Your mother doesn't want you tracking mud in from the bank, either.'

'Is something going on, Daddy?'

'Oh, Mother and I have our little discussions sometimes. It's nothing.' He smiled at me over his coffee cup.

I almost always obeyed my father, but that morning I found ways to put myself among the trees on the bank of the bayou. First, I went down on the dock to empty the rainwater out of my pirogue, then I threw dirt clods at the heads of water moccasins on the far side, then I made a game of jumping from cypress root to cypress root along the water's edge without actually touching the bank, and finally I was near what I knew my father wanted me away from that day: the old houseboat that had been washed up and left stranded among the oak trees in the great flood of 1927. Wild morning glories grew over the rotting deck, kids had riddled the cabin walls with .22 holes, and a slender oak had rooted in the collapsed floor and grown up through one window. Two sets of sharply etched footprints, side by side, led down from the levee, on the other side of which was the tractor shed, to a sawed-off cypress stump that someone had used to climb up on the deck.

The air among the trees was still and humid and dappled with broken shards of sunlight. I wished I had brought my .22, and then I wondered at my own foolishness in involving myself in something my father had been willing to lie about in order to protect me from. But I had to know what he was hiding, what or who it was that would make him choose the welfare of another over my mother's anxiety and fear.

I stepped up on the cypress stump and leaned forward until I could see into the doorless cabin. There were an empty dynamite box and a half-dozen beer bottles moted with dust in one corner, and I remembered the seismograph company that had used the houseboat as a storage shack for their explosives two years ago. I stepped up on the deck more bravely now, sure that I would find nothing else in the cabin other than possibly a possum's nest or a squirrel's cache of acorns. Then I saw the booted pants leg in the gloom just as I smelled his odor. It was like a slap in the face, a mixture of dried sweat and blood and the sour stench of swamp mud. He was sleeping on his side, his knees drawn up before him, his green-and-white, pin-striped uniform streaked black, his bald, brown head tucked under one arm. On each wrist was a silver manacle and a short length of broken chain. Someone had slipped a narrow piece of cable through one manacle and had nailed both looped ends to an oak floor beam with a twelve-inch iron spike. In that heart-pounding moment the length of cable and the long spike leaped at my eye even more than the convict did, because both of them came from the back of my father's pickup truck.

I wanted to run but I was transfixed. There was a bloody

tear across the front of his shirt, as though he had run through barbed wire, and even in sleep his round, hard body seemed to radiate a primitive energy and power. He breathed hoarsely through his open mouth, and I could see the stumps of his teeth and the snuff stains on his soft, pink gums. A deerfly hummed in the heat and settled on his forehead, and when his face twitched like a snapping rubber band, I jumped backward involuntarily. Then I felt my father's strong hands grab me like vice grips on each arm.

My father was seldom angry with me, but this time his eyes were hot and his mouth was a tight line as we walked back through the trees toward the house. Finally I heard him blow out his breath and slow his step next to me. I looked up at him and his face had gone soft again.

'You ought to listen to me, Son. I had a reason not to want you back there,' he said.

'What are you going to do with him?'

'I haven't decided. I need to talk with your mother a little bit.'

'What did he do to go to prison?'

'He says he robbed a laundromat. For that they gave him fifty-six years.'

A few minutes later he was talking to mother again in their room. This time the door was open and neither one of them cared what I heard.

'You should see his back. There are whip scars on it as thick as my finger,' my father said.

'You don't have an obligation to every person in the world. He's an escaped convict. He could come in here and cut our throats for all you know.'

'He's a human being who happens to be a convict. They do things up in that penitentiary that ought to make every civilized man in this state ashamed.'

'I won't have this, Will.'

'He's going tonight. I promise. And he's no danger to us.'

'You're breaking the law. Don't you know that?'

'You have to make choices in this world, and right now I choose not to be responsible for any more suffering in this man's life.'

They avoided speaking to each other the rest of the day. My mother fixed lunch for us, then pretended she wasn't hungry and washed the dishes while my father and I ate at the kitchen table. I saw him looking at her back, his eyelids blinking for a moment, and just when I thought he was going to speak, she dropped a pan loudly in the dish rack and walked out of the room. I hated to see them like that. But I particularly hated to see the loneliness that was in his eyes. He tried to hide it but I knew how miserable he was.

'They all respect you. Even though they argue with you, all those men look up to you,' I said.

'What's that, Son?' he said, and turned his gaze away from the window. He was smiling, but his mind was still out there on the bayou and the houseboat.

'I heard some men from Lafayette talking about you in the bank. One of them said, "Will Broussard's word is better than any damned signature on a contract."'

'Oh, well, that's good of you to say, Son. You're a good boy.'

'Daddy, it'll be over soon. He'll be gone and everything will be just the same as before.'

'That's right. So how about you and I take our poles and see if we can't catch us a few goggle-eye?'

We fished until almost dinnertime, then cleaned and scraped our stringer of bluegill, goggle-eye perch, and sacalait in the sluice of water from the windmill. Mother had left plates of cold fried chicken and potato salad covered with wax paper for us on the kitchen table. She listened to the radio in the living room while we ate, then picked up our dishes and washed them without ever speaking to my father. The western sky was aflame with the sunset, fireflies spun circles of light in the darkening oaks on the lawn, and at eight o'clock, when I usually listened to 'Gangbusters,' I heard my father get up out of his straw chair on the porch and walk around the side of the house toward the bayou.

I watched him pick up a gunny sack weighted heavily at the bottom from inside the barn door and walk through the trees and up the levee. I felt guilty when I followed him, but he hadn't taken the shotgun, and he would be alone and unarmed when he freed the convict, whose odor still reached up and struck at my face. I was probably only fifty feet behind him, my face prepared to smile instantly if he turned around, but the weighted gunny sack rattled dully against his leg and he never heard me. He stepped up on the cypress stump and stooped inside the door of the houseboat cabin, then I heard the convict's voice: 'What game you playing, white man?'

'I'm going to give you a choice. I'll drive you to the sheriff's office in New Iberia or I'll cut you loose. It's up to you.'

'What you doing this for?'

'Make up your mind.'

'I done that when I went out the back of that truck. What you doing this for?'

I was standing behind a tree on a small rise, and I saw my father take a flashlight and a hand ax out of the gunny sack. He squatted on one knee, raised the ax over his head, and whipped it down onto the floor of the cabin.

'You're on your own now. There's some canned goods and an opener in the sack, and you can have the flashlight. If you follow the levee you'll come out on a dirt road that'll lead you to a railway track. That's the Southern Pacific and it'll take you to Texas.'

'Gimmie the ax.'

'Nope. You already have everything you're going to get.'

'You got a reason you don't want the law here, ain't you? Maybe a still in that barn.'

'You're a lucky man today. Don't undo it.'

'What you does is your business, white man.'

The convict wrapped the gunny sack around his wrist and dropped off the deck onto the ground. He looked backward with his cannonball head, then walked away through the darkening oaks that grew beside the levee. I wondered if he would make that freight train or if he would be run to ground by dogs and state police and maybe blown apart with shotguns in a cane field before he ever got out of the parish. But mostly I wondered at the incredible behavior of my father, who had turned Mother against him and broken the law himself for a man who didn't even care enough to say thank you.

It was hot and still all day Sunday, then a thunder-shower blew in from the Gulf and cooled everything off just before suppertime. The sky was violet and pink, and the cranes flying over the cypress in the marsh were touched with fire from the red sun on the horizon. I could smell the sweetness of the fields in the cooling wind and the wild four-o'clocks that grew in a gold-and-crimson spray by the swamp. My father said it was a perfect evening to drive down to Cypremort Point for boiled crabs. Mother didn't answer, but a moment later she said she had promised her sister to go to a movie in Lafayette. My father lit a cigar and looked at her directly through the flame.

'It's all right, Margaret. I don't blame you,' he said.

Her face colored, and she had trouble finding her hat and her car keys before she left.

The moon was bright over the marsh that night, and I decided to walk down the road to Tee Batiste's cabin and go frog gigging with him. I was on the back porch sharpening the point of my gig with a file when I saw the flashlight wink out of the trees behind the house. I ran into the living room, my heart racing, the file still in my hand, my face evidently so alarmed that my father's mouth opened when he saw me.

'He's back. He's flashing your light in the trees,' I said.

'It's probably somebody running a trotline.'

'It's him, Daddy.'

He pressed his lips together, then folded his newspaper and set it on the table next to him.

'Lock up the house while I'm outside,' he said. 'If I don't come back in ten minutes, call the sheriff's office.'

He walked through the dining room toward the kitchen, peeling the wrapper off a fresh cigar.

'I want to go, too. I don't want to stay here by myself,' I said.

'It's better that you do.'

'He won't do anything if two of us are there.'

He smiled and winked at me. 'Maybe you're right,' he said, then took the shotgun out of the wall rack.

We saw the flashlight again as soon as we stepped off of the back porch. We walked past the tractor shed and the barn and into the trees. The light flashed once more from the top of the levee. Then it went off, and I saw him outlined against the moon's reflection off the bayou. Then I heard his breathing – heated, constricted, like a cornered animal's.

'There's a roadblock just before that railway track. You didn't tell me about that,' he said.

'I didn't know about it. You shouldn't have come back here,' my father said.

'They run me four hours through a woods. I could hear them yelling to each other, like they was driving a deer.'

His prison uniform was gone. He wore a brown, short-sleeved shirt and a pair of slacks that wouldn't button at the top. A butcher knife stuck through one of the belt loops.

'Where did you get that?' my father said.

'I taken it. What do you care? You got a bird gun there, ain't you?'

'Who did you take the clothes from?'

'I didn't bother no white people. Listen, I need to stay here two or three days. I'll work for you. There ain't no kind of work I can't do. I can make whiskey too.'

'Throw the knife in the bayou.'

'What 'chu talking about?'

'I said to throw it away.'

'The old man I taken it from put an inch of it in my side. I don't throw it in no bayou. I ain't no threat to you, nohow. I can't go nowheres else. Why I'm going to hurt you or the boy?'

'You're the murderer, aren't you? The other convict is the robber. That's right, isn't it?'

The convict's eyes narrowed. I could see his tongue on his teeth.

'In Angola that means I won't steal from you,' he said.

I saw my father's jaw work. His right hand was tight on the stock of the shotgun.

'Did you kill somebody after you left here?' he said.

'I done told you, it was me they was trying to kill. All them people out there, they'd like me drug behind a car. But that don't make no nevermind, do it? You worried about some no-good nigger that put a dirk in my neck and cost me eight years.'

'You get out of here,' my father said.

'I ain't going nowhere. You done already broke the law. You got to help me.'

'Go back to the house, Son.'

I was frightened by the sound in my father's voice.

'What you doing?' the convict said.

'Do what I say. I'll be along in a minute,' my father said.

'Listen, I ain't did you no harm,' the convict said.

'Avery!' my father said.

I backed away through the trees, my eyes fixed on the shotgun that my father now leveled at the convict's chest. In the moonlight I could see the sweat running down the Negro's face.

'I'm throwing away the knife,' he said.

'Avery, you run to the house and stay there. You hear me?'

I turned and ran through the dark, the tree limbs

slapping against my face, the morning-glory vines on the ground tangling around my ankles like snakes. Then I heard the twelve-gauge explode, and by the time I ran through the back screen into the house I was crying uncontrollably.

A moment later I heard my father's boot on the back step. Then he stopped, pumped the spent casing out of the breech, and walked inside with the shotgun over his shoulder and the red shells visible in the magazine. I knew then that neither he, my mother, nor I would ever know happiness again.

He took his bottle of Four Roses out of the cabinet and poured a jelly glass half full. He drank from it, then took a cigar stub out of his shirt pocket, put it between his teeth, and leaned on his arms against the drainboard. The muscles in his back stood out as though a nail were driven between his shoulder blades. Then he seemed to realize for the first time that I was in the room.

'Hey there, little fellow. What are you carrying on about?' he said.

'You killed a man, Daddy.'

'Oh no, no. I just scared him and made him run back in the marsh. But I have to call the sheriff now, and I'm not happy about what I have to tell him.'

I didn't think I had ever heard more joyous words. I felt as though my breast, my head, were filled with light, that a wind had blown through my soul. I could smell the bayou on the night air, the watermelons and strawberries growing beside the barn, the endlessly youthful scent of summer itself.

Two hours later my father and mother stood on the front lawn with the sheriff and watched four mud-streaked deputies lead the convict in manacles to a squad car. The convict's arms were pulled behind him, and he smoked a cigarette with his head tilted to one side. A deputy took it out of his mouth and flipped it away just before they locked him in the back of the car behind the wire screen.

'Now, tell me this again, Will. You say he was here yesterday and you gave him some canned goods?' the sheriff said. He was a thick-bodied man who wore blue suits, a pearl-gray Stetson, and a fat watch in his vest pocket.

'That's right. I cleaned up the cut on his chest and I gave him a flashlight, too,' my father said. Mother put her arm in his.

'What was that fellow wearing when you did all this?'

'A green-and-white work uniform of some kind.'

'Well, it must have been somebody else because I think this man stole that shirt and pants soon as he got out of the prison van. You probably run into one of them niggers that's been setting traps out of season.'

'I appreciate what you're trying to do, but I helped the fellow in that car to get away.'

'The same man who turned him in also helped him escape? Who's going to believe a story like that, Will?' The sheriff tipped his hat to my mother. 'Good night, Mrs. Broussard. You drop by and say hello to my wife when you have a chance. Good night, Will. And you, too, Avery.'

We walked back up on the porch as they drove down the dirt road through the sugar-cane fields. Heat lightning flickered across the blue-black sky.

'I'm afraid you're fated to be disbelieved,' Mother said, and kissed my father on the cheek.

'It's the battered innocence in us,' he said.

I didn't understand what he meant, but I didn't care, either. Mother fixed strawberries and plums and hand-cranked ice cream, and I fell asleep under the big fan in the living room with the spoon still in my hand. I heard the heat thunder roll once more, like a hard apple rattling in the bottom of a barrel, and then die somewhere out over the Gulf. In my dream I prayed for my mother and father, the men in the bar at the Frederic Hotel, the sheriff and his deputies, and finally for myself and the Negro convict.

Many years would pass before I would learn that it is our collective helplessness, the frailty and imperfection of our vision that ennobles us and saves us from ourselves; but that night, when I awoke while my father was carrying me up to bed, I knew from the beat of his heart that he and I had taken pause in our contention with the world.